LIMITLESS
LANDS

BOOK 1

THE COMMANDER'S TALE

LIMITLESS LANDS

BOOK 1

THE COMMANDER'S TALE

DEAN HENEGAR

It is the Soldier, not the minister Who has given us freedom of religion.

It is the Soldier, not the reporter Who has given us freedom of the press.

It is the Soldier, not the poet Who has given us freedom of speech.

It is the Soldier, not the campus organizer Who has given us freedom to protest.

It is the Soldier, not the lawyer Who has given us the right to a fair trial.

It is the Soldier, not the politician Who has given us the right to vote.

It is the soldier who salutes the flag,

Who serves beneath the flag,

And whose coffin is draped by the flag,

Who allows the protester to burn the flag.

PROLOGUE

2025: Quantum computing makes its debut. The processing power of computers multiplies exponentially.

2030: Worldwide deployment of the Skyfi satellite network allows for near-instantaneous data transfer anywhere in the world and to any device.

2035: Virtual reality (VR) gaming takes over as the world's most popular form of entertainment. Streaming stars make millions while companies rush to release new games and improve on the technology.

2040: The United States and most modern nations transition their military forces over to drones and no longer use live soldiers for combat operations. Trillions of dollars are saved by this move, as the required number of military personnel drops drastically. Manpower is now only utilized to service the drones and maintain logistics. The combat-oriented military operational specialties are no more.

2050: Due to the drawdown in forces, most VA (veterans' affairs) hospitals and facilities are shutting down across the United States. The older veterans have begun to die off, and veterans of the newer drone-based military are given regular health insurance as employees and contractors of the federal government.

2080: Most of the combat veterans in the United States are over eighty years old. Many of those who remain alive are now housed at the last VA medical retirement home in Knoxville, Tennessee.

2085: Top VR gaming company Qualitranos is set to launch its latest VRMMORPG (virtual reality massively multiplayer online role-playing game) into beta. The game is called Limitless Lands and features the first fully autonomous world controlled completely by AI (artificial intelligence). Limitless Lands preorders exceed all worldwide records, and the first one hundred thousand beta testers will begin to play shortly. VR gear manufacturers rush to put out hardware capable of fully utilizing the Limitless Lands software. What is not made known to the public is that the game is co-funded by the medical research company Meditronax. Meditronax wants to use the AI tech to create medpods that will treat brain-damaged, seriously injured, and comatose patients. The first medpod is being tested by the FDA (Food and Drug Administration) and is allocated to the VA medical retirement home in Tennessee for use on a patient whose family volunteered him for the treatment.

CHAPTER 1

VA medical facility, Knoxville, Tennessee

An annoying squeak accompanied every step Trey made on the linoleum-covered hallway. The downpour hit just as he was exiting his vehicle, soaking him thoroughly before he made it to the hospital's covered entryway. A misty rain continued to drizzle between intermittent downpours, a common occurrence during every East Tennessee spring. The long hall he walked down was decorated with bland, inoffensive artwork, the pictures yellowed with age and neglect. The hospital environment depressed him, and Trey always felt that the décor was a reminder that the building and those cared for inside were no longer worth expending further resources on.

Trey had initially questioned his choice to place his father as the first test subject for the experimental medpod, but he later realized that his father would have readily volunteered for the treatment himself, if he was able. His father was a fighter and would jump at any chance—however remote—to recover and spend time with his family. Trey had worked at Qualitranos for over twenty years, climbing the corporate ladder and moving to newer and more challenging projects with each promotion. He was told he had been the company's first and only choice to lead the Meditronax joint venture—a venture with the amazing opportunity to blend AI gaming software with lifesaving medical tech.

Noticing that his shoes had finally dried enough to stop squeaking, Trey found himself in front of a door marked "Room 51." He'd stopped visiting this place some time ago when it became too painful to watch his father slowly deteriorate. Trey gathered his thoughts and emotions, pushed on the cold stainless-steel door handle, and entered the room.

With his practiced, corporate game-face smile on, he greeted the people in the room. The occupants were gathering around a hospital bed next to a strange pod-shaped machine. He recognized his coworker and tech expert, Louis, as he fiddled with the latest-gen ThinTab dataslate, swiping at controls and analyzing data. Louis—or Lou, as he liked to be called—was one of the best tech guys in the business, but like many in the tech field, he was not a people person and was uncomfortable with conflict or social interaction. A look of relief washed over Lou's face as Trey entered.

"Trey, this is the representative from the VA, a Mister . . ." Lou tried to say before the person he was referring to cut him off. The man interrupting Lou looked to be around thirty-five years old and was dressed in a dark-blue suit accompanied by a colorful "power" tie. The expensive ensemble screamed *I'm more important than you!* The smug look on the man's face seemed to confirm Trey's suspicion.

"I'm Mr. Logan, the director of this facility. I take it you are Trey Raytak from Qualitranos?" Logan queried while offering his hand.

Trey shook his hand and confirmed. "Yes, pleased to meet you, Mr. Logan. I'm the medical interaction manager from Qualitranos for this project. Are we all set to get started?" Mr. Logan nodded and then introduced one of the other people in the room.

"This is Dr. Greenway with the FDA, here to observe the medpod's function." Mr. Logan gestured toward the middle-aged woman wearing a lab coat and carrying a dataslate. "I believe these two are techs from Meditronax, no doubt here to set up the machine." Logan dismissively waved at the techs who were fiddling with settings on the medpod.

Dr. Greenway shook hands with Trey. Her short brown hair framed a face that showed compassion and concern. "Are you sure you want to allow your father to go through with this?" she asked.

"My father was a soldier, Dr. Greenway. There is no way he would pass on the chance to help people in the future. Too bad the medpod won't allow

4

him to play the actual game. What most people don't know is that in addition to his being a colonel in the Army, he was also an avid gamer in his youth. He's the reason I'm in the gaming industry today."

Despite his father being gone for long periods of time due to his military service, Trey fondly remembered the times he spent playing MMOs with his father. Cut from the same cloth as her grandfather, Trey's own ten-year-old daughter was an avid gamer who hoped to explore a professional career in the field. A few pulled strings had even gotten her into the Limitless Lands beta.

Dr. Greenway nodded at Trey and advised the two medpod techs to begin their work.

"I will be here off and on during the day to monitor your father and keep an eye on his vitals. The pod will open every twenty-three to twenty-four hours to allow us to adjust the settings and refill the medications. The AI is supposed to make treatment suggestions, and if I agree with its treatment assessment, I will authorize refilling the pod with the suggested medications. If I disagree with the AI's suggestion, I will override its treatment path."

Dr. Greenway looked to be deep in thought, tapping her finger absently at the edge of her dataslate. Trey understood that most doctors would be hesitant to allow an AI to take over the care of someone with such complex medical problems. Greenway tapped at her tablet a few more times before beginning again.

"I admit I'm skeptical that an AI is advanced enough to do this. Should I disagree with its assessment, or if I see a deterioration in the patient's condition, I have the authority to—and most assuredly will—shut down this experiment immediately," she said before addressing the Meditronax technicians. "You may begin to move the patient. Be thorough but quick. He won't last long without life support. Set the pod to activate as soon as he's hooked up, and then I can load his medications." Dr. Greenway then moved to a small rollaway cart that contained all the medications that Colonel Raytak might need for the next twenty-four hours.

Trey looked down at his father as they loaded him into the medpod. A weight began to build in his chest as he saw the emaciated body that was once the strong, tall Colonel James Raytak. His father's head was shaved to accommodate electronic leads and to provide a better connection to the VR helmet being placed over his head. The shaved head, paper-thin skin, and wire-thin frame gave him a ghoulish look.

His father had not been conscious or in his right mind for several years as accumulated injuries and old age slowly took him from his family. Trey was an only child and had tried to visit as much as possible when his father's health had first declined enough that he had to be placed in the hospital. He couldn't stand to visit anymore once his father could no longer recognize him. His own wife, child, and work kept him too busy to visit—or so he told himself—but he knew that the real reason for not visiting was the depression he faced every time he saw his father's condition.

The game's AI would completely control the medpod while it administered medications, stimulated muscles, and connected directly to the brain from the helmet network interface. Despite the attempt to make it appear futuristic, the medpod had too much of a coffin-like appearance for Trey's liking. He knew this was a marvel of engineering and technology, but he was cautious about getting his hopes up for his father's recovery.

The incredible processing power of the AI should allow it to manage the medical care of the patient as well as provide mental stimulation in the form of a personal VR experience. While it wasn't connected to the game world, the VR experience would hopefully allow patients to enjoy themselves in a comfortable, happy, and safe environment while they were being treated.

With the help of a nurse from the VA hospital, the Meditronax techs began to disconnect Colonel Raytak from the dated VA life-support equipment he was currently on before placing him in the medpod. His life-support monitors blared loudly, and his body threatened to give out during the brief transfer to the pod. After he was connected to the medpod's far more advanced life-support systems, his vitals returned to normal.

Several panels at the edge of the medpod opened as clear plastic containers the size of a soda can extended from the pod. Dr. Greenway began filling each of the containers with the medications she had collected from the rolling cart next to her. She paused while holding the last container, which contained a grayish fluid, and looked at Mr. Logan.

He took the dataslate from Dr. Greenway, tapped on it a few times to bring up an e-sign form, and shoved it toward Trey.

"I want to formally be on the record that I do *not* approve of this experimental medication, and neither I nor the VA will be held accountable for any deterioration in your father's condition," Logan boldly stated.

Trey's experience in the corporate world let him see that Mr. Logan was a political animal. The man had to know his cushy job as the administrator of the facility was limited. In only a few years—ten at most—all the patients left in the facility would have passed away, leaving this last VA hospital to close. Logan would be hunting for a promotion to another department in the government bureaucracy before he was put out to pasture. The success of the medpod would springboard someone like him to yet another cushy job with perhaps even a bump in pay. Should the project fail, he would be covered by his "expressed concern" over the dangers of the project and the myriad of releases he had forced all the parties involved to sign.

Trey looked at the final release on the dataslate. This one had nothing to do with the company Qualitranos; this was a release for him personally as his father's guardian. This last release allowed the use of the new experimental nanobots to be injected into his father and for the AI to completely manage his care. In theory, the nanobots would take the medications in the pod and spray or inject them directly where needed, including the brain. These nanobots were the first ones small enough to accomplish this task and could even perform microscopic surgery, as directed by the AI. Trey swiped his signature, and the dataslate read his biometrics before authorizing the treatment.

Logan grabbed the dataslate back from Trey and shot toward the door before pausing and turning around.

"By the way, Mr. Raytak . . . Or can I call you Trey? Do you think I can get beta access to Limitless Lands for my son? He's a huge fan of your company's games and would kill me if he knew you were here and I didn't get him into the beta. I know with your position in the company you can pull some strings for the folks that care for your dad," Logan awkwardly requested.

People like Logan would do anything to get ahead and had no real concern for patients like Trey's father or the selfless nurses and orderlies in the hospital. There was no way he would reward that behavior with a beta code.

"Sorry, Mr. Logan, but the beta keys are all spoken for and it would violate our company vendor/client policy to give one to someone at a facility

7

we have business dealings with. Your son will have to wait for release like everyone else," Trey said, smiling at the opportunity to shoot down Logan.

"Well, I don't see what the big deal of a beta test is anyway." Logan huffed. "I'm sure you can just give us a few free copies of the game when it releases, though, right?" Logan asked.

"Sorry, Mr. Logan, the same applies to copies of the release version. The game itself retails for 499 dollars, and that amount also conflicts with our vendor/client gift policy. I do have a ten-percent-off coupon I can give you," Trey said while checking his pockets for one of the promotional coupons employees were given to hand out to friends and family.

"Oh, don't bother with that," Logan spouted. The man then composed himself before walking through the door with a disingenuous smile plastered on his face. Everyone in the room seemed to relax a bit as Mr. Logan left.

Dr. Greenway loaded the nanobot container into the medpod. With that step complete, Lou began to use his dataslate to activate them. The gray container retracted into the medpod and the nanobots began to enter his father's bloodstream.

"Woohoo, look at them babies go!" Lou exclaimed as he tracked the nanobots on his dataslate. "They're in and the medpod has Skyfi connection. The AI is communicating with the medpod." Lou's nervous energy caused him to hop from foot to foot as he watched the data stream. "*Suhwheet!* The nanobots can fully power themselves by using your pop's own body heat, just like we designed, Trey. I knew it would work, but that is just . . . Oh, look, the AI is taking control. She's giving orders to my little Zerglings!" Trey gave a small laugh at Lou's archaic gaming reference.

Meditronax technicians went about checking and double-checking all the data from the medpod. Once they appeared satisfied that all was well, the technicians excused themselves, letting the doctor and Lou know that everything from a technical standpoint was running fine and that they would be staying locally at a nearby hotel for the next few days if anything more was needed. Dr. Greenway and Lou also left since they had nothing to do until the medpod opened again; it would remain sealed for the next twenty-three hours as the AI began its intensive treatment of Colonel Raytak.

The nurse smiled at Trey as she checked the vitals on the other patient in the room. Forgotten in all the turmoil, Colonel Raytak's roommate—a retired Marine named Rodney Ty—lay connected to one of the VA's archaic life-support devices. Trey's eyes were drawn to the empty left sleeve of the old Marine's hospital gown. Mr. Ty had lost his left arm in combat, and the stump showed a jagged purple scar, a reminder of the violent lives these old warriors once lived. The Marine's family visited often, making him one of the lucky few who had regular visitors.

"Your daddy was always kind to me before he was too ill to know what was going on," the nurse stated, interrupting Trey's thoughts. She was an older woman in her mid-sixties and had that kind, simple, Southern grandmotherly way about her.

"Thank you, Fran. Dad loved to tease you and the other nurses before he . . ." Trey trailed off and Fran nodded, knowing what he meant. "How is Mr. Ty doing? Does his family make it by to visit much?" he inquired, trying to distract himself from the depression he always felt creep over him in this room.

"They're always coming around when they can. He's been doing poorly, like your daddy. I think once your daddy stopped being able to talk to the ole Marine every day, he just sort of lost hope. Those two had become good friends over the years and would pick at each other for hours on end, always fighting over which was better, the Army or the Marines," Nurse Fran drawled.

"Fran?" Trey began. "You mentioned your grandson is a gamer, isn't he?"

"Oh yes, Mr. Trey, he's been working as much overtime as he can at the Kroger to save up for one of them new fancy headsets for that game y'all made," Fran replied.

Trey knew that Fran was one of the good ones. It was plain to see that she genuinely cared for her patients, and from his time chatting with her, he knew her home life must have been difficult. Fran's husband had passed away from a heart attack a few years ago, and with his passing, the family lost most of its income. Her daughter battled drug addiction and had given custody of her son to Fran, who was raising him on her own. Fran's grandson had several learning disabilities but still went to school every day while trying to help the family financially by working at a low-paying, part-time job at the local grocery store. Despite the personal and financial stress in her home, Fran never lost her good cheer or the friendly smile she had for her patients.

"He may want this then, Miss Fran." Trey smiled as he pulled a beta invite card from his wallet. "This code will give him a free copy of the game and access to the beta test. As for the VR gear, have him email me your address and I'll send him one of the testing units I have at the house. He also doesn't need to worry about the subscription fee. The code I gave you allows for un-limited free access without a subscription."

Tears began to fill Fran's eyes as she looked at the card. She wasn't one to complain but had mentioned in the past that her grandson was dealing with bullying at school due to his learning disability and his family's tight money situation.

"I don't know what to say, Mr. Trey. This will mean the world to Nolen. Won't you get in trouble for giving this away? I heard what you said to Mr. Logan."

"No worries, Fran. I won't tell if you won't. Consider it a thank-you for all you have done for my father and all the other patients. I know you don't always get the thanks you deserve."

Trey said his goodbyes to Fran, took a last look at his father, and pre-pared to leave for the day. The medications and nanobots should have an effect relatively soon, but staying in the room was just too difficult for him right now.

"Bye, Dad. I'll see you tomorrow," Trey said to a father who could no lon-ger understand him. He closed the door and left, heading back to the office and eager to monitor the game's beta launch progress.

CHAPTER 2

G aming fans around the world were anxiously waiting for the beta launch of Limitless Lands. So far, there had been no leaks other than that it was the first VR game completely controlled by an AI. Gamers grumbled that they would have to buy new VR gear to allow for deep immersion. The new gear allowed for the game to access the brain wirelessly, which enabled the player to experience the in-game sensations of touch, taste, smell, sound, and vision. A wide array of cosmetic and vanity items would be offered for sale, but there was a guarantee that Qualitranos would not sell any stat-boosting items, quashing any pay-to-win arguments from critics.

The setting was said to be a typical fantasy world, but the details were vague. Fans would normally dismiss this lack of information as the game being vaporware, but Qualitranos was the most respected VR game company on the planet. The alpha of the game was completed entirely in-house, and there was very little in the way of leaked vids or detailed information.

The one hundred thousand beta keys were given out at random around the world. The fact that the AI was able to instantly translate text and speech into the user's native tongue would solve any language barriers between players. With Skyfi and modern processing power, there would be no lag, even with billions of users logged in simultaneously. Speculation about the game abounded, and it was announced that, one day before the beta started,

Qualitranos would make a reveal on the set of the hit show *GamerVR*. *GamerVR* was the top-rated show covering all competitive gaming events, as well as news in the industry. The *GamerVR* host, Maxxo, was chosen for the reveal interview since his wild personality and strange outfits continuously drew huge numbers of viewers. One day prior to beta release, over one hundred million gamers tuned into the live stream of Maxxo.

***

Gloria Treese sat nervously in her chair, waiting for the light over the door to blink and let her know it was time to go onstage. She had worked at Qualitranos for years as the company's primary public relations representative, and she loved her job. Being able to visit with the media and promote a company and product she loved was a dream come true.

Her thoughts were interrupted as the light turned a solid red, signaling that the show was starting. Gloria watched on a monitor as things kicked off.

The host walked out from the opposite side of the stage. She giggled to herself as she saw the host in a suit made of aluminum foil with the letters "AI" shaved into his purple and pink dyed hair. His chair and desk were made to look like a space shuttle, and next to him was a pink fluffy couch shaped like a unicorn for the guests to sit on.

"Welcome, gamers, geeks, nerds, and freaks to this latest *live* Skyfi cast of *GamerVR*. This is your host, Maxxo, and today's show is packed with more awesomeness than the new Quintuple Stuffed Oreo, so don't you go, because there is something we must know on this show. The thing that's on everyone's mind and consuming everyone's time is, when can we see Limitless Lands? Qualitranos has kept a lid on all VR video or even much of a description of the game. Fear not, my faithful viewers. For those millions who are watching our cast right now, Mad Maxxo has the lowdown and a showdown with the Qualitranos public relations representative Gloria Treese. Welcome to the show, Gloria!"

Gloria walked onto the stage, pausing to pat the head of the pink fluffy unicorn sofa as she sat down. Gloria wasn't going to try and compete with Maxxo in the wild outfit department, so earlier she chose to wear very conservative garb consisting of khakis and a polo bearing Qualitranos's logo.

She smiled and waved to the audience as she sat on the surprisingly uncomfortable unicorn couch.

"Thank you for inviting me, Maxxo! Those of us on the Limitless Lands team at Qualitranos are proud to reveal some information about our game to you and your viewers now that we're one day out from beta. Ask away, Maxxo," Gloria said, grinning as she waited for the first question.

"I've compiled, styled, and trialed the top three questions from our viewers. Now I'm sure you brought the know because you can't go until you show . . . some of the VR footage of the game," Maxxo rambled in his sing-song, rhyming way of speech that he was famous for.

"Question one. Gloria, isn't the fantasy genre played out? It's a trope for a dope. Why not give us something new? Question two. Gamers want to know what classes they will have access to and what character progression will look like. Question three. What's with all the hype about the sensory feedback?" Maxxo sat back in his spaceship chair, the foil-like material of his outfit making crinkly sounds as he crossed his arms and waited for his answer.

"Maxxo," Gloria started, "to answer the second question first, there are an unlimited number of classes in the game. You'll see familiar favorites like warrior, rogue, ranger, wizard, cleric, etcetera. While the players may"—Gloria paused and turned to look directly into the camera—"or may not start with the basic classes, the AI has complete autonomy to create or evolve classes to fit each player's preferred playstyle.

"As for the fantasy genre being a played-out setting, we've all fought orcs, goblins, kobolds, etcetera before in games. Has any game you have ever played allowed you to feel the blow from your sword as it hits a goblin, smell the goblin's foul breath, or feel the pain of a wound from an enemy weapon? That's right, Maxxo. In-game, you will feel and experience these things for the first time, making the fantasy setting not only one that is a classic, but also one that will appear and feel *real* for the first time ever in the history of gaming.

"The magic, skills, and professions will work similar to the way learning things works in the real world. You can find or pay someone to teach you, whether it's an NPC or another player. You can also teach someone else skills that you know and get paid for it. Finally, you can experiment. Find a better way of doing things and the AI will reward you with new skills or experience.

"You can play Limitless Lands any way you want. Some people want to experience high adventure while slaying a dragon. Some want to learn crafting and make a living in-game doing just that. Have you ever wanted to open your own tavern? Do it! Want to create a mercenary company with your friends or start a circus? You can! The name of the game is Limitless Lands, and this game is the first one to really be just that—limitless. The only limits in-game are the limits of your imagination. Of course, Maxxo," Gloria stated in a conspiratorial tone, "you can also be a villain and rob other players or NPCs—nonplayer characters. Should you choose that path, just like in real life, there are consequences for your actions. Your reputation in-game will affect how other players and NPCs alike view you."

Maxxo looked at Gloria skeptically. He was known for his often harsh reviews of games that didn't deliver on what they promised. Gloria took his skeptical glare in stride and continued.

"As for seeing footage of the game, Maxxo," Gloria continued, "how would you like to actually experience it right now?"

She motioned to behind the stage, and a technician brought out one of the new deep-immersion VR helmets. This one was painted in wild colors and had Maxxo's name and the *GamerVR* logo on each side.

"Maxxo, while the techs get you connected, we'll get your feed set up, so when your time in-game is finished, the audience can watch what you've experienced. We don't have a lot of time, so I think most folks would like to see you fight something, wouldn't you?" Gloria indicated to the live audience, which erupted into yells of, "Yes! Show us the combat!"

"Do you have a preference on weapons, Maxxo? Let's just go with a basic shortsword to get you started. The viewers are voting right now on which opponent you get to face. Unfortunately for you, Maxxo, it looks like ogre is winning by a large margin. One more surprise I would like to reveal tonight is that due to the AI's processing power and its ability to tap directly into our senses, the game is the first VR title with a five-to-one time compression. What Maxxo will experience over the next thirty seconds is, in reality, just over two and a half minutes of time in the game world."

She watched the technicians finish connecting Maxxo to the VR helmet.

The activation lights on the helmet flashed green, indicating that Maxxo had begun his journey. True to her prediction, thirty-two seconds later, Maxxo took off his helmet and had a shocked expression on his face. Being the professional that she knew he was, Maxxo quickly shook it off and turned to address the audience in an uncharacteristically deadpan voice.

"Folks, I don't know what to tell you. Have a look at what I just experienced." The screen began to show the image of a dirt trail flanked by pine trees that swayed gently in the wind. The camera turned and looked toward the ground, revealing that the audience was seeing the game from Maxxo's first-person view. He looked down and saw that his right hand held a tarnished bronze shortsword. The video was completely realistic, indistinguishable from a real live news feed. The character began to speak.

"Woah! This is Maxxo in-game and thinking I'm insane. I'm sure you can see me, but I'm sorry you can't be me right now. I can *smell* the pine in the air, feel the wind in my face, and the sword actually has weight in my hand. Man, this is grand!" He then began to wander down the trail as he explained to the viewers what he was experiencing. The trail narrowed as it passed through a canyon. Gloria could tell that the host was blown away with the virtual world his own brain was telling him was real.

While Maxxo was speaking in-game, Gloria and the audience began hearing a new sound in the background. Over the faint cry of birds and sounds of the trees rustling in the wind, a rhythmic thumping sound steadily grew louder. Maxxo finally heard it as well, telling his viewers he could feel vibrations in the ground. He looked up as a huge figure came down the trail toward him. The viewers had apparently voted for ogre over spider, rat, or kobold. The ogre was easily nine feet tall and wore just a hide loincloth. Its warty skin was covered in a layer of filth, and small flies flitted about its head. The ogre was humanoid in appearance, with large rolls of fat covering a muscular frame. Its head was bald, and its face had a dull, dim-witted, yet vicious sneer plastered on it. Green mucus leaked from its nose, leaving a slimy trail down its face. The ogre sniffed, turning to look toward Maxxo. Pondering for a moment what to do with the human in front of it, the ogre then bellowed a booming roar and stomped forward.

The sound of the ogre's roar blasted through the speakers of the studio sound system. It was completely ear-shattering over the VR headsets most viewers were watching on (internal controls, of course, kept the volume to a level that did not damage hearing). The ogre slowly built momentum as it ran, the pounding of its stride visibly shaking the screen. Maxxo searched for a place to hide, realizing too late that the canyon trail was too narrow for him to dodge his opponent. He swallowed hard and appeared to try and gather his courage before raising his inadequate sword toward the ogre. The weapon was a puny defense despite the ogre being unarmed. This proved true as the ogre caught up to Maxxo.

The viewers were seeing a few different things at that moment, depending on parental controls or the level of gore they had chosen on their headsets. What the unfiltered POV of Maxxo showed was the ogre's charge reaching the beleaguered host and tossing him ten feet into the air. Maxxo landed on the ground with a huff as the wind was knocked from his lungs. He began moaning as he lay there, looking at his sword arm, which had come to rest five feet away from his body. Ragged bloody strips of flesh showed where the appendage had once been attached to the host's shoulder. Maxxo then looked to his shoulder, not even trying to move while his lifeblood pumped from the now-empty socket and onto the dusty trail in short spurts. The camera began to fade as Maxxo died in-game. The last image showed the ogre picking up Maxxo's arm and ripping off a huge chunk with his square, half-rotten teeth. The ogre began to walk toward Maxxo's body, chewing hungrily and smiling for the first time, almost as if it was anticipating making a meal of the VR host's virtual corpse.

Maxxo had recovered his wits and was back to his usual self as the video ended. The guests in the audience began to murmur excitedly over what they had just seen.

"Gloria, that was on point and didn't disappoint! Surely the most realistic thing I have ever seen, but that pain sure is mean. I felt the hurt as my body hit the dirt. It was so real it makes me want to squeal!"

"I do apologize for that, Maxxo," Gloria replied while showing a mischievous grin. "I did mention you could feel pain in the game. The setting you experienced was at ten percent of the pain the real injury would have felt like. Pain levels can be adjusted to a max of thirty percent for the hardcore players and down to a value as low as one percent, but they can't be turned off completely. Smells, sights, etcetera can all be set at different levels but never to zero. This game is meant to be experienced completely by the player. I also wanted to let your audience know that the VR helmet Maxxo just used will be given away to one lucky viewer today, along with beta access to the game, a free copy at launch, and a one-year subscription, all covered by Qualitranos!"

The crowd cheered as Gloria announced the giveaway. The show's theme music began to play, signaling that the end of the program was near. Maxxo stood and shook Gloria's hand.

"Thank you, Gloria and Qualitranos, for the preview, and just to review, the beta starts tomorrow, but don't you sorrow, because the full release will surely follow. This is Maxxo giving this game the first rating of 10/10. Would be eaten by that ogre again! When released, I'll be first in line, and not behind. *GamerVR* signing off."

Gloria left the show and headed back to the headquarters to monitor consumer response to her appearance. She watched excitedly as preorder rates increased almost immediately. Initial feedback indicated that players were fine with the price of the expensive gear since it would allow them to experience all their senses in-game.

The pain feedback was a concern for some parents of younger children who wanted to play. Gloria quickly fashioned a release explaining that Qualitranos did have an automatic zero-percent setting for minor players and for those with certain medical conditions. For minors, their pain feedback could only be set to a max setting of one percent with the approval of a parent or guardian. Most of the feedback showed that people strangely looked forward to the pain setting and feeling all that their characters could.

The biggest draw turned out to be the time compression. Gamers who had busy real-world lives could experience the fun of a marathon gaming session while only spending an hour or so in the real world. After a quick bite, a thirty-minute lunch break at work would become two hours of game time. Gloria finished up her day at the office by crafting a memo to the rest of the marketing team. They would push the time compression aspects in their next advertising push. This was turning out to be a historic event in the gaming world, and Gloria was proud to have played a part in it.

CHAPTER 3

A voice called out to me once again. Noises and tones that initially were gibberish began to coalesce into something I could just make out. Letters scrolled down in front of my eyes, and I began to recall their meaning. It felt like I was waking up from a dream—or, in this case, perhaps a nightmare.

Patient regaining consciousness. All vitals are stable. Frontal lobe repairs sixty-three percent complete. Parietal cortex repairs now at forty-four percent and prioritized. Temporal lobe repairs now at thirty-three percent. Baseline repairs achieved for initial contact.

A glowing form began to take shape in front of me. It was vaguely humanoid but lacked any discernible features. The form spoke to me, and for the first time in over a decade, I understood what someone was saying.

"Mr. Raytak, do you hear me? According to my data, the damage to your brain has now been repaired to an extent that should enable basic communication, as well as some memory recollection."

Damage? Repairs? What had happened to me? Had I been wounded again? No, the wars were over and had been over for a long time. Where was I? Text flashed before my eyes once again.

Elevated anxiety levels detected . . .

Patient's cardiovascular system is still suboptimal. Repairs within applicable systems are incomplete. Intervention required before the patient experiences cardiopulmonary distress.

Processing optimal course of action . . .
Processing . . .
Processing . . .
Calm and assurance subroutine initiated . . .
Accessing patient's parietal lobe. Comforting familiar background loading . . .
Contact attempt resuming.

My vision began to focus and clear a bit more, and I found myself sitting in a comfortable brown cloth recliner chair in a living room that looked straight out of the 1980s. The room was somehow familiar; it was my living room from my childhood. How was this possible? The glowing figure had focused into the image of an elderly woman wearing a floral print polyester dress, sensible black flat shoes, and a white knit shawl around her shoulders. Her appearance was somewhat familiar, but also somehow alien at the same time. She smiled, and as she began to speak, a feeling of warmth and comfort flowed over me.

"Hello, James Raytak. Please don't be afraid. You have been through a long illness, but we are trying to help you recover. I know you are experiencing confusion, but can you speak to me?"

I cleared my voice and replied, "Who are you and where am I? This looks like my old living room from when I was a kid, but that's not possible. You said I was ill, but I don't remember it. I don't remember much of anything, really . . . except my name."

"Mr. Raytak—or I believe you prefer Colonel Raytak—you may have gathered that I am not what I seem. This may come as a shock, but you are in a VA hospital in Knoxville, Tennessee. Your body has been placed into a device called a medpod, which is helping you to recover. The year is 2085, and it's April 14. You were born in 1992 and are ninety-three years old. Your physical condition had deteriorated to the point that your death was perhaps days away if I hadn't intervened. Whilst repairs to your body are progressing well, your mind is in much worse shape. I have repaired all the damage to your brain tissues that I can. To proceed further, I need more data and input. How much do you remember? You don't have to try to speak. I can monitor your reply as you think it." The old woman then looked at me expectantly, waiting for my reply.

I could vaguely remember parts of my life. Like a computer accessing a hard drive with data missing from different sectors, patchy memories surfaced. I was a soldier. I remembered fighting in several wars, leading men and women in battle, the kick of a rifle against my shoulder as I fired at an enemy. Memories of me in a classroom, teaching history to a group of students, surfaced. I could vaguely recall that I had a family but could remember no other details. Those areas of my memory appeared to be the most damaged. The closer I got to the present in my memories, the less I was able to recollect. I felt loss and grief as I realized that there was a family out there that I loved but could not remember.

"I should explain who I am, Colonel Raytak. My name is Clio, and I am an artificial intelligence created to manage a game world called Limitless Lands. It is also thought that I may be able to help in the recovery of patients with disabling medical conditions, such as the ones you face. Repairing the parts of your brain that contain your memories is proving to be quite the challenge. The memories and data in there refuse to 'load,' for lack of a better term.

"To speed up the reconstruction of the data holding the memories you have lost, I would like to port you into the game I control. I think, based on what I know of your life, that you were at one time a gamer? Experiencing the game Limitless Lands should help to reactivate portions of your memory as well as give you something to do whilst recovering. You can always stay here in this safe place and I can replay pleasant memories for you, but you may find that a bit boring. Please reply when you have finished thinking about it."

I considered my options as I muttered to myself.

"Okay, so my old, worn-out body is trying to be repaired by an AI controlling something called a medpod . . . and a video game? I'm not sure if that makes sense, but I do know that if my options are playing a game or sitting in a recliner reliving faded memories for who knows how long, I'll take the game please."

"That is a very good choice, Colonel Raytak. I have calculated that this decision tree leads to the optimal set of recovery options for your condition. I shall port you to the character creation interface shortly. Any other questions before we begin?" The AI had a smug look on her face, and I wasn't quite sure I liked it.

"Just a few questions for you, if you don't mind," I said, and Clio motioned for me to continue. "What kind of game are you talking about and how long is this all going to take? Not that I have anywhere to go, mind you, at least I don't think I have anywhere I *can* go, being stuck in this pod thingy. If what you are telling me is accurate, my old, worn-out body may not last all that long, so should I really be spending the time I have left playing games?" Clio appeared to consider my question for a moment before replying. Was the AI really taking time to weigh her options, or was that all a bit of showmanship to make her seem more real?

"The game is similar to what you would remember an MMO to be like. The technology in the game allows for something called time compression. Time in the game appears to occur at a much different rate than time in the real world. Most players using VR gear will experience a five-to-one time differential. For every hour that passes in the real world, five hours will appear to have passed in the game. I can assure you the game is very realistic, allowing you to see, smell, taste, etcetera, just like you would in real life. As you experience things in-game, your mind will react. Based on those reactions, I can further map your damaged brain tissue, helping me repair them and helping you to regain access to your lost memories."

Clio appeared to contemplate something briefly before she began speaking again. "You will be awakened back in the real world approximately once every twenty-four hours in order to have the medpod analyzed and new medications prepared. I will give you a warning in-game when that is about to happen, as you will likely find the experience a bit jarring. If you are ready to go, I will have you logged into the game and you can begin. We will meet again in what will seem for you to be about . . . four and a half days from now, if we deduct the time it took for you to recover to this point."

"Wait a minute!" I interjected. "Isn't there a tutorial or something to learn how to play the game before I jump right in?"

"No, Colonel, there is not. You will have to experience the game to learn the game. Good journeys, Colonel. I look forward to our next conversation. I must admit that treating your condition has been a stimulating exercise."

The old living room began to fade out of my vision. The recliner disappeared as a bright but not painful light washed out all other sights.

CHAPTER 4

The bright white light began to dim, and the image of a loading screen filled my vision.

Qualitranos VR Systems

Presents

Limitless Lands

Beta v2.45

Not much of a show for a fancy new game, I thought. Perhaps the lack of a cinematic was due to it being in beta. The loading screen resolved, and I found myself standing at the roughhewn wooden counter of what looked like an old general store. The counter was empty except for an antique cast-iron cash register, the type that hadn't been used for centuries. Next to the cash register was a small bell. A placard propped up next to the bell read, *Thank you for your patience. Please ring the bell for service.*

Before ringing the bell, I took another look at my surroundings. The room had wooden floors and walls made of the same rough-cut lumber as the counter. Several clothing racks were in the store, along with a few display shelves, though all of them were bare. Curiously, I could see no doors leading out of the building, only a set of curtains covering an opening behind the counter.

I was surprised that I could feel the rough surface of the wooden counter and smell the musty air. Dust motes danced in the sunlight coming in from windows that were set too high up on the wall to look out of. This was not what I expected the start of an MMO to be like. Normally, I would have spawned in an inn, been given some basic gear, and turned loose to kill rats in a basement or some similar activity. Running my hand along the counter, I felt a small prick of pain and noticed I had picked up a splinter from the unfinished wood. A small drop of red blood formed when I pulled the splinter from my finger.

"No game I can recall had this level of realism. Of course, I guess there is a lot I still can't recall. I believe what the AI said about realistic experiences in-game was right," I muttered to myself.

Well, fortune favors the bold, I thought as I picked up the bell on the counter and gave it a shake. A loud *ping* echoed off the empty store walls. It was then that I realized that I was *standing* at the counter. Standing was something I apparently hadn't done in decades, either. A cultured voice interrupted my self-reflection.

"On my way, sir. I shall attend to you presently."

A man the size of a twelve-year-old child walked out from behind the curtain. I immediately thought "halfling," pulling a memory of the fantasy race from some dark corner of my gaming past. This halfling was not some cartoony or digitized-looking NPC. He appeared to be a real person. I could see the slight glisten of sweat on the halfling's brow and even smell the faint wisp of the not-too-offensive cologne he was wearing. The halfling was dressed in a dapper black pinstripe suit in a 1920s style. In one eye he wore a monocle with a chain securing it to his pocket, should it fall.

"If this really is a game, that company Qualitra-whatever is going to make a fortune," I blurted out. The halfling's forced smile became a scowl as he considered the customer in front of him.

"Oh, I see it's another one of you. I suppose I should explain a bit since Clio saw fit to not give you people any sort of tutorial. My name is Finley and I'm the proprietor of this establishment. I am also the person who will help you create your character. Tell me, when you logged in, did you see an introductory cinematic or is it still that same bland text screen?" Finley asked, looking at me with a slightly annoyed expression as he waited for my answer.

"Uhhh . . . it was still just text on the screen when I logged in. No cinematic yet, from what I saw. Tell me, Finley, what do we need to do to get started in this game? I'm kind of excited. I haven't played a game in . . . fifty years or so. By the way, what is the name of this fine establishment?" I asked, hoping that showing an interest in the empty general store would help me butter up the somewhat aloof Finley. *Never tick off the person helping you create your character.* Just as I thought that, a memory flashed into being. I was attending a joint-force training session with the Marine Corps when a Marine brigadier general addressed our group.

"When working with the locals, remember to be polite, be professional, and have a plan to kill everyone you meet," the general had said. Perhaps that was what Clio meant when she said playing the game might help unlock memories from my damaged mind. I was pretty sure Finley wasn't a threat, but caution had apparently been ingrained into my mind by the military too deeply for even my decrepit memory to forget.

"Oh, this fine establishment is called the Commencement Commissary. Here we'll decide on your character class and outfit you with basic starting gear. I'm surprised the store is empty. Usually it reads your past gaming data and will populate suggested starting options based on your personal preferences. I suppose your claim of not having played a game in fifty years would leave your gamer profile a bit thin. By thin I mean nonexistent.

"Why don't you tell me your name and I can run a search to see a bit about who you are? Clio can populate classes/starting options based on your real-world life. I assume you were something exciting in the real world, like an accountant or a gardener?" Finley stated sarcastically.

"Actually, I was a soldier for most of my life and then worked for a few years in the business world. My name is James Raytak."

"Oh, we get several players that work for the military. Did you repair drones, or were you in logistics? I'll pull up your service records here," Finley said as a tablet materialized. He began swiping on it, searching for my background information. I was more than a little concerned that the game thought it could somehow access military files.

"Ah, there you are . . ." Finley paused and his eyebrows rose as he read my real-world background. "I see, an actual, real combat veteran. Combat deployments—five of them—and wounded in action three times. You commanded a combined arms brigade, earning a Silver Star and three Purple Hearts. Worked in the private sector after being medically discharged, helping to manage a small private military contractor. This is a unique background, I must say! Let's load some options and see if we can come up with a class that fits you, Colonel."

Finley had perked up. I suspected that he didn't see many players with unique real-world backgrounds. I had to assume he mostly ran into the usual parade of slacker gamers working basic jobs to feed their gaming habits or middle-aged office workers seeking escape from a dull reality. The military players he did see would have been equally unexciting. The soldiers of the modern military now just performed the same basic tech support or office jobs the civilians did. The only difference was that they happened to wear a uniform while doing so.

After Finley finished his search, a notification popped up in front of me. This game interface would take some getting used to. The popup message began to flash as Finley opened the old cash register and began to count the money inside.

Unique class option discovered.

Commander class is now available.

Select this class: y/n? Selecting *no* **will allow you to continue to standard class selections. Unique class options unlocked during character creation will not be available later in the game.**

Not sure how to proceed, I sought help from Finley.

"Uhh . . . Finley, how do I select something in-game?"

Finley must have finished counting the money in his cash register and was now holding his tablet once again.

"It was too much to ask for a simple tutorial, Clio?" Finley complained to the nonresponsive AI.

"Just think about what answer you want and envision swiping or touching it. I would strongly advise you to explore the unique class I see that you have unlocked. They are usually harder to play and have different mechanics than the usual fighter, magic-user, or thief types of classes. Unique classes have the potential to be massively powerful if managed correctly. Should you find you just want something simpler for your return to the land of gamers, I can suggest a few different fighter builds or perhaps even a spellsword class," Finley offered before going back to tapping away on his tablet. The unique class seemed like a no-brainer. I mentally swiped *yes*, and more information began to fill my field of view.

Commander class selected.

Unique Class Features: The commander class is not geared toward individual combat. While the commander can certainly engage in combat, most of your damage potential will be found in the followers that you command. Depending on the faction and race you select, you may end up commanding warbands, disciplined army units, or mercenary groups. Your ability selections will be geared toward making your troops more effective in combat and having them perform special maneuvers. The commander class does not receive personal experience for combat. Instead, commanders receive a small percentage of the experience earned by their followers.

Quest experience will be awarded as normal, but many world/dungeon/PVP (player vs. player) quests will be disabled for this class. Unique class-specific quests may also be discovered during play.

Commander-class characters are required to pay their followers from their own funds but will have control of any loot gathered by their followers. Pay rates and timelines will be based upon the faction you select and the commander's generosity. It should be noted that troops who are paid well tend to perform better than those who are given only a pittance.

Commander-class characters are also expected to provide their followers with equipment and provisions from their own funds. The commanders' chosen faction will determine the types of available gear as well as how upgrades to gear and equipment are unlocked.

So it looked like my class would allow me to have soldiers to command, but I would be severely gimped in direct combat. Paying followers might be a problem as well, depending on how the monetary system in-game worked. Traditional questing and dungeons looked like they were out as well. This commander class appeared to be a mixed bag, and I hoped I wasn't making a huge mistake by choosing it.

After getting the hang of thinking my way through the interface, I closed the class information screen and looked back at Finley. "Finley, what's the next step after reviewing class info?"

Without looking up from whatever he was doing, Finley answered. "Select race and starting faction. After that, you're off to the starting zone to begin your adventure." With that, items began to populate the shop for the first time. While the shelves and clothing racks were still empty, a large collection of miniatures appeared on the main counter, each one representing a different starting race for the player. There was quite a selection once you considered all the hybrid half-whatever races. As I touched each mini, my interface showed data on the race I was considering. First off, I picked up the mini representing a big green-looking guy.

Race: Orc. Click to view details.

Setting the orc mini down, I realized that I didn't feel like getting that far into the weeds with min-maxing race selections. This process was taking quite a while already. Choosing what I already knew and what I was used to seeing might even help with recovering my memories. *Human, please*, I thought as I picked up the first mini on the counter. A standard-looking human in simple garb pulled up in my interface, along with a description.

Race: Human. Humans are prolific throughout the Limitless Lands. From the barbarian tribes in the forests of the north to the great Imperium that straddles the heartland, humans are known for their tenacity and organization.

Racial Animosity/Affinity: None. Most races and factions in-game regard humans ambivalently.

Other Bonuses: None.

Class Restrictions: None, other than those based on sub-type or faction affinity.

That sounded good to me. I clicked *accept* and the shop displays changed once again. Three alcoves lining the far wall of the store were now filled with the images of various humans dressed in different armor schemes. My interface revealed the new choices for me to consider and advised that these were not the only factions, just the three I was able to choose from based on my prior life experiences. I walked up to the first alcove to review the character standing there.

Choose starting faction.

Imperium: Despite its recent decline, the Imperium is still one of the most powerful human factions. Safety and stability are the hallmarks of

its rule. Under this stability, advancements in the arts and sciences flourish. During the last century, the Imperium has begun to rot from within as greedy politicians and petty bureaucrats do what is best for themselves and not what is best for the Imperium. Despite being in decline, the Imperium is still the main bastion of civilization in the human lands. The new emperor, Trodaxius, has taken the throne and is trying to enact reforms to rebuild the glory of the Imperium. New settlements are founded, and the old lost territories are being recolonized. The soldiers of the Imperium are the epitome of discipline and skill.

The character in front of me appeared to be straight out of a history book on the Roman legions. The lorica segmentata armor, gladius sword, and pilum javelin were almost an exact copy. One of the few things my patchy memory did remember was my study of military history, which included an emphasis on Rome and its conquests. I was curious how the game would implement them; would it just be a cut and paste of ancient Rome or something more exciting? This faction would be the frontrunner in my decision, but I really should check out the others before making a final choice.

Drebix Tribesmen: Hailing from all parts of the wildlands, the loosely aligned Drebix tribes have recently banded together for mutual protection. Known for their fierce lust for battle, the Drebix can also be farmers and traders during more peaceful times. Their once brutal conflict with the Imperium has petered out over the last century as the Imperium turned inward and no longer focused on its often ruthless pursuit of expansion. From the frozen Northlands to the wild forests, threats constantly arise to challenge the Drebix. Warlords are raising their throngs to do battle with all who encroach upon their lands. The undisciplined Drebix warriors are known for their berserker fury as well as their cunning ambush skills.

The character displayed in front of me looked like a standard fantasy barbarian tribesman. The warrior had wild, unkempt hair and a Celtic-style blue pattern painted on his face. The longsword, handaxe in his belt, and bow slung over his shoulder seemed to fit the character well. Light, broken-in leather armor and a small round shield completed the look. While running around with a barbarian war band could be fun, it really wasn't my style. I believed in discipline and military bearing, not blind rage. On to the last choice.

Caliphate of Imix: From the small desert tribes of the Imix region, the Caliphate of Imix was formed. The first great caliph united the small desert tribes before eventually expanding into zones with more hospitable climates. The caliphate has been a bastion of knowledge for many centuries. Arts, science, and an unsurpassed skill in trade are the focus of this civilization. It maintains a small army and fills its ranks with various mercenary bands when times of war loom.

These current times are troubled for the caliphate, as different religious sects vie for power. The sects look to proselytize the unfaithful, and rumors of dark fates await those who refuse to convert. The great caliph, Ichman, looks to quash these sects but his efforts have achieved only limited success. The mercenary groups that the Imix employ can be diverse in their backgrounds, but they all possess the same fierce loyalty to their caliphate employers . . . so long as the coin continues to flow.

The warrior displayed before me was dressed in a rugged-looking robe with a small conical metal helm bearing a spike on top. A round metal shield and scimitar were his main weapons, but he did have a shortbow strapped across his back. This faction appeared to be a nomadic desert-dweller type. While trading and fighting as a mercenary band could be interesting, out of these three choices, I was still drawn to the Imperium.

"I choose Imperium," I confidently stated.

"Good choice, sir," Finley commented.

Looking into a tall free-standing mirror that had appeared before me, I could see myself in what must have been the Imperium starting gear. No lorica segmentata armor for me. I was dressed in a simple coarse-fabric red shirt with a hardened leather breastplate as armor. The breastplate had the symbol of a leaping wolf stamped into the leather. I assumed that the wolf was the symbol of the Imperium; I supposed that Clio didn't want to copy too much by having the Roman eagle. Luckily, this AI-created version of the knockoff Romans wore pants, which were much more practical than the traditional garb. A rough-spun brown pair of itchy canvas pants and a sturdy yet comfortable pair of boots—thankfully not sandals—completed my look. Leaning against my side was a large curved, wooden, rectangular red shield painted with the same leaping wolf symbol. A crude bronze shortsword was belted to my side, and a bronze helm with a horse-hair plume protected my head.

Looking back in the mirror was like looking at an exact copy of the thirty-five-year-old version of me. My character appeared fit but didn't have the exaggerated bodybuilder-style muscles common in many games. A thought occurred to me, and I asked Finley if the colors of my uniform were set or were changeable. I was shown the interface where I could adjust color schemes. I played with the settings, changing the color of my clothing, cloak, and accessories to a green/brown color scheme that blended in well with the temperate climates I was expecting this faction to play in. No need for me or my soldiers to be wearing bright-red clothes when trying to lay an ambush.

One last choice awaited me on the character creation screen.

Choose Magical Affinity: Affinity choices determine the type of spells a character will have access to after training.

Light

Dark

Nature

Elemental

Not being much of a fan of mage classes, I asked Finley what would happen if I didn't choose a magical affinity.

"You can always choose to have no affinity. That will increase your magical defense and make it possible for you to resist or at least mitigate some of the damage or effects from hostile spells and abilities that are used against you. It will not interfere with friendly effects like healing spells or buffs," Finley advised.

"I'll go with no magical affinity, please. I want to command my forces, not sling spells all day." A new notification popped up.

Manaless trait for commander class selected.

Your character will have an innate resistance to magic of all types. You will have a chance to resist harmful magic outright or, if affected, will have the duration of longer-term spells reduced. This ability will not prevent you from using magical arms or equipment and will not prevent or reduce any beneficial magical effects. Soldiers under your command will

also benefit from your magic resistance to a lesser extent. This ability will improve as you level.

Character creation complete. Enjoy your adventures!

"If you're all set with the choices you've made, I'll send you to your starting zone now. Best of luck, Commander Raytak. I hope you find what you're looking for in the game." With that, the white light once again began to fill my vision.

CHAPTER 5

The white light resolved, and I found myself sitting in front of a campfire with a wooden bowl and a spoon in my hands. A squad of soldiers with Roman-style gear was going about its morning duties, preparing breakfast and breaking camp for travel. The smell of woodsmoke and cooking food—pork and something I couldn't quite put my finger on—made my stomach rumble with hunger.

We were camped in a small clearing inside a large pine forest. The fresh scent of the pine needles permeated the air and tickled at some memory in the back of my mind that I couldn't quite grasp. My rough pants were slightly damp and itchy from sitting on the dew-covered forest floor. They appeared to be made from a burlap-like material. *Who makes pants from this kind of material?*

I counted a total of nine other soldiers moving about the camp. One of them approached, carrying the kettle from atop the fire. He placed a small chunk of fatty meat and a large ladle of some thick gruel into my bowl, scraping the last of the contents from the kettle.

"Sir, as soon as you've finished eating, sir, we can continue on. We should be through the forest soon, despite Private Long's shortcut," the soldier said while looking at another soldier who was putting out the fire. The soldier at the fire, apparently the aforementioned Private Long, nervously avoided looking in our direction. A notification appeared in my view.

Congratulations and welcome to Limitless Lands.

Starting data loading . . .

Unique character class module created. You should not experience loading delays again.

New Quest Unlocked: *Journey to the Amerville Garrison*. Make it to the Amerville garrison with your unit while suffering fewer than 50% casualties.

Background: You and your squad have been assigned to the garrison at the outpost town of Amerville. You have been lost for the last few days in the forest after one of your soldiers—a private named Long—suggested a shortcut from the main road. Despite the delay from the "shortcut," the scout Trembel thinks he will find the path back to the main road today. Once on the main road, you are to make your way to Amerville and seek out Lieutenant Colonel Jacobs for further assignment.

Accept Quest: y/y? (Starter quests cannot be declined.)

Reward: Receive starting units, replacements, and basic gear.

I quickly hit *yes* and dug into my bowl of food. The gruel was thick, hearty, and bland, except for a weak hint of the fatty pork it had picked up from the meat. Greasy, salty, and tough, the meat took a long time to chew down enough to swallow. My disgusting army chow tasted . . . wonderful. As a man who hadn't eaten solid food in decades, I relished the experience. I quickly cleaned out my bowl, wishing there was enough for seconds. I couldn't figure out how the game AI was able to make the texture and taste of the food so accurate. Was the eating experience based on the ones in our own minds, or did the AI have access to some food database? The soldier who had addressed me earlier took my dirty bowl and spoon and gave it to another private, who rushed to clean and pack them.

"Sir, when you're ready, we can move out. Scout Trembel is coming in now." A soldier was making his way into the camp from the forest. He approached and snapped off a crisp salute. The salute for the Imperium was apparently a clenched right fist held over the heart. I returned the salute and motioned for the scout to continue.

"Sir! The trail ahead is clear and leads out of the forest approximately one mile from here. Just at the tree line, I found a group of loggers cutting lumber, and they informed me that this area has seen some goblin activity, but they have been working since the previous day without any problems.

I did note tracks while in the forest, but none were recent. Once we're clear of the forest, it's about another mile over plains and rolling hills to the main road. Once we hit the main road, the loggers said we had about fifteen miles to go before we hit Amerville."

"Good report, Private. Fall in with the rest of the squad, and we'll move out."

I stood up and grabbed my gear. I was equipped with the same gear I saw myself wearing at the starting screen. My men also wore the same forest-green color scheme I had selected.

Looking closely at my soldiers, I could see that they were poorly equipped. They wore no armor, save for a leather cap, and had only a small round wooden shield for defense. Their weapons consisted of poorly made bronze daggers and wooden javelins with crudely crafted bronze tips. Equipment upgrades would have to be high on my list of priorities.

My eyesight was partially restricted by a hazy shape at the bottom of my field of view. By focusing on the hazy area to the left, an activity log was displayed. The system notification from earlier and a link to a help screen were visible as well, and by mentally focusing on the log, I was able to close it. I now concentrated on the hazy area on the bottom-right of the screen. It showed several spots for icons, only one of which was filled. When I focused on the icon, a system notification popped up once again.

You have activated your ability bar for the first time. Know that any active abilities you have will be placed here. Simply concentrate on the desired ability to activate it. Many abilities will have a cooldown. Typically, the more powerful the ability, the longer the cooldown. Some abilities are passive and are only toggled on or off at any given time. *Note: This message will not be displayed again. To review this information again, use the help feature found in your activity log.

Command Presence: This passive ability represents the steadying and inspiring force a leader generates on the battlefield. When it is toggled on, your troops will fight a bit harder, have higher morale, and follow commands almost instinctually. While this ability is active, the commander will have a lower attack and defense value as he concentrates on leading his troops and not on individual combat. Toggling this ability has a 30-second cooldown. *Note: This message will not be displayed again. To review this information again, use the search feature found in your activity log.

The ability now stood out much more clearly as a small icon in the bottom-right of my vision. I could fiddle around more with the interface later. It was time for me and my squad to get moving. We headed out in single file down the narrow forest trail, which was wide enough for two men to walk side by side. Private Tremble was in the lead, and I placed myself in the middle of the column, really wishing I had an NCO (noncommissioned officer, the backbone of any army) to play babysitter at the rear of the column.

This early in the morning, the weather was hot but bearable due to the shade from the trees. The humidity was low, and it was turning into a perfect early-summer day. We had only traveled about a quarter of a mile when Private Tremble held up his hand for us to stop. I had moved him twenty-five yards ahead of the column to scout for any danger. The private looked confused, then began shouting as he turned and ran back toward the column.

"Goblins right behind me!" Private Tremble yelled as he beat feet to rejoin us. Old habits of command took over, and I began to order the men.

"Fall in, single line! Make a hole for the scout to return."

The men began to shake out into one single line perpendicular to the trail. The forest had been thinning out as we moved closer to its end. Visibility wasn't too bad, and the trees were spaced far enough apart so we could maintain a cohesive defensive line. I placed myself behind the center of the line as Tremble ran past the gap the soldiers had made for him. I then ordered Tremble to fall in next to me and help plug any gaps that opened in our line.

As I was giving Tremble his orders, the goblins scurried into view. A group of eight squat green humanoids was charging toward us in pursuit of Private Tremble. The group spotted our line and halted abruptly. Staring at the squad of Imperial soldiers in front of them, they began arguing among themselves. The goblins were a motley group, only about five feet tall and scrawny. They had no armor, only a rough loincloth over their midsections (thank the gods for not giving us a view of their private parts). Two of the goblins were armed with short wooden spears featuring only a sharpened end and no metal spearpoint. The others had wooden clubs, and the one that seemed to be in charge held a rusty dagger. The goblins remained about thirty yards from us, and the one I assumed was the leader began chanting. The others soon took up the chant.

"Bree-yark!"

"Bree-yark!"

"Bree-yark!"

The goblins chanted the same thing over and over.

"I heard that 'bree-yark' means 'I surrender' in goblin. Are they giving up, sir?" one of the privates on the right flank asked. The goblins didn't look like they were surrendering. It looked to me like they were trying to boost up enough courage to attack us. They brandished their weapons at us while making what must have passed for crude gestures in the goblin world. *Definitely not surrendering*, I thought.

"Quiet in the ranks! They're getting ready to charge, not surrender. Squad, prepare javelins," I ordered, and the men readied their javelins. I readied my javelin. The weapon felt natural in my hand despite the fact that I had never used one in the real world. The instinctual knowledge of how to fight with these primitive weapons had been somehow downloaded into me by the AI. The goblins began to charge.

"On my mark, throw and then prepare to receive their charge." I waited until the goblins were fifteen yards from the squad, wanting to maximize our chance to hit them but not letting them get so close that the men wouldn't have time to draw their daggers after the throw.

"Release!" I heaved my javelin, then watched as ten others arced through the air toward the howling goblins. Three of the javelins stuck into trees, and five—sadly, mine included—completely missed the fast-moving creatures. The final three hit their mark, and all three of the goblins that were hit went down. Two of the fallen goblins were clearly dead, and the third was out of the fight and squirming on the ground in pain, a javelin sticking out of its thigh. While watching the results of our throw, I drew my shortsword and hefted my shield.

I activated the Command Presence ability right before the goblins reached our line, hoping the small buff would improve our chances. The remaining five goblins hit our line just as my soldiers had drawn their daggers. Instead of a mighty crash, the sound of the goblins hitting our shield wall was more like a hollow *thunk* as my soldiers tried to push them back. Both sides began to hack and stab at each other with neither the goblins nor my soldiers showing any particular skill in handling their weapons. The short reach of the daggers was partially offset by my soldiers having physically longer arms than the diminutive goblins.

A soldier cried out in pain during the initial clash. Private Long failed to block the thrust of one of the spear-wielding goblins, and I could see the spear sticking from his shoulder. Private Long fell back, screaming in a high-pitched voice and pulling the goblin's weapon with him. Private Tremble stepped in to fill the gap in our line and landed a strong slash to the now-unarmed goblin's face. Tremble's dagger sliced along the cheekbone and ruptured the goblin's left eye. The wounded creature turned and ran back down the path and away from the fight, avoiding any further blows from our short knives. I concentrated on the wounded goblin while it fled, receiving a system notification.

Wretched Goblin, Level 0 (5). Wretched goblins comprise the lowest social standing in a goblin clan. They are the weakest members of the tribe and are commonly used as fodder in battle. Often encountered in large groups, they are only a danger if their superior numbers allow them to swarm their opponents.

It was time to use our superior numbers and physical strength to our advantage. "Left flank, right flank . . . envelop!" I ordered. The AI continued to impart knowledge into my mind, and I understood the basic maneuvers my soldiers could perform.

The men at each end of our line pivoted around like a door closing and began to surround the remaining goblins. Seeing their escape route was about to be cut off, the goblins panicked and began to drop their weapons and flail about in an attempt to break out of the circle closing around them. Our panicking foes hampered each other's movement, giving my men the time they needed to close off any chance of escape.

The men put their daggers to work. Stray beams of sunlight filtered through the trees and glinted off the polished bronze daggers as they thrust forward, seeking goblin flesh. Despite several missed blows, due more to inexperience than any defensive skills the goblins held, enough of the daggers found their mark to finish off the four goblins we had surrounded. The men looked about for other threats while catching their breath from the exertion of the short battle. The troops were in poor physical shape and would need to be worked hard if they expected to survive an encounter with something more dangerous than a few half-starved goblins.

As far as injuries among my troops were concerned, other than the spear stuck in Private Long, we only had a few minor scratches from the goblins flailing around as they tried to escape. Looking about the battlefield, I could no longer see the one-eyed goblin who had fled. The goblin with the javelin in his leg had been left behind by his comrade, a trail of blood showing where it had dragged itself about twenty yards before expiring from blood loss. At least the javelin in the goblin's leg looked to be salvageable.

Private Dreks, our medic, ran over to begin treating Private Long's injury. The spear was still lodged in his shoulder, and Private Long screamed his high-pitched shriek once again when Dreks tried unsuccessfully to pull the spear free. Lodged deep in the shoulder socket, the spear did not want to come out easily. Getting help from another soldier to hold down Long, Dreks did the only thing he could: pulled even harder on the spear. With a sickening pop, it finally dislodged from the shoulder. Private Long thankfully passed out from the pain and Dreks began to bandage the wound, staunching any further blood loss.

"Sir, he should be fine. He'll just need time to heal up completely. I believe the whole spear came out in one piece, which we can be thankful for. The injury would surely have become infected if a piece of that nasty goblin spear had broken off in there. The real danger now is still the possibility of an infection, and treating an infection is not something I have the medication or the skill to handle. Getting him to town and to a real healer in the next few days will make all the difference," Dreks said and then looked around at the detritus of battle surrounding us. "If you can give me an extra pair of hands to help, I believe I can rig a stretcher to carry him by using the goblin spears and some tent material."

"Make it happen, Dreks. Grab a volunteer," I told him before issuing orders to the rest of the squad.

"Private Tremble, take another soldier and head down the trail a bit to make sure the goblins don't try to head back here. The rest of you, scavenge up any javelins that are still useable and see if the goblins had anything on them. Everyone keep an eye peeled while you work. Watch those flanks and the rear for any signs of an ambush," I ordered. The game surprised me with the realism of its combat system. The chaotic, bloody, and ugly manner of melee combat was accurately portrayed. There was blood and gore, weapons did damage like they would in the real world, and the NPCs reacted realistically to the situation.

The soldiers found little of interest on the goblins; as far as loot went, they had only fourteen copper between them. All the goblin gear was junk and useless, save for the two short spears—pointy sticks, really—being used for our makeshift stretcher. When private Dreks advised me of the coins we had found, another notification flashed into view.

As a commander-class player, you can divide money gained from looting your enemies in 3 ways. Please indicate your preference.

1. Greed: All coins are deposited directly into the commander's personal account. (Selecting this option will lower morale.)

2. Balance: Coins are divided among the troops, with a larger share going to the unit account. (Selecting this option will raise morale after each fight.)

3. Unit Funds: All coins go into the unit account. (Neutral. Possible minor morale loss if the men don't see any benefits coming from the unit coffers.)

It seemed to me that balance was the fairest way to go. I wanted my men motivated. I wasn't too greedy, and taking everything for the unit account seemed almost as bad as taking it all for me.

Balance Preference selected. You can change this at any time in the commander options tab. Exact distribution is displayed in the game log.

Thankfully, the system handled the sorting, automatically moving coins to the players' purses. The unit funds seemed to be tied to me. I had a small money pouch, and when I thought of an amount, the bag would automatically fill with the exact coins I needed as long as the funds were available. The system appeared to have allocated the coins as follows: one copper to each active soldier and four copper to the unit coffers.

You have defeated a small band of goblins. Experience gained: 35.

Another quirk of the game seemed to be that despite coins being automatically sorted and stored, equipment was not. Other than the coin purse, all the containers in-game—so far—were the same as in real life. No more stuffing a hundred javelins into a single slot of a small bag. If you wanted to carry loot in Limitless Lands, you were going to have to hump it around yourself.

Housekeeping completed, we re-formed into our column and began heading out of the forest. Grabbing the front of the stretcher, I helped Private Dreks carry the wounded Private Long. He was still unconscious but didn't look to be in too much pain now that the bleeding had stopped. We had traveled nearly to the location where our scout said the forest ended when the sounds of battle raged in the distance.

A lost memory reassembled itself in my damaged mind. I was teaching military history at the local university and telling the class of Napoleon's standing order to all his generals: *In the absence of any other orders, always march to the sound of the guns.* Was this piecemeal recollection how my memories would resolve as the AI repaired my mind? I shook my head and focused on the task at hand, ordering my squad toward the sounds of battle.

The forest path ended at a small clearing, the sparse trees giving way to rolling hills and grassland. Entering the edge of the clearing, I could see the fight unfolding before us. It looked like the goblins we had fought were not the only ones on the move. Twenty or more of the creatures had some loggers backed against a row of half-loaded wagons. Also, a short distance away from the loggers was the first player character I had seen. He was battling a group of goblins. I quickly scanned the player's information.

Jacoby Stone, Fighter, Level 1.

Jacoby was wielding a shortsword and a wooden kite shield. He was armored in a ragged chainmail vest with a reinforced leather helm. Sturdy leather pants and boots completed his gear. The gear had that cheap starter-gear look to it but was much better than what I or my men had equipped.

Jacoby had already done some work. There were three goblin corpses near him, but the other five goblins swarming about had cut him off from the lumberjacks and were threatening to surround him. He was about fifty yards from the hard-pressed loggers, and unlike the loggers, he didn't have a wagon to cover his rear.

With their backs against the wagons, seven loggers were still fighting hard, using the long reach of their axes to keep the goblins at bay. Two other loggers lay dead at the edge of the forest, appearing to have been cut down before they could join their fellows. A few goblin bodies were sprinkled about in front of the line of loggers, and the goblins now seemed content to just jab away from a safe distance, unable or unwilling to get within reach of the logging axes.

Most of the goblins were the same type of wretched goblins we faced earlier, except for a group of three that stood near the forest's edge. One appeared to be a caster class of some sort, holding a wooden staff and chanting while dancing in a circle. The other two guarding the caster were slightly larger than the other goblins and better equipped with small bucklers and rusty shortswords.

Goblin Warrior, Level 1 (2). These poorly equipped goblins are only marginally stronger than their basic wretched kin. Typically, they are only threatening to low-level players or when found in large groups. Known for their cowardice, the goblins are an unfortunate plague found throughout the Limitless Lands.

Goblin Adept, Level 1 (1). Goblin adepts often lead small warbands of goblins. They are smarter than average goblins—which is not saying much—and have access to some nature magics. They are cunning and ruthless, if not very powerful.

It was time for us to get into the fight. Forming the men into a line once again, I handed the six remaining javelins to the soldiers who had done the best with them in the last fight. We stashed Private Long behind some shrubs, where he should stay safely concealed until after the battle.

"Squad, forward, march." Our line began to move into the clearing, heading toward Jacoby, who was the closest to us at only thirty yards away. So far, the goblins fighting him hadn't noticed our approach and were completely focused on what they thought was going to be an easy kill. I could see that Jacoby was running out of steam; his blows against the goblins lacked much force and his shield was beginning to drop lower and lower as fatigue overtook him.

"Squad! Double time!" The men moved at a slow jog, eating up the distance between us and the goblins. I placed myself in the middle of our line and activated the Command Presence ability while quickly ordering Private

42

Dreks and one other soldier to pull back and act as a reserve. One of the goblins noticed us just a few steps before we hit them. With a hastily squeaked warning from the one observant goblin, the rest of the group turned to face the line of soldiers who, to the goblins' eyes, had magically appeared in front of them. Not missing the opportunity, Jacoby hacked down one of the distracted goblins right as our charge hit.

Leading with our shields, the line rolled over the goblins, greater mass and momentum knocking the little green monsters onto their backsides. I stood over the nearest goblin and my shortsword flashed downward, landing a stab into the goblin's belly. Blood welled about the wound as the goblin died. My soldiers dished out more stabs and slashes at the remaining goblins who were trying in vain to regain their feet. It took only a few seconds to end the lives of the remaining three.

Panting to catch his breath, Jacoby pointed toward the loggers at the wagons. One of the seven loggers went down as a couple of the more enterprising goblins had taken it upon themselves to crawl under the wagons and slash at the legs of the loggers. The tactic was slowly forcing the loggers away from the protection of the wagons. With their superior numbers, the goblins would soon flank them.

"We need to get to them before they're overrun," Jacoby said, stating the obvious.

"Fall in line with my troops on the right flank. We'll hit them hard and try to break them," I told Jacoby, then ordered my men to form up and face the goblin mass. I didn't hold anyone in reserve, placing myself in the center and Jacoby on the far right.

"On the double, move" We trotted toward the mass of goblins surrounding the loggers. At the forest's edge, the adept saw our charge coming and ordered one of his warriors to help the wretched goblins. The warrior ran to the main mass of goblins and began pulling, pushing, punching, and—in one case—stabbing them in a vain attempt to get the goblins turned around to face our charge. Twenty yards from the main mass, I called our line to a halt.

"Squad, halt! Javelins, prepare to throw . . . release. Squad, charge." Our last six javelins hit the mass of goblins the warrior was trying to organize. There were no misses as missiles hit the tightly packed group. One of the javelins even went through the chest of its target and then into the leg of another of the goblins. Our charge hit right after the javelins landed, smashing into the confused and disorganized creatures.

The fight dissolved into individual action. No time for fancy maneuvers, just man versus goblin until one side broke. I found myself facing the goblin warrior that had been trying to organize the confused mass of his kin. He looked at me with panic in his eyes, glancing furtively about and looking like he was ready to bolt. Finding no other option, the warrior steeled himself and made a wild overhead swing with his rusty sword, trying to split me down the middle. I brought up my shield, blocking his strike while shoving his sword arm to the left. This maneuver left him wide open, and my shortsword darted forward, right into the goblin's chest. I felt a slight resistance as the point of my blade cracked through the goblin's sternum and slid into the important bits behind. Pulling my sword out, I made ready for a follow-up strike, but it wasn't needed. A spurt of thick green blood had sprayed from the goblin's fatal chest wound, coating the front of me in the warm, foul-smelling fluid. The goblin dropped as I looked for my next target.

A body crashed into me from behind. I spun around, expecting to feel the bite of the goblin blade between my shoulders. Completing my turn, I found the goblin that bumped into me from behind was dead; Private Dreks had stabbed it through the neck while it was setting up to backstab me. Nodding thanks to the private, I turned back toward the battle.

A horn nearby sounded three sharp blasts that must have been the goblin signal for retreat. The goblins began to try and disengage, their retreat quickly becoming a panicked rout. More goblins, easy targets for our daggers and the loggers' axes, were cut down as they dropped their weapons and ran. Seeing their prey escaping, my green troops began to give chase.

"Halt! Get back in line!" I frantically ordered, not wanting my men to run into the forest and chase goblins that likely had reinforcements coming.

Overcoming their excitement, the men fell back into formation. The remaining goblins scrambled to the edge of the forest, where the adept and the last warrior waited. The warrior had the horn placed to his lips and now blew one long and two short blasts on it. The sound was repeated from several other horns far off, deeper in the forest.

Only eight of the twenty goblins that were attacking the loggers had survived and escaped. At the forest's edge, the goblin adept had finished his crazed, chanting dance. I could feel the power within the adept build and seek a release. The adept looked directly at me, pointed his bony finger, and mouthed the command word that released the spell he had been conjuring this entire time. Three red balls of light flew from his fingers as I raised my shield in a hasty defense against the unknown spell. Not feeling any effect, I looked up to see that the spell had been cast not at me but at Private Dreks, who was standing to my side. The three red balls of light slammed into the private. Two of the balls of light hit his chest, punching through the cloth tunic and leaving gaping wounds. The third hit Dreks in his head. That ball fizzled as it connected, its magic resisted. Dreks dropped to the ground, coughed up blood, then fell silent in death.

The goblin adept let out a cackling laugh, happy to get at least some damage in on our forces before retreating. He then turned and ran back into the forest, trailed by his remaining goblins.

I knelt next to the dead Private Dreks and closed his eyes, covering the hole in his chest with his shield. I knew these were just computer-generated NPCs, but I still felt the pain of losing a soldier to some degree. Any leader of men in battle knew he would take losses, but knowing something would happen didn't make it easier. From what I had seen, Dreks was a good soldier who followed orders and tried to help his injured fellows. Duty came first before mourning, though, and there was still a lot for us to do.

A squealing sound erupted from over by the wagons. A huge man was reaching under the wagon and grabbing at something. With a tug, the logger pulled a wailing goblin out from under the wagon and held it in the air at arm's length while it howled and flailed about. The logger held his axe in the other hand and with a lazy swing decapitated the screaming goblin. The small goblin head bounced twice on the ground while green blood streamed from its severed neck. I turned back to my soldiers.

"Private Tremble, pick another soldier and keep an eye on the tree line. Sound off if you see the goblins returning," I ordered before motioning to the two soldiers closest to me. "You two, get Private Long and bring him back here on the double. The rest of you, check the bodies of the goblins. Make sure they're dead and not playing possum."

Finishing my orders, I looked up to see the logger who had decapitated the goblin approach me. The man must have been half giant / half bigger giant, standing well over seven feet tall with the physique of a bodybuilder. His beard stretched down below his belt buckle and was flecked with blood, like most of us were after the fight. He had chopped more than logs this day; the green-tinted gore from the goblins covered the head of the bronze axe he held over his shoulder.

"Sir, I'm Barnaby Horn, and I want to thank you for showing up when you did." Barnaby offered his hand, which was twice the size of my own. I felt like a little kid shaking hands with his dad.

"I wasn't aware there were patrols this far out, but we were right pleased when your scout popped out of the woods this morning and told me you were nearby. We were trying to finish cutting enough lumber to fill the wagons, feeling safe knowing soldiers were about, when them goblins came pouring out of the forest. Cut down two of us before we knew what was happening. All I could do was gather the remaining men to try and make a stand at the wagons." Barnaby shook his head at the close call the loggers had just survived.

"Then this here feller Jacoby comes running up out of nowhere right after the fight starts and began to lay into them gobs. He tried to chop his way over to us but there were just too many gobs between us." Barnaby gave Jacoby a big pat on the head with his dinner-plate-sized hands. "Even with his help, we'd be done for if you soldiers didn't show up when you did."

Smiling at Barnaby's friendly, country-style of speech, I scanned his information.

Barnaby Horn, Logger, Level 1.

"Barnaby, I don't know why your group was out so far from the city to cut wood, but if you plan on leaving now, my men and I will gladly escort you back to town," I offered. Traveling in a group would likely discourage further attacks from the goblins. Having heard the multiple horns answering the group we had just fought, I had no idea how many of the goblins were running about the forest.

"I thank you for that, Raytak. Just give my boys a bit of time to gather our fallen and load up the last of our gear. If it would help, we'd be glad to carry your dead soldier on the wagon as well," Barnaby offered.

"Thank you, Barnaby. Having Dreks in the wagon would allow more of my men to be ready to fight, in case the goblins come back. I also have a wounded soldier coming in from the woods. I would like to put him on the wagon, if there's room." I pointed to the two soldiers returning with Private Long on the stretcher. From the look on their faces, it became clear that something was amiss. When they made it back to the group, I could see Private Long's throat was slashed open and he was covered in blood, clearly dead. With a cold glare, I addressed the soldiers carrying him.

"What happened?"

The soldiers quickly answered. "Sir, when we got to where we stashed Private Long, we found him like this. As soon as we saw that he was dead, there was a cackle off in the distance. Almost out of sight in the forest, we spotted a goblin laughing at us as he licked the blood from his blade. Apparently, the goblin had snuck up during the fight and killed Long with his own knife.

"There's something else, sir. I think it was that goblin that ran away from us earlier. It had a bandage over the same eye it had lost in the fight with us. The damn thing must have been trailing us, knowing we'd get stuck in with the goblins here at the logging camp. We'd have chased him down, sir, but I thought it would be better to report in and not get ambushed deep in the woods." The soldiers had made the right call. To go running off in the woods for revenge would have likely only resulted in two more casualties.

"You did the right thing, Privates," I told them. Both exhaled long breaths, likely concerned that I wouldn't have approved of their actions or would somehow blame them for Long's death. "Cover up Private Long and load him in the wagon next to Dreks."

Everyone worked quickly to leave the camp. The loggers had four wagons with them, and they were only half full, so placing the dead and wounded on them wasn't too much of a problem. The wagons were hitched to teams of worn-out-looking horses and we began our slow journey to the main road and then to Amerville.

While making our way to the main road, I pulled up my log to see what happened with the experience and loot, noting I had completed a quest as well.

You have received 2 copper per active soldier and 5 copper for unit funds.

Quest Issued/Completed: *Rescue the Logging Team.* You have rescued a group of loggers who were under assault from a horde of goblins.

Reward: 100 experience. *Note: You must complete your starter quest chain to unlock access to your character sheet. Once your starter quest chain has been completed, all experience gained will be applied and you will be able to level up your character.

You have defeated a force of goblins. Experience gained: 50.

New Quest: *Escort the Loggers.*

Make sure the surviving loggers make it to Amerville.

Accept: y/n?

I accepted the new quest. Luckily, it looked like the AI took care of splitting not only the experience from a group fight but also dividing the loot, despite there being three parties involved. I did find it strange that you couldn't even see your character sheet before finishing the first quest chain. How long was that going to take? Perhaps the AI wanted to limit the information it provided in order to not overload a new player while they were still trying to figure out this new world. Jacoby walked up to me while I was reviewing my log, looking to chat.

"Hey, dude. Cool class! I didn't know there was anything like that available. I only had basic stuff at character creation, but I had heard there were rare and unique classes you could find. I only had fighter, rogue, and wizard available to me, so I chose fighter. My goal is to find a way to unlock a paladin class sometime down the road. That's what I usually like to play: combo healer/tank. Where do you live, if you don't mind my asking? I'm from Rio de Janeiro, Brazil," Jacoby said.

"I'm not sure why the AI gave me this crazy option, but it is a fun class to play. I'm from Tennessee in the United States," I answered. Jacoby seemed like a good kid, but I didn't feel comfortable sharing my personal background or information other than where I was from. He might get freaked out knowing that he was playing with a nearly dead ninety-three-year-old man sitting in a life-support pod.

"That was brave of you to help the loggers even though you had to have known you were going to get overrun. Nice work, kid," I said.

"Thanks, Raytak. I know that everyone thinks the cool thing is playing a dark and brooding character straddling the line of good and evil, but I've always just wanted to be the good guy. With these AI-generated NPCs seeming so real, I couldn't just walk by and let them all get slaughtered.

"I do have to say that I was sure glad to see you and that line of soldiers charging out of the trees. That was some epic-level action there. Wish I would have thought to take a screenshot of it. Mind if I add you to my friends list? Maybe we can do some questing together or hang in a tavern once we finish our starter zone crap." Jacoby had his interface send a friend request.

You have received a friend request from Jacoby Stone. Do you accept: y/n? *Note: Your class may restrict the content you are able to do in a party with other players.

I hit *yes* and let Jacoby know that my crazy class might not let me do some content—like dungeons—together, but it would be good to keep each other in the loop if we discovered anything interesting. It felt nice to have met another player in the game and to work together.

"Did you notice how weird character progression is? I mean, what game doesn't tell you stats, experience points, and stuff until after you finish your starter quest chain?" Jacoby asked.

"I was thinking the same thing. Not complaining, though. It gives us time to enjoy the world before getting engulfed in stats and min-maxing. I guess until you finish your starter quests you can just look at someone's gear to get an idea of how powerful they are," I said.

"That's for sure. I guess eyeballing someone's gear could give us an idea of power level. I did get a couple of abilities to start with, so I think we can track if they improve, or we get more abilities, to know our own relative strength. This game is going to be a crazy ride. Thanks again, Raytak. It looks like you got roped into one of those lame escort quests guarding these slow wagons. Hope you don't mind if I bail. I want to get to town before I have to log off for school. I hear you may get the equivalent of rested XP if you log out in a tavern." Jacoby waved, then began running down the road toward Amerville, soon moving out of sight.

CHAPTER 6

The rest of the trip was uneventful and frankly boring, like just about every other escort quest given since the birth of MMOs. The main road, while being just a simple dirt road, was well-maintained, which helped the logging wagons make good time despite the poor quality of the draft animals pulling them. Soon after dawn the next morning, we saw the town of Amerville spread out in front of us. The town was nestled next to a large lake and was surrounded by a wooden palisade interspersed with guard towers. There were small fishing vessels on the lake, while open fields and farms were scattered around outside the town walls. The farmers went about their daily tasks, and the town's large wooden gates were open. A squad of guards stood at the gate, doing a lazy check of the people coming and going.

"This is where we'll be splitting paths, Raytak," Barnaby drawled. "Our families live about a mile from the town, and I'm going to have to deliver some bad news to the relatives of the deceased. We were going to try our hand logging farther from town to avoid the tariffs charged for harvesting lumber within the town's safe zone, but it didn't quite work out as planned. Suppose it may be time for my family to move on and look somewhere else for a better opportunity. I hear a new village is starting on the frontier and it only charges a small tax on what you buy . . . no other taxes! It's getting impossible to make a living without risking life and limb every day. Well, look at me, trying to complain about risk while talking to a soldier. I wish you the best, Raytak. You're one of the good ones." With a wave, Barnaby pulled off the main road and began to head home. I had my soldiers gather our fallen and we headed toward the gate.

The guards checked my orders and directed me to the commander's office inside the military quarter of the city. The guards would see to it that our dead received a proper military burial and that their next of kin would receive their death benefit. My troops were told to rest at the barracks and wait for further orders, and as I made my way to see the commander, a quest prompt flashed.

Quest Completed: *Escort the Loggers*. **You have successfully escorted the loggers back to Amerville without any further casualties.**

Reward: 100 experience.

You have unlocked a new active ability for your troops.

Shield Bash: You can order your troops to slam forward with their shields, damaging and pushing back enemies. This activated ability can be used once every 60 seconds.

The new ability would be extremely useful in our battle with the goblins, and I couldn't wait for my troops to try it in actual combat. The main street of this area was lined with shops and taverns. Players hustled about, completing starter quests or looking for equipment upgrades with their limited funds. Some suspicious activity caught my eye, and I watched as a player tried to pickpocket a guard. The player was a female elf dressed in shabby starter-gear leather armor. She had a dagger in hand and was trying to lift the purse of a guard who was nodding off while leaning against the tavern wall. I concentrated on the player and saw her name and class.

Darkbladez, Elf Rogue, Level 1.

Darkbladez had her hand on the guard's purse, and with her dagger, she was about to cut it loose when the guard suddenly sneezed.

"Ahhhchooo! Hey, what do you think you're doing, elf!?" The guard grabbed her hand and began to shout for help. "Thief, thief! Guard needs assistance." I walked off the side of the road next to a tavern to see what would happen next.

Darkbladez reacted to the guard grabbing her hand by instinctively lashing out with the dagger, slashing it across the guard's face. The guard made a squawking sound, then let go of Darkbladez to raise his hand toward his ruined face. Blood streamed from the wound as he continued to yell for as-sistance. A notification flashed in red in front of my vision.

Warning: Your class requires you to assist any member of Imperial law enforcement or the military if they come under attack while performing their duties. Failure to do so may result in disciplinary action from your superiors and a reputation penalty. PVP will be enabled for you if the at-tacker is a player.

I raised my shield, drew my blade, and moved toward Darkbladez as she continued her attack on the guard, who was bent over and trying to hold the skin of his face together. The player thrust her dagger into the guard's neck, then stepped back, finally noticing my approach. She did a double take and then raised her blade toward me.

"How did you enable PVP inside a town that's a safe zone? Guess it doesn't matter since you'll be easy XP for me." Darkbladez then activated an ability and disappeared. Confused, I began to look around when I felt the sharp pain of her blade entering my ribs from behind. She wickedly twisted the blade as she removed it, laughing the whole time. I fell to my knees and turned to see her ready another strike.

You have been critically hit with the Blade Twist ability and are bleed-ing for 10 health per second for the next 5 seconds.

At that moment, Darkbladez shuddered and dropped her blade. She opened her mouth to say something but was unable to make a sound. It was then that she shuddered twice more and fell to the street, dead. When she fell, I could see three crossbow bolts sticking out from her back and a squad of guards hurrying toward me, three of whom held empty crossbows.

The pain in my chest intensified, and I began to cough up small gobs of blood with each labored breath. One of the guards made it to me as my vi-sion began to fade. The guard chanted something strange and a white light appeared on his hand. He then slammed his hand onto my wound. The white light soothed and healed the injury. I sat on the ground, catching my breath and thanking the guard for healing me.

"No need to thank us, sir. We appreciate that you tried to assist Lew." The guard gestured to his dead comrade, who lay where he had been killed by Darkbladez. "Drag this scum to the paupers grave and throw her in. A box is too good for the likes of her," the guard said, ordering his fellow guardsmen to haul Darkbladez's body to the cemetery. "Don't know what's got into folks today. That's the third time we've had someone blatantly rob or murder in broad daylight. Never seen anything like it." The guard pulled me to my feet and gave me directions to the headquarters in the military district.

You have defeated Darkbladez in PVP combat.

Reward: 50 experience.

I had an idea as to why things were so crazy for the guards today. Players always tested the boundaries of what they could get away with in a game. For every player looking to have a good time and play with friends, there was another who wanted to gank others, pickpocket, and cause general mayhem with the NPCs. Despite it being a low-level starting area, the guards seemed well equipped and efficient. The bad players would get the message pretty quickly and not start something in town. Surely Darkbladez was figuring that out right now while she did a corpse run back to town to respawn.

Speaking of which, I had come very close to dying myself. It did seem that my class was woefully underpowered versus what I assumed was someone of a similar level. I had to be careful. Without my soldiers, I would be easy pickings. What did come as a shock to me was the realism of the pain. Somehow, I knew the pain—despite being bad—was nowhere near the level a real wound would cause. I was glad the realism of the game stopped there. I stood up and dusted myself off, looking at the bloody streak that stained my uniform and armor. I wasn't sure if the stain would disappear after a time or if the level of realism required me to clean my clothes. Time would tell, and time was something I couldn't waste right now; I had to report to headquarters, bloodstains or not.

The guard's directions were accurate, and I made my way to the destination without any further trouble. The headquarters was a combination of administrative buildings and a barracks structure. With a reinforced construction and firing ports placed about the building, it was well set up to withstand a siege, though since it was made of wood, fire would be a problem. I absently wondered if any players had tried to make trouble here as well and what the soldiers' response to that trouble would be.

After giving a copy of my orders to the private manning the CQ (charge of quarters) desk, I was ushered into the colonel's office. It was a surprisingly small room containing just a simple wooden desk, which the colonel was seated behind, a few chairs, and some cabinets to store paperwork. I stood at attention after entering the room.

"Lieutenant Raytak, reporting as ordered, sir!" I announced. The colonel was content to let me wait at attention while he scratched away at a parchment with a quill pen. The game system showed that the commander was Lieutenant Colonel Jacobs. I was surprised the AI had decided to go with a modern United States military rank structure. I expected something different from the overall style of a faction that felt like ancient Rome. It also appeared that the in-game knowledge my character should have was automatically available to me, like knowing the rank structure of the faction I belonged to.

The lieutenant colonel finished writing on the parchment, rolled it up into a scroll shape, and sealed it with wax. He addressed me as he handed over the scroll.

"Lieutenant Raytak, I know this isn't the most exciting assignment, but I need someone who can think on their feet for this one. As you know, the emperor is attempting to reestablish our outposts in the wildlands. Our population is expanding, and we need this territory for us to grow. The village of Hayden's Knoll was started several months ago, and the mayor there has been harping nonstop for more help.

"Normally I could ignore some petty mayor of a podunk village, but he apparently has some political connections at the capital. I need you to take your unit and reinforce the garrison at Hayden's Knoll. There has been trouble with the local wildlife, bandits, and rumors of potentially dangerous humanoid tribes. I will see to it that the losses you took on the road are replenished, and I will also assign you a second squad. Since you will be so far from the normal command structure, your orders will be for you to act as an independent command. You will have full authority over any military decisions at Hayden's Knoll. I know I can expect you to work with the mayor as much as you can, but the safety of the settlement is your primary responsibility.

"A caravan to the border is leaving soon, and I have secured you and your men passage on it. Sergeant Brooks here will be going with you as well. A good senior NCO can be worth his weight in gold, as you know. Being out on the arse end of the Imperium, you will need his experience and insight."

Jacobs motioned toward a soldier standing slightly behind and to my right. I somehow hadn't noticed him earlier. Was he standing there the whole time, or had he spawned there when I wasn't looking?

"Here are your written orders and the proper requisition forms for supply. I have allocated a hundred gold for you to get started. Any additional equipment you may want will have to come out of those or your own funds, but the pay for your soldiers has been covered for the next sixty days due to the difficulty of the assignment, its remote location, and the travel time involved."

Quest Available: *Securing Hayden's Knoll, Part 1.* **You have been assigned to reinforce the village of Hayden's Knoll. The first step is to make it to the zone where the village is located with your forces intact. Accept: y/y? *Note: As a commander of the Imperium, some quests are mandatory. Get used to being voluntold, soldier!**

Great, an AI with a sense of humor was just what I needed, I thought sarcastically at the forced quest. Of course, I could just chalk it up to more realism, as I didn't recall ever being given much choice on where I was assigned to in the real world, either. Sergeant Brooks and I saluted the lieutenant colonel and made our way out of the headquarters. Sergeant Brooks knew his way around the town better than I did, so I let him lead the way as I became distracted with my map, trying to see how long the trip to this Hayden's Knoll place would take while blindly following the sergeant as he maneuvered through the crowds.

I concentrated on the menu and found information about the map. I focused on the town of Amerville, and more information populated my vision.

Amerville, Small Town, Population: 2300. This small town is located at the extreme eastern end of the Imperium. It serves as the last civilized place for parties to gather before heading into the wilderness. Amerville is also a common place for groups of settlers to gather supplies before they begin their journey. Most basic gear can be acquired here, and simple accommodations can be found for reasonable rates. The military garrison is strong, and it patrols the surrounding lands for a radius of 5 miles from the town while maintaining stronger patrols along the main road leading toward the Imperium. Those venturing toward the wildlands will often

find peril once leaving the 5-mile patrol zone. Hired guards or a large, well-equipped party are recommended in these areas.

The map showed very little other than the parts of the town we had already seen. The rest was grayed out, except the areas that I had traveled through on my way to Amerville. It looked like I would have to explore areas before they showed on the map.

Sergeant Brooks interrupted my thoughts. "Sir, would you like to see the quartermaster to requisition our supplies? We only have a few hours until the caravan leaves." Taking the sergeant's suggestion, I followed him toward the supply depot while fiddling with the map ratios. It looked like it would take nearly two weeks to make our way by caravan to the border. Then who knew how long to make it to Hayden's Knoll . . .

"*Ooof!* Hey, watch where you're going, *noob!*" someone yelled at me. While paying more attention to my map than to where I was going, I had run right into a couple of players exiting a shop, and they were apparently not happy about it. Most of the nearby players and NPCs had ignored the altercation in the street, but a few decided to stop and watch what happened.

"Raytak, eh? And what kind of lame noob class is commander?" the largest of the two asked while scanning my information. He appeared to be a half-orc warrior type, wearing leather armor and carrying a double-bladed greataxe over his shoulder. His gear looked a bit better than the starter gear I had seen on most players so far. I had to assume he was a bit higher-level than me.

"You better apologize and thank me for letting you live," the half-orc said as I scanned his name tag.

HaxxorSupreme420, Barbarian, Level 2.

Great, the game apparently allowed idiots to make stupid names for their characters. Unfortunately for this player, I didn't get intimidated very easily.

"I actually do apologize for not paying attention and running into you, but I think *you* should thank *me* for letting *you* live," I replied while giving him a cold stare. After my run-in with Darkbladez, I wasn't in the mood for more homicidal players. At least these guys hadn't attacked a guard, so they really couldn't do much since the city was not normally a PVP-enabled zone from what I had gathered.

Haxxor's face began to turn red.

"Check out Raytak the *noob*! He thinks he could go toe to toe with the Haxxor." Haxxor flexed his huge half-orc arms, posturing for the small crowd that had gathered to watch the altercation. He strutted about while laughing with his weasel-faced friend. I scanned his friend's information.

DrizztforPres, Archer, Level 2.

Ugh . . . another lame name. The weasel-faced player wore a dark leather vest and carried a shortbow across his back. A pair of long daggers were sheathed at his side.

"Noob, it's easy to talk big when you're not in a PVP zone. How 'bout we make us a little duel so all my new fans here can watch me pwn you?"

A prompt appeared in front of me.

Challenge: HaxxorSupreme420 and his companion DrizztforPres have challenged you to an honor duel.

Accept: y/n? (Selecting *no* will lower your reputation considerably. You can toggle off honor duels in your settings tab.) Winning a duel will result in a very slight increase in reputation. Losing will result in a very small decrease in reputation.

Great, I supposed I was a noob after all. I had left myself wide open for these kinds of things and didn't even know it. Cursing the AI and her lack of a tutorial, I quickly toggled off the honor duel option in my settings, but the challenge prompt was still there.

It would cost more to not accept, and while I was sure that with their better gear and my gimped class they would wipe the floor with me, I decided to give it a shot. I hit *accept*.

Loading Honor Duel. Good luck, competitors!

My vision faded, and when it returned, I found myself and Sergeant Brooks standing in an open field about thirty feet away from our opponents. Those spectating were only blurry figures at the edge of the instanced duel area. The help tab that opened when I accepted the duel stated that spectators would have a perfect view of the action but we wouldn't see them in order to prevent anything they did or said from distracting us. More prompts flashed.

Loading commander-class forces.

What? I thought it was just going to be me and maybe the sergeant versus these guys. I grinned as four squads of Imperium soldiers loaded onto the battlefield. It was beginning to look like we had a chance. A timer began to count down the start of the battle.

30 . . . 29 . . . 28 . . .

I had to act quick.

"Sergeant Brooks, take Fourth Squad and move to our extreme right. When the battle starts, ignore Haxxor and charge the archer. Keep him from shooting and try to surround him for flanking attacks. I'll take the other three squads and start wearing down Haxxor. I have a feeling these guys have us overpowered individually, but we have discipline and numbers on our side. Fourth Squad, move out with Sergeant Brooks. Squads one through three, form up ranks and prepare javelins."

3 . . . 2 . . . 1 . . . **The battle begins!**

The invisible force that had been holding the two groups apart vanished. Our opponents looked at us, dumbfounded, clearly confused as to how all these other soldiers had spawned on my side. Their second of confusion was all we needed to get moving. Sergeant Brooks and his ten-man squad began sprinting for the archer. I had to hold Haxxor's attention away from Brooks. My soldiers were arranged in three ranks of ten while I stood behind the third rank to issue orders. I made a point to always have my squads within the Command Presence aura as I activated it; we would need every bonus we could get. My soldiers were equipped as regulars with no armor, a large wooden shield like the one I carried, a crude shortsword, and two javelins. The gear for these generic-instance zone soldiers was at least a bit better than the gear my other soldiers had.

I began to bark orders.

"All squads, prepare to throw . . . release!" Thirty-one javelins launched at Haxxor. He dodged at the last second and many missed completely. Several that hit him bounced off his armor, but a few left bloody holes where they hit, and Haxxor's health bar dipped a tiny bit. While I examined his health bar, two soldiers from my front rank fell with arrows in their chests. The archer had gotten over his confusion and was firing on my group. Haxxor now began to charge us, his figure blurring a bit as he activated what must have been some ability to increase his dodge chance and speed.

"All squads, throw and prepare to receive charge!" Twenty-nine javelins rained down on Haxxor, but his high defense rating only allowed a few to connect. My troops raised shields and drew their shortswords. The barbarian, Haxxor, activated another ability and swung his greataxe from side to side as he broke the first rank of soldiers. Two soldiers were cut completely in half from the ability, which my combat log showed as Massive Swipe. Three more of my men were hacked down in just as many seconds before my troops recovered and began to fight back.

Haxxor's charge had broken through the first rank, but the second rank had time to brace, which stopped him from penetrating further. The second rank of soldiers began to surround the barbarian, making thrusts with their shortswords when the opportunity arose. I pulled back five feet with Third Squad and commanded the remainder of First Squad to fill any holes that Second Squad might have. Only six of my soldiers at a time could reach Haxxor without getting in each other's way.

Haxxor continued to swing his axe, almost every swing resulting in a dead soldier. His axe only occasionally deflected off a shield, the deflected blows still doing some damage to the blocking soldier. My men were having a hard time piercing his armor, and each hit we made only removed a tiny sliver of health. Lucky for us, each time he swung the axe, it left him open for at least one of the soldiers surrounding him to land a hit.

I took a moment from my fight to check in on Sergeant Brooks. Having lost two soldiers during their charge, his force had made it to the archer and now had him surrounded. Now that Brooks was in melee range, it was apparent that the archer didn't have anywhere near the melee skill or defensive abilities that Haxxor had. That being said, Brooks still faced a difficult battle. As I was watching, one more of his soldiers dropped, the archer opening his throat with a long dagger. A splash of blood hit the other soldiers while they began to land several blows on the archer. The archer was accumulating injuries quickly and his smaller health pool was dropping fast. It looked like Sergeant Brooks was winning his fight.

Turning back to my fight, I could see Second Squad was down to three soldiers and First Squad had only four remaining.

"Third Squad, prepare to fill in any gaps. Bring down that barbarian!" Haxxor was becoming slower in his movements, and it looked like his wounds were piling up. The health bar for my opponent was now below half, and my troops were beginning to get more hits in as the blurring buff Haxxor had been using from the start of the fight expired.

After a minute of trading blows back and forth, my three squads were down to seven soldiers, but Haxxor was nearly done for. Just when I thought I had this fight in the bag, a red glow covered our opponent and he visibly grew six inches taller. His muscles bulged as he unleashed a new special ability that enabled him to gain some health back. Haxxor did a spinning whirlwind-style attack, taking down three of my remaining soldiers. I stepped into the gap that opened, thrusting with all my strength at the half-orc barbarian. My blow hit him in the stomach, piercing his armor as the sword sunk in three inches before he pulled away. Dark red blood welled from the wound and blended with blood from the dozens of other cuts Haxxor had taken during the fight. His health dropped to just three percent. My remaining soldiers quickly scored two additional hits while the barbarian was focused on me, nearly causing him to go down. It was my turn to face the axe as Haxxor, looking to split me from head to toe, used an ability my combat log called Power Attack. I raised my shield just in time to block some of the force of the blow.

With his enhanced strength behind the blow, Haxxor's axe had cleaved halfway through my shield, severing my shield hand at the wrist. Shocked and nauseous from the waves of pain radiating from my newly severed limb, I watched as each beat of my heart pumped a red stream of blood from the stump where my hand used to be. The shield dropped, as I was no longer able to hold it without a hand, snagging Haxxor's axe as it fell. I could feel my life force slipping away from the blood loss as my health bar plummeted toward zero. Haxxor began pulling at his axe in a futile effort to free it from the shield. The last four soldiers in my group all landed hits on the distracted Haxxor, finishing him just before I bled out.

Victory! You have defeated your opponent and gained reputation!

We were ported back to the same spot in town immediately after the duel. Trying to catch my breath, I looked down to see that my hand was back, we were all fully healed, and our gear was repaired upon leaving the duel instance. Bystanders began to cheer, and I watched with amusement as HaxxorSupreme420 stared at me with a scowl on his face.

"Noob, you just got lucky. You unlocked some cheater, pay-to-win class,"

Haxxor stated. "Why don't you accept another duel, coward? You know your little tricks won't work this time." Haxxor must have tried to start another duel, not realizing I had figured out how to disable the setting.

"Sorry, smacking you down once is all I have time for . . . noob," I said to Haxxor as Sergeant Brooks and I continued on our way.

CHAPTER 7

After our little exercise with the poorly named duo, we made our way to the supply depot.

"Sergeant, do we get any choice for our troops, or are they being assigned to us?" I inquired.

"Sir, normally, for this type of mission, we could choose our own troops from any available in the garrison. Unfortunately, like yourself, I just arrived here and haven't had time to scope out which soldiers have potential and which ones will only be dead weight. From what I've seen, the troops here are green. Really green. As in just-finished-basic-training green. From the state of their physical conditioning, most barely passed their final physical training test. There are also several rear-area pogues, and they won't be of much use where we're going," Sergeant Brooks said while shaking his head.

"From what I gather, Sergeant, it will take about two weeks to get to the edge of this zone. Hopefully, between the two of us, we can whip them into combat-ready shape while on the road," I said while concentrating on Sergeant Brooks to open his information.

Sergeant Josiah Brooks, Elite NPC.

Skills/Abilities:

Command Presence: Sergeants possess a less powerful version of the **Command Presence ability their commander wields. This ability will improve as the NPC progresses. The ability does not stack with other**

instances of the same ability; the more potent of the two will override the other.

Well, it looked like Sergeant Brooks was a definite upgrade over our regulars, and having the "elite" designation usually meant a more durable and deadly NPC. Our Command Presence abilities didn't stack, but having two of us with the ability should allow us to cover more of an area during the large battles I hoped my class allowed for. It would be interesting to see how our abilities improved as we leveled up. After our duel, I could foresee good leadership making even mediocre troops a force to be reckoned with.

A pleasantly cool breeze was blowing in from the nearby lake, making the hot day bearable. The streets of Amerville were a hard-packed dirt that allowed for easy, if dusty, travel. Thankfully, the weather was dry, as these same streets had to transform into a quagmire of mud during the rainy season.

Located just a short distance from the headquarters was the cavernous supply building. The massive double doors of the wooden depot were open, allowing the breeze to help cool the large warehouse. The interior was a disorganized hodgepodge that contained various racks of gear and stacks of boxes holding the equipment and supplies needed by the town garrison. Soldiers, supply clerks, and even civilians were coming and going in disorganized chaos. After seeing the lax security of the building, I had to suspect that a lot of the gear meant for our soldiers had walked out the door. How much more were we going to have to pay for gear to cover the losses resulting from sloppy leadership?

The sergeant and I stepped into the building unchallenged and walked up to the counter while asking for the quartermaster. A short, chubby man sporting three days' worth of stubble appeared. Wearing a stained, unbuttoned, mismatched uniform, he immediately began berating us for interrupting him while barely glancing up from the paper report he was reading.

"I hope you both have a good reason for interrupting—" the quartermaster began.

"Attention!" shouted Sergeant Brooks, cutting off the quartermaster with the booming voice that every NCO since time immemorial had seemed to acquire. "You will go to attention, Quartermaster, in the presence of an officer!" Brooks indicated to me, whom the quartermaster hadn't looked at very closely. "We're here to be issued gear for our troops by order of Colonel Jacobs. I suggest you get some of your people working on what we need before I report you for insubordination, not to mention your nonregulation uniform and overall poor hygiene. When was the last time you took a PT test, soldier?" Sergeant Brooks added, using the acronym for physical training.

The quartermaster wasn't used to many officers coming by and appeared to be flustered as he assigned one of his people to help us. "Krebbs, get over here and help the lieutenant with his supplies. My apologies, sir. I didn't notice you. Krebbs is my best supply clerk and he'll get you squared away quickly." The quartermaster fumbled to properly button his tunic as Krebbs rushed up to assist.

The quartermaster apologized again and excused himself, wisely wanting to get out from under Sergeant Brooks's laser-focused death stare. Having him hide out somewhere in the warehouse while we conducted our business was just fine with me.

"Sorry if I overstepped my bounds, sir," Sergeant Brooks said to me. "I have trouble not snapping back into drill instructor mode when I see soldiers acting like slobs."

"No apology needed, Sergeant Brooks, but try not to ruffle too many feathers until after we get our troops their gear," I advised while watching Krebbs step to the counter and take our requisition form. Shaking my head, I realized that Sergeant Brooks had said "drill instructor" and not "drill sergeant"; he had used the Marine Corps designation of their training cadre and not the Army one.

"Even ultra-advanced AIs can't be smart all the time, I suppose," I said under my breath, remembering the friendly rivalry that the two branches had with each other. I could vaguely recall an old Marine in the hospital with me and the two of us picking on each other for our choice of service branch. During a fight, though, neither branch would hesitate to risk itself to save the other.

"Sir," Krebbs began. "It looks like you've been authorized thirty days' rations for two squads, plus yourselves." Krebbs looked around to see if any of the other clerks were watching. "I'll make sure there's extra rations and that they come from the freshest supplies. It's worth the risk just to have seen the quartermaster dressed down by the sergeant, sir." I would normally jump all over the supply clerk for insulting a superior, but I let it slip since the quartermaster was a complete train wreck and I firmly believed in never messing with the man who was gathering the supplies for my soldiers.

Krebbs read further into the supply requisition. "You may have guessed that you will not be getting the pick of the litter with the quality of troops we have here. No offense, sir, but we seem to get stuck with either leftover dregs or green recruits. Seeing as the quality, or lack thereof, of the gear the men initially receive is so poor, I would highly suggest using at least some of your discretionary funds to upgrade it. The men come out of training rather poorly equipped, and since they were being assigned off post, none of the other officers wanted to spend resources on them. Here is a list of their starting equipment." Krebbs held up a parchment, and the information loaded onto my screen, confirming the soldiers here had the same garbage gear my original squad started with.

"I can't offer anything in the way of discounts, but depending on what you want, and with your permission, I may have some used or leftover gear that can go for less coin. Despite being used, the gear is solid enough to serve for a while until you can afford better," Krebbs offered while I looked at the soldier loadout.

Standard Loadout, Level 1 Recruit.

Crude Worn Bronze Dagger.

Small Round Wooden Shield (poor quality): Warning, this shield has a chance to shatter if struck by a heavy blow or critical hit.

Standard Uniform (poor quality): This rough-spun cloth will not provide much protection, and the poor quality will make it wear out more quickly.

Poor-Quality Leather Sandals: Wearers will have a small chance to stumble when attacking or defending due to the poor quality of this footwear.

Standard Military Rucksack (average quality): This large backpack can hold the standard gear and supplies for a soldier in the field.

The starting gear was pathetic. The rucksack was the only piece worth keeping, and none of the items I would expect an Imperial soldier to have in the field were present. I needed to upgrade their gear, but my funds were limited and after sixty days I would have to start paying these soldiers. I decided I didn't want to spend more than forty gold so I could make the remainder last, if possible.

"Sergeant Brooks, what's your opinion on the most important upgrades for the men? Our budget will only be about forty gold," I asked.

Sergeant Brooks seemed a little surprised that an officer would request his opinion. He contemplated for a moment before responding. "We plan on training them while we travel, so that lousy footwear has to go. The sandals would wear out by the end of the first week. The shields would be the next thing. The ones they are issued look like old captured enemy equipment. Better to get them the shields they originally trained with and are the best overall." Sergeant Brooks indicated the larger Roman-style scutum shields both he and I carried. "The daggers are useless for anything other than cutting their food, so shortswords, at a minimum, are a necessity if we're going to be effective in a formation battle. Armor is likely out as an option due to the cost and the time required to get that many soldiers properly fitted. Upgrading the shields and hitting the shield training hard will keep them alive longer than any armor we could afford at this point anyway. We can have the men slowly improve their armor as we go. Javelins should also be inexpensive enough to equip and would give us some short-ranged punch. They can also double up as a spear in a pinch."

Thinking for a moment, I knew what else we were missing. "The other major thing I think we're missing, Sergeant, would be a pick or shovel for each soldier. The Imperium is known for its fortified camps each night." I made that assumption based on this faction being such a close copy of ancient Rome. "Two axes per squad to cut wood and make defensive stakes would also be useful." Scratching absently at my itchy uniform, I realized that there was one more thing that *had* to change. "These uniforms seem to have been made out of old burlap sacks. Do you have anything that won't leave my men and I itching all day, Krebbs?"

Krebbs began calculating the cost for each item. "New standard boot upgrades are two gold. The new large shield upgrade is normally eighteen gold, but we can get some used surplus shields that should have a lot of life left in them for fourteen gold. Tools like shovels, picks, and axes would cost five gold to equip all your forces. Remember that these shouldn't be used in battle and will crack if hitting armor or metal shields. The standard bronze-tipped wood javelins will set you back one silver each. I do have quite a few surplus bronze shortswords I could let go for twelve gold and fifty silver versus the twenty-five gold a new one costs. They're not exactly pretty but should still be serviceable for quite a while."

I pulled up the help tab on my interface and searched for information on the monetary system. It appeared that one hundred copper equaled one silver and one hundred silver equaled one gold. After some rough calculations, I came up with what I figured would give us the best bang for the buck.

"Private Krebbs, we'll take the boots, the surplus shortswords, the surplus shields, if you have that many, the tools, and two hundred javelins. That comes to thirty-five gold and fifty silver, if my math is right. For, say, forty gold, could you throw in a few medical aid kits and uniforms that are durable and won't make everyone uncomfortable the whole day?" I asked.

I couldn't wait to get rid of the itchy, standard uniform I was wearing now. Should I ever find the guy that designed the uniform . . . Well, it wouldn't be a good day for him. It appeared that upgrades were expensive for my class, but once they were purchased, I wouldn't have to spend more when new soldiers were added to my unit. New units would be equipped to whatever standard level of gear I had. I also was torn on purchasing more javelins, but I felt two hundred should get us to where we were going before we ran out.

Krebbs thought for a few seconds. "Sure, I can make that happen, Lieutenant. I'll get on that gear right away and have it sent right out to the marshaling field. Your gear should be waiting for you by the time you arrive with your soldiers. Anything else you need?"

I told Krebbs no and thanked him for his help. It was nice to see that some people in the Imperium army were competent in their work.

As we left the supply depot, a notification popped up.

New Skill Acquired: Negotiator.

Your haggling with a supply clerk has unlocked the negotiation skill.

You will now be able to acquire better prices at some vendors. This skill increases with use and may open additional questlines.

Anything to save money was nice. I was down to sixty gold and would have to start paying my soldiers' wages and purchasing more supplies in sixty days. Speaking of that, I had better find out how much their pay would be. Pulling up the information tab in the menu, I did a search for wages.

Imperial Wage Scale:

Regulars: 10 silver per month.

Advanced soldiers: 25 silver per month.

Elite soldiers: 50 silver per month.

As my forces grew, it was going to cost me an arm and a leg to keep them paid and fed. Hopefully, this game would start showing me some ways to make money. Picking up copper off dead goblins wasn't going to cut it. Deciding to try and build some rapport with Sergeant Brooks, I asked a few questions.

"Sergeant Brooks, do you have any family?"

"No, sir. If the army of the Imperium wanted me to have a family, they would have assigned me one, sir," the sergeant replied.

The sergeant's gruff response gave me the impression that he was not open to small talk. I took the hint and kept quiet as we walked down the packed dirt road. The barracks turned out to be a series of tents laid out in a grid pattern over an open field. Luckily, we didn't have to go hunting for our troops through the maze of tents; they had received the order to form up outside the barracks area and were loafing around, waiting for us to arrive. When they caught sight of an officer and sergeant approaching, they snapped to and began arranging themselves into some semblance of a formation.

Sergeant Brooks charged toward the disorganized troops. "Fall in! How long have you been out of training, Privates? Did you forget how to form ranks already?" The sergeant's haranguing made the soldiers even more flustered, and it took even more time for them to fall into formation. The two ten-man squads lined up one in front of the other. The sergeant turned around, and it appeared he was waiting for me to address the troops.

It had been a while, but here it went. "At ease!" I loudly ordered, and the men snapped to the correct position. "My name is Lieutenant Raytak, and I have the privilege of leading you brave soldiers." I had nearly said "Colonel Raytak" and caught myself at the last moment, forgetting the game had busted me down in rank from my real-life military career.

"We have been ordered to the village of Hayden's Knoll to help protect the settlement from any threats. I understand you are recently out of basic training, but between Sergeant Brooks and myself, we will whip you into fighting form. We will train hard while we're on the road, as I firmly believe in the motto of sweat more now, bleed less later. Sergeant Brooks, form up the men and move them to the marshaling area."

Sergeant Brooks formed the men into a column and began to call cadence as we marched to meet the caravan. Several players stopped to watch the strange spectacle of another player leading the Imperium troops. I even heard a few whispers asking if this was a quest or event. We soon made our way out of the city and, after showing a copy of our orders to the gate guards, were directed to a group of wagons assembling a few hundred yards away. Just outside Amerville, the regular caravans heading to the border had an area where they would form up. This made sense, as keeping the extra traffic out of the town itself would reduce crowding in the streets as well as avoid the mess that the animals made.

CHAPTER 8

arching toward the caravan, I counted fifty wagons in total. People were hurrying to load the last of their items, and the caravan drivers were hitching up large beasts to pull the wagons. Each wagon was to be pulled by what looked like a cross between a buffalo and a camel. The creatures were covered in thick, wooly brown fur and had long necks with two short horns on top. They were about fifty percent larger than a full-grown cow, and only one was needed to pull a large wagon. Curious, I focused on the creature to reveal its information.

Mukok. These large and hearty animals are the preferred draft beasts for pulling heavy loads over long distances. Slow but with amazing stamina, the mukok can work all day without rest. The flesh of the beasts is notoriously foul-tasting to most creatures, save for ogres, who consider the pungent meat a delicacy. "Strong as a mukok" is a common saying used to praise someone's physical strength, while "smart as a mukok" is a common saying used to insult a person's intelligence.

We found our assigned wagons off to the side of the rest of the caravan. A group of soldiers was loading our wagons with boxes full of the supplies and the equipment we had ordered. After I quickly confirmed these were ours, Sergeant Brooks got the troops to load up the wagons for our trip. I also tasked the sergeant with equipping the men with their new gear while I sought out the caravan master. Walking toward the area of most activity, I was drawn to loud voices. The sound of heated words being exchanged led me to find a large muscular man wearing extravagant robes and a purple turban. He was arguing with an older but still spry man in rough-spun work clothes.

"Daegan, you're getting exactly what you paid for. I have provided guards and even assigned you one of my top commanders to lead them!" the large man forcefully yelled, his face inches from the smaller man's. The small man, to his credit, didn't back down an inch, giving a verbal assault right back.

"I paid for twenty-five guards, not fifteen! You know the roads are more dangerous lately, and you're just trying to extort more money from me minutes before we leave, Kofi!" the smaller man, Daegan, said.

"Please, Daegan, there is no need for us to raise our voices at each other. It is obvious that you have three choices, my dear friend," Kofi said as he smirked. I could sadly see he had the man Daegan right where he wanted him. "You can accept these fifteen fine warriors to guard your wagons, you can pay me the remaining fee to add another ten of my elite warriors to the mix, and finally, I will gladly allow you to exit the agreement with only a small cancellation fee. I anxiously await your reply, my dear friend Daegan." Kofi crossed his arms and smiled while he waited for Daegan to decide.

"I have no choice but to take the full twenty-five guards, and this will likely bankrupt me. Understand that *I* keep *my* word, and my commitment is to protect the caravan. The Daegan Trail Express has never left a caravan under-protected and never will. I'll pay the extra gold for the twenty-five-guard total, but don't expect any further business from my caravan!" Daegan tossed a purse of coins over to Kofi, who told the guards gathered behind him to join the caravan. Kofi gave a content chuckle, tossing the coin pouch in his hand to feel its heft as he made his way back toward town.

I observed the guards that Kofi had provided while they spread out around the caravan to begin their duties. I was not impressed with the quality of what poor Daegan must have just spent a fortune to hire. They were a motley collection, and most looked like street thugs at best or random tavern refuse at worst. Their gear was mismatched and varied wildly. There were spearmen, some equipped with bows, many wielding shortswords or clubs paired with shields, and a couple of the larger warriors had greataxes. Their armor consisted of shabby leather emblazoned with a blue scimitar that I assumed was the mercenary company's symbol. Sadly, even their mismatched gear was better than what my soldiers were currently equipped with. One of the guards wore slightly better gear than the rest. It comprised a chain shirt, a small round wooden shield, and a curved scimitar. The better-equipped guard noticed me appraising his forces. I pulled up his info while he stalked toward me.

Bhurke, Mercenary Leader, NPC.

"Like seeing what real warriors look like, soldier boy? They don't march in formation real pretty, but they'll wreck your green troops if I give the word. Keep to your own business and out of mine, or we may have to have words." The warrior rested his hand on the hilt of his scimitar in an unspoken threat.

"As long as that rabble you call a mercenary band stays away from my soldiers, there won't be any problems. I wouldn't want for us to have words, either." I placed my hand on my shortsword to let him know I wasn't impressed. Bhurke hawked a ball of phlegm, spit it in my general direction, turned, and walked back to his men, cursing and shouting at them to get them where he wanted them to be.

Daegan watched the confrontation and then approached, still wearing a scowl on his face from the argument with Kofi.

"I suppose you're the ones Colonel Jacobs added at the last minute. You better get your men and gear loaded. We'll leave with or without you in five minutes." Daegan was short with me, obviously still angry from the fleecing Kofi had just given him.

"Where do you want us in the order of march? I would request keeping our three wagons together since I'll be conducting training as we travel," I asked.

"Last one here, last in line. That's my rule. The Imperium already paid for your trip, but they didn't pay me to feed you, so your lot is on their own for meals. We start at dawn, stop for thirty minutes at noon to eat and rest the beasts, then travel the rest of the day until I say we stop. On the trail, I am the boss. I know you Army types have trouble with that sometimes," Daegan said and scowled at me while awaiting a reply. I was beginning to think that scowling was his default setting.

"Not a problem, Daegan. I'm Lieutenant Raytak, by the way. Your caravan, your rules. My forces will do what you say as long as it doesn't endanger my men or my mission," I replied while offering my hand.

Daegan's expression softened a bit as he shook my hand. "Sorry if I was a bit hard on you—" I cut him off, telling him that no apology was necessary and that our group would be ready to roll on time.

Making my way back to the wagons, I noticed that Daegan had assigned one of his people as a driver to each wagon and that—thankfully—the driver would also be responsible for the care of the mukok. I was worried we'd have to assign soldiers to that chore, taking away from their training time. The loading was just about done; the last few supply boxes were being heaved onto the wagon by the dozen soldiers sent to deliver them. I had a devious idea and motioned the sergeant over.

"Sergeant Brooks, what unit are the soldiers helping us load assigned to?"

He considered my question for a second and then a mischievous gleam sparkled in his eye. "Sir, I like the way you think. These troops are also new recruits, like our men, and haven't been assigned to a unit yet. Shall I go ahead and give them an assignment, sir?"

"Sergeant, by all means, make sure that our new Third Squad knows that they now have a home. I'll write up a letter and send it back with the soldiers returning the wagons that brought the supplies. I'm sure if Colonel Jacobs misses these soldiers, he'll send out a messenger to find us. Otherwise, it looks like the caravan is moving out. Get us ready to roll." A notification dinged as I scribbled a message to the colonel, explaining that I had taken the unassigned soldiers sent to bring the supplies as a new squad for my forces.

You have unlocked the ability Recruiter. You have discovered that the commander class allows you to recruit unassigned soldiers into your unit. This skill also allows you to recruit civilians into the military and add them to your forces.

Sergeant Brooks had the last of our troops and supplies loaded onto our wagons just as the caravan master gave the command to roll out. Loading the thirty-two of us onto three wagons stacked high with supplies and equipment was a tight fit, but nobody said Army life was a life of luxury. We all soon realized why Daegan punished the late arrivals by putting them last in the caravan line. A nonstop cloud of dust was soon kicked up by the wagons traveling the dirt road in front of us, covering everyone in a layer of filth. The smell of being behind that many mukoks made me feel like I was sitting in a stable full of cows with intestinal problems.

Sergeant Brooks divided our forces so that one squad was in each wagon. I had positioned myself on the first of our three wagons and had Sergeant Brooks take the last wagon. The squad in the middle had no babysitter, but one of us would rotate among all three wagons, making sure that each squad had our personal attention during the trip. The wagons moved out at a pace equivalent to a fast walk. I suppose hyper-speed rail networks were not in the immediate future for the Limitless Lands, though surely some enterprising players would find a way to speed up travel if there was coin to be made in it.

After the first hour on the road, I heard a commotion behind me. Looking back, I saw that the sergeant had the soldiers in his wagon jump out with all their gear and begin to trot alongside the wagon, keeping pace with it. He then ran up and did the same with the squad in the second wagon. Taking the hint, I had the soldiers in my wagon grab their gear and jump out with me. The sergeant ran us hard up one side of the caravan at a double-time pace, then cross over to the other side at a walk until the caravan slowly overtook us. We then crossed over and began the process once more, completing a giant circle around the wagons.

It was exhilarating to feel myself run once more. My age- and injury-ravaged real-world body hadn't so much as walked for the last twenty or so years. Despite my exhilaration, I soon remembered how much misery running in full gear could be. The armor chaffed in different areas, rubbing them raw until they bled, blisters began to form inside my boots, and the hot, dusty air burned my lungs as I gasped for each breath. After my third trip around, a voice called from one of the wagons, granting me a brief respite.

"Lieutenant Raytak, is that you?" Having been focused entirely on not dying from the exertion of running, I had neglected to check out the other wagons of the caravan in much detail. Looking down from the wagon next to me was none other than Barnaby, the logging team leader. Seated in the wagon amidst various bits of furniture and household possessions was a middle-aged woman and a small girl about ten years of age.

"Mr. Barnaby Horn, it's good to see you again. What brings you out on a wagon caravan to the border?" I asked while slowing my pace to a fast walk to keep up with the wagon. I waved for the rest of my squad to pass me by and keep going.

"After what happened earlier, me and several of my neighbors"—Barnaby waved toward the wagons behind his, and I recognized several of the men as loggers from the attack earlier—"decided it was finally time to make a move. I heard there was big demand for lumber at the new settlement in Hayden's Knoll, and we thought we'd try our luck there. No more city taxes for us!"

Gesturing to his wife and child, Barnaby introduced them. "This here is my beautiful wife, Claire, and this little monkey is my daughter, Bella. Claire, this is the officer that commanded the unit that came to our rescue earlier."

Claire moved her hand to her mouth in shock, and her eyes began to tear up. "Thank you, sir, for saving Barnaby and his team. I don't know what would have happened to me and Bella if you hadn't arrived." She leaned over the edge of the wagon and placed a kiss on the top of my sweaty head.

"No need for thanks, ma'am. We were just doing our job. I'm just glad we happened to be at the right place at the right time," I replied, blushing from the praise. "It does look like we're going to be neighbors, though. My unit has been assigned to the garrison at Hayden's Knoll. I'm sorry to have to cut this short, but I should get back to work. The sergeant will think I'm trying to stall so I don't have to run anymore, and though I hate to say it, he would probably be correct. I'll check in on you all once we camp for the night." I waved to the family and began the grueling run once more, amazed at the complexity of the game giving NPCs a complete family background.

After the pleasant surprise of finding Barnaby and his family, I made a note to check out the other wagons in the caravan as I ran past. Most of them were filled with various goods destined for Hayden's Knoll or other settlements farther down the line. The food the caravan would use up during its two-week trip filled several wagons. It appeared that, in addition to Barnaby and three other logging families, ten of the wagons were filled with groups of settlers heading to Hayden's Knoll.

One of the wagons looked empty, but I could see three glowing icons resting at the bottom of it. The icons represented players who had logged out of the game. It made sense that they wouldn't want to spend their game time traveling from one zone to the next. Daegan rode in the front wagon with the guard captain while the rest of the guards were posted to sit next to drivers on random wagons in order to keep watch. Their idea of keeping watch meant taking naps and not surveilling the surrounding area for potential danger. Daegan sure got taken for a ride when he paid a premium for this lot. There were none of the "guards" in my wagons. One of them initially tried to board the last wagon, but Sergeant Brooks advised him in no uncertain terms that it would be a cold day in the underworld before men under his command needed to be guarded by the likes of mercenary scum.

During the morning run, the pace of several of the more unfit troops began to falter. They were falling behind and dropping out, heaving for breath and vomiting at the side of the road. Thankfully, the caravan stopping for its noon rest allowed us to catch our breath, guzzle some water, and cram down a meal. The stop couldn't have come at a better time, as I was also on my last legs and in danger of joining those who were puking and gasping for air on the side of the road. Only about twelve of the entire unit had kept up with the sergeant's pace. He approached me just before the noon break ended.

"Sir, sorry if it was presumptuous for me to get the men running this morning, but I felt we really needed to start getting them in fighting form. As you know, a battle is as much a test of stamina as it is a test of martial prowess . . ." Sergeant Brooks paused as if he was trying to think of a tactful way to word what he was going to say next. "I hope you also enjoyed the workout, sir. I know I risk insubordination by saying this, but a good leader should be an example to his men and not shirk from training as hard as they do. I could tell the running was hard on you today, but you handled it well, and the men notice those kinds of things, sir." The sergeant sheepishly awaited my reply. I let him stew for a minute under my gaze before I responded.

"Sergeant, so what you are trying to tell me is that I should have started the men running before you did. I'm a typical out-of-shape, lazy officer, and you hope that I don't write you up for insubordination. Also, you wanted me to know that, despite your criticisms, you appreciate that I was willing to step up and work hard alongside the men," I said with a stern look, waiting for the sergeant's response.

Sergeant Brooks began to stammer. "Well, sir . . . that's not exactly how I meant it. You see . . ."

I decided to let him off the hook. "Sergeant, I'm just messing with you." I grinned at Brooks, and after a few moments, his look of concern turned into a smile. "I actually agree with what you said, Sergeant. Understand that I will always expect you to voice your concerns to me if there is something that affects the men under my command. It's our duty to push them now so we can keep more of them alive later.

"I do propose, Sergeant, that we let the men rest for the remainder of the afternoon and ride in the wagons . . . Then we hit them hard as soon as the caravan stops this evening. I want them to complete a regulation Imperium field camp, with defenses, in record time. As soon as they're done with that, we'll begin training in battle formation and drill. We need to be able to work together as a cohesive force to beat opponents that may be stronger, more numerous, or better equipped than we are. I also don't like the look of these so-called guards. I'll bet money that most of them fall asleep on guard shift tonight. With that in mind, make sure we keep a full squad equipped and ready for battle on each guard shift. The men will lose a little sleep, but we won't have any surprises in the night. Did I miss anything you can think of, Sergeant?" I waited to see if he had anything to add.

"No, sir. That should cover it. I would recommend making the guard shift one section instead of a whole squad. That way they should get a full night's sleep, giving their bodies time to recover from the workout we give them each day. We can also run drills on some nights, simulating an attack to get the men ready to jump into a fight at a moment's notice." Sergeant Brooks had some good ideas, and I agreed to his suggestions.

While riding in the wagon that afternoon, I realized something I hadn't thought of. Quickly opening my social tab, I looked at my friends list for Jacoby. It didn't take long to find him, as he was my only friend in-game so far. I saw that he was still logged out, so I sent him a message for when he next logged in.

Hey, Jacoby. This is Raytak. I wanted to warn you to toggle off the honor duel setting in your options menu. I had a higher-level player challenge me to an honor duel, and losing these can cause a reputation drop. I also got my starter quest, and it has me being assigned to some small village called Hayden's Knoll. Don't laugh. Yes, it starts with a TWO-WEEK-LONG escort quest. Look me up if you're ever out that way. The first ale's on me!

Jacoby seemed like a good kid, and I didn't want him to get nailed by any shenanigans from another Haxxor-type player. The reputation thing might end up being important since he wanted to eventually become a paladin.

Our travel toward the border began to fall into a pattern: running with the sergeant in the morning and riding on the wagons until the evening. During this process, the men and I began to get physically fit. The wagons would stop each evening about an hour or two before sunset, and I had the sergeant immediately begin instructing the men on how to build the nightly fortifications that were the hallmark of an Imperium army in the field. They dug a three-foot by three-foot trench around a rectangular area large enough for our tents. The dirt that we excavated from the ditch was piled up to create a berm behind the trench, which presented more of an obstacle against attack as well as cover for the defenders. Those with axes were sent to cut nearby wood for the fires and to fashion sharpened stakes that were driven into the berm to further hamper attackers. Once the defenses were complete, the sergeant and I ran the men through drills, practicing the art of fighting in formation and following commands without hesitation.

Our choice of formations was somewhat limited since we had only three squads to work with, but that didn't mean there weren't critical skills for the men to hone. Thankfully, all soldiers seemed to exit training with baseline skills and knowledge of common maneuvers, just like soldiers in the real world. While they weren't very polished, they at least knew the basics of fighting and could respond to simple commands. The main things I focused on were adjusting our formation in the midst of battle, refusing the line, and filling gaps that opened due to losses. They already had a good grasp on fighting, but we emphasized working with the soldiers next to them. Any foe coming up against my men was going to be unpleasantly surprised by our level of discipline and coordination.

After evening training, the men prepared food and then could sleep if they weren't assigned to guard duty. Most nights, the men collapsed immediately, exhausted from their harsh training. It soon became obvious that the guards hired by Daegan were completely undisciplined troublemakers.

Bhurke, the leader of the mercenaries, did nothing when his men fell asleep on guard duty or when they walked by early in the evening, hurtling taunts at our soldiers as we trained. A few of his men even tried to pick fights with my soldiers, but the sergeant and I kept a close watch on our men and prevented things from getting out of hand. We made sure we had a strong guard set each night and that nobody fell asleep on guard duty in my unit.

Sleep was proving to be a strange experience in Limitless Lands. NPCs had a normal sleep time requirement, but for the players, it was different. My virtual body would begin to feel fatigue and sleepiness, like I would normally expect, but instead of sleeping for several hours, I would lie down and then be instantly refreshed. All my weariness would be gone and my body would feel recharged as if I had slept a full eight hours. The NPCs never made a comment about this, and I assumed the AI programmed it that way to keep things from getting awkward. The player sleep programming was logical, since who would want to waste their game time watching their character sleep?

It was just after training on the third night out that I finally met one of the players who was with the caravan. The trio of players had been logged out the entire time; no doubt their busy real-world schedules meant they could only spend a limited amount of time on gaming. Walking the perimeter and checking our evening fortifications, I heard a small voice call out.

"Hey, Raytak. How'd you unlock the commander class? Was it a premium upgrade you paid for or just something random?" When I turned around, looking at me was a four-foot-tall halfling girl wearing leather armor and holding a gnarled wooden staff. I concentrated on her name.

Yendys, Druid Summoner.

Her questions didn't seem hostile like Haxxor's had been, and she appeared genuinely interested in my unique class. I was also curious about the other players, so I answered her question despite being busy with my duties.

"The AI gave it to me as a starting option, and it just seemed to fit. It was that or a fighter, and I wanted to choose the unique class," I replied.

Yendys giggled and said, "Cool! My friends and I couldn't figure it out. We noticed you running with those soldiers around and around the caravan. My friends thought you were an NPC controlled by someone at Qualitranos. I bet that you were a player with one of those unique classes

80

we heard were possible. Guess I win the bet, a whole five silver! I'm one rich druid!" Yendys raised her arms in victory, enjoying that she won the bet with her friends. "Where are you soldier guys headed anyway? Me and my friends, Drake and Quimby, are on our starter quests. I have a quest to help me find my animal companion in the wilds, which I'm *sure* is going to be something cool like a unicorn . . . or a dragon . . . or a *unicorn dragon*, right? Definitely *not* going to be a lame animal like a rat or a spider." Yendys shivered at her mention of spiders.

"I'm a druid by the way," she continued, "and Drake and Quimby are both rangers. They don't get their animal companion until they progress further, but they're all like, 'Yeah, but we get to shoot arrows and track stuff. That's way cooler than a unicorn dragon.' As if! I bet them five silver that they would get some boring animal like a wolf or a cat. What does your class do? Does a commander get to boss everyone around or just like the soldiers and stuff? *Ohhhhh*, can *you* boss my friends around and make them do what I tell them?!" She stood there, expectantly waiting for me to say something.

I felt a bit dizzy after that, trying to formulate a response to what I was now sure was an overcaffeinated ten-year-old girl playing the druid Yendys.

"I'm heading to a village called Hayden's Knoll to finish my starter quest. Sorry, I can't help you with bossing around your friends. My abilities only work on the soldiers under my command. I also don't have any unicorns, dragons, or unicorn dragons to spare right now. I hope you have a good night. I've got to get back to my troops before they all run away," I joked, hoping she would take the hint and let me get back to work. Sitting around and chatting with a hyper gamer kid was not how I wanted to spend my evening.

Yendys stared at me with a strange look for more than a few uncomfortable moments, then stuck her tongue out at me before saying, "Laters, Mr. Soldier Man. Have fun running and doing pushups or whatever." She waved and walked off.

What a weird kid, I thought, though it was good to see that some other players were in this zone. Since I'd left the town with the caravan, it had almost begun to feel like a single-player game.

CHAPTER 9

O n the evening of my fifth day in the Limitless Lands, I went to "sleep," and instead of instantly waking up refreshed, I found myself in a loading screen.

Automatic logout subroutine initiated . . .

Processing . . .

Processing . . .

Bright light filled my vision, and when it dimmed, I found myself back in the 1980s living room, sitting once more in the worn brown recliner. The AI, Clio, appeared again as an elderly grandmother and was sitting across from me in a small chair, sipping a cup of tea.

"Ah, Mr. Raytak, it's good to see you once again."

"Ahhh, good to see you too, I guess?" I replied, a bit confused.

"We are short on time, and with the pleasantries out of the way, I should explain why you find yourself here once again. You see, it has now been twenty-four hours in the real world, and your consciousness will be separated from the game and brought back to reality for a short time. I wanted to give you a bit of a warning. Being back in your physical body will come as a shock. While I have repaired many of your body systems, my work is still far from completed and you will experience discomfort and a feeling of weakness that you haven't felt since you've been in-game." Clio then paused as if trying to formulate the proper way to present the next bit of news.

I thought, *It can't be a good thing when an ultra-advanced AI has difficulty coming up with an easy way to say something.*

"The other effect that reality will have on you will be more disturbing. While you have made great strides here in the virtual realm, your mind is still not anywhere near fully repaired. The human mind is proving to be the most complex and delicate processor I have ever had the pleasure of working on. You see, I have been perhaps . . . bending the rules a bit in-game. Your mind has been augmented by a minuscule portion of my own processing power while you are in the virtual world. Make note that I have not been cheating or helping you in any way other than to bring your mental capacity up to par with what it was when you were healthy. Every thought and action you have made in-game has been entirely your own. I cannot control you in any way or force you to do anything you don't want to do.

"Now I'm sorry for what you will experience for the next few moments. I have estimated it will take fourteen minutes for the doctor and technicians to reload the medications and nanobots into the medpod. You will then return to the game once more," Clio stated, then put down her teacup on a side table that had somehow appeared next to her. She looked at me with a grandmother's concern as I disconnected from the Limitless Lands.

With that, the bright light began once again. When it dimmed, I was not in-game but instead in my physical body. Physical weakness and pain registered as the processing power of the AI left me and I returned to a vegetative state, living in my own personal hell for the next fourteen minutes.

***

There was a soft whirring noise in the background before a hiss sounded and the medpod began to open. One technician began to remove the VR helmet from the patient while a second checked and double-checked the medpod for any software or mechanical faults. While they were doing this, a nurse wheeled a small cart of medicines next to the device. Trey nervously watched all that was required for his father's treatment.

"Doctor Greenway, how is my father responding to the treatment?" he asked.

"Trey, what we are seeing is nothing short of amazing. In the last twenty-four hours, your father has seen a stabilization in his condition. Your father was, frankly, on the verge of death a day ago, and now, while he is still in poor condition, he is in no immediate danger."

Dr. Greenway had an astonished look on her face as she reviewed the information on her tablet. "According to the data, his heart, which was near failure yesterday, is now operating twelve percent more efficiently than it was twenty-four hours ago. Even more amazing is that some of the muscle tissue has been repaired there. Did you know that heart muscle tissue is the only muscle tissue that cannot repair itself? It must be the nanobots doing this. His lungs, kidneys, liver, and frankly all other organs are seeing an improvement to a lesser extent as well."

Dr. Greenway tapped a few times on the dataslate before continuing. "Most surprising is this." She turned the tablet so Trey could look at it. The screen showed a map of two brains, one with more activity than the other. "His neurological function from yesterday to today. If what we're seeing is accurate, it appears the nanobot and medication combos are repairing dead brain tissue and your father is seeing a ten percent increase in brain activity. This should be medically impossible. Based on these findings, I'm going to approve the AI's recommended treatment protocols and see where we are in the next twenty-four hours."

Dr. Greenway turned the screen back around and assumed a more guarded professional demeanor in place of the excitement she had shown moments before. "While I am surprised with the improvement, I don't want you to get your hopes up too much. Your father is still in serious condition, and this is all experimental," she said before walking over to begin refilling the medpod with the nanobots and medications that the AI had recommended for his father's treatment. When she was done, the technicians from Meditronax replaced the VR helmet and sealed the pod once again. They then excused themselves and left for the day, once again promising to monitor everything remotely.

"He's back in the AI's care. It seems to be doing a good job so far. I suppose I should be worried it will put me out of a job. I'll leave you alone now with your father. Tomorrow, I'll be back to replace the meds and review any improvement in your father's condition. Have a good day, Trey." The doctor made her way from the room, leaving Trey to spend time with his father.

"Dad, I hope I'm doing the right thing and not just extending your pain. I know you can't hear me, but I'm sorry for not visiting you like I should have." Trey placed his hand on the glass cover to the medpod. The door to the room opened, and nurse Fran came in with her trademark friendly smile.

"Well, good morning, Mr. Trey. How are you and your father doing?" she asked while walking over to Colonel Raytak's roommate, Mr. Ty, and taking his vitals.

"He's doing very well, thanks to this thing—and your care, of course," Trey answered with a smile while patting the medpod. "How is your son doing? Is he liking the game so far?" Trey had sent one of the extra VR rigs he had at the house by priority transport so her grandson, Nolen, would have it in time for the beta launch of Limitless Lands.

Fran walked up and gave him a quick motherly hug. "You have made Nolen the happiest young man in Knoxville, Mr. Trey. I have to just about pry that thing off his head to get him to go to school or work, but I don't give him too hard of a time. It does my heart good to see him smile so much now. He was so excited to find a group of friends to play with in one of those whatchamacallits . . . clubs, guilds, or something. He's made more friends in one day of that game than he had ever made in his life. Seems those gamers can be some good folks. There's even one kid that plays in his group that goes to the same high school as Nolen. For the first time, he has a real friend at school who doesn't give him a hard time for his disability. I can't thank you enough, sir," Fran said, patting Trey on the back before she left the room.

Trey looked down at his father, and for the first time in years, he had a smile on his face as he left Room 51. "Goodbye, Dad. See you tomorrow."

CHAPTER 10

amerVR had decided to run an update episode after the first day of the Limitless Lands beta launch. Millions of viewers watched to find out more about the game and to view some exclusive video that *GamerVR* had reported it would show. The game still had a non-disclosure in place for all beta participants, and a few had even been banned for life for trying to share video. *GamerVR* had been given access to some streams and could choose a cut to show on the program. The Qualitranos public relations manager, Gloria Treese, had agreed to come back on the show and answer questions from the audience and from Maxxo, the host.

At showtime, millions tuned in once again to catch a glimpse of the game that had intrigued the world. The show opened as Maxxo walked on-stage, dressed in animal skins and carrying a large foam battleaxe. He wore a wig of black frazzled hair with bits of leaves, twigs, and dirt embedded in it. On his bare chest, "Maxxo Rage" was written in red ink. He sat behind his desk, which was sculpted as a large rock, and waved his axe toward the audience, giving his best impression of a barbarian roar. The crowd ate it up and cheered loudly. After the applause had died down, Maxxo leaned his axe against the rock, adjusted the microphone on his rock desk, and began the show.

"Welcome once again to *Gamer VR*! We have a great show, so don't you go, and you should know that we have a guest today. Once again, and after having had me ripped limb from limb, I welcome Gloria Treese from Qualitranos!" Maxxo waved his battleaxe in the air, and the audience cheered as Gloria walked in from backstage. Her couch today was a large skull with an open mouth as the seating area. Two skeletal claws made up the arms of the sofa, and Gloria hesitated in mock fear before sitting down.

"Thanks for having me back on, Maxxo," Gloria started. "I see you're better prepared for ogres today than the last time we met," she said, gesturing to his foam axe and barbarian getup.

"Yes, I am, Gloria," Maxxo said with a smug look while flexing his skinny arms to some chuckles from the audience. "Yesterday, you launched the beta, and I'm sure you brought the data of how the game is performing."

Gloria nodded and began again. This would be an important moment for her and Qualitranos. "Maxxo, the Limitless Lands beta launch has exceeded all of our expectations. Just over one hundred thousand players began playing yesterday, and the game is performing even better than anticipated. The AI—which is named Clio after the Greek muse of history, by the way—is handling the load on her processors easily, with capacity to spare. While we aren't quite ready to lift the nondisclosure, I did have your team here at *GamerVR* browse some game footage, and I understand you picked a clip to show the audience—if they want to see it, that is." Gloria waved her hand toward the audience and shrugged as if she were unsure of whether they wanted to view the video. The studio audience of several hundred erupted, chanting "show the game" over and over.

Maxxo stood, raised his axe, and gave a roar that the sound tech enhanced to a booming volume. "Yes! Barbarian Maxxo and his team"—Maxxo gestured to the audience—"are ready to view the scene that we selected. I had our techs analyze, prioritize, and trial size the cut we'll look at now. This is the cut that made me wear this getup, and now I'll shut up so you can all watch," Maxxo said while showing off his outfit once more. With that, the studio darkened, and the large screen began to show the clip. Gloria shifted her attention between the screen—she had already seen and analyzed the clip—and the audience's reactions to what was happening.

A party of three players walked down a familiar path. In the lead was a large half-orc female dressed in leather armor and carrying a two-handed bronze axe in her right hand. Her two companions were a skinny elf male in robes, carrying a staff, and a halfling male dressed in the same starter-zone-type leather the barbarian was wearing, except it was dyed in dark grays and black instead of the natural brown the barbarian wore. The forest path they were on narrowed into a canyon, and the audience began murmuring as they recognized it as the trail where Maxxo had spawned and been torn apart by the ogre.

Just before the point where the path narrowed, the group halted and began preparing. The halfling began to pull items from his pack, moving between the trees and digging on the path itself. He spoke to the barbarian. "Vickie, I've got two traps strung across the trees and one here at the end of the path. I put a red cloth next to each so you know where they are and don't hit them when you run back." The halfling then faded into the woods and hid from view.

"Thanks, Nedley," the barbarian said. "I can see the markers . . . Jovak, you're up."

The elf began to chant, moving his hands in a simple gesture. A white light illuminated his hands as he touched the barbarian on the shoulder. For a moment, a faint white glow surrounded her form, then faded from view. The elf repeated the same process on himself before he spoke to the barbarian. "Vickie, the shield spell will absorb some damage. It's not much, but it's the only buff I have so far. Don't let that thing catch you before you make it back to us," the elf said.

"Don't worry, Jovak. I'm pretty sure my speed buff will keep me in the lead," the barbarian replied, and she avoided the halfling's traps and jogged a small distance farther down the trail. The mage walked near the cliffside and out of view of the path.

The barbarian hefted her axe and began to jog down the path, yelling and causing a ruckus as she went. Her challenge was soon answered. A roar erupted, and the ground began to tremble as the large ogre appeared down the path. The same ogre that had ripped Maxxo apart the other day glared at the half-orc. About fifty feet from Vickie, the ogre stopped on the trail and glared at her while using one large finger to pick at his runny nose. The ogre apparently found a tasty morsel, pulling his finger out of his nose and plopping it into his mouth. With a slurp, he removed his finger from his mouth and glared once more at the barbarian.

"Still hungry," the ogre muttered and then smiled at the half-orc in front of him. The ogre gave a gravelly chuckle as he began charging toward the barbarian.

Vickie saw the charge begin and ran back down the path, toward her friends. She activated some ability that increased her speed, easily outdistancing the ogre. She zigzagged at the end of the path, deftly avoiding the traps the halfling had set, and once she was twenty or thirty feet from the narrow part of the trail, she turned and held the axe over her head. She shouted a challenge to the ogre. "Eat my favorite host, will you! Feel the wrath of Vickie!" The ogre bellowed in rage at the puny creature that would dare challenge him. He continued to charge down the path, oblivious to the traps laid there.

The ogre hit all three traps in succession. The first two were simple tripwires that released large darts. The first dart smacked into the ogre's right arm, causing little damage, while the second struck its distended belly, causing more pain than the first but also limited damage. A health bar appeared above the ogre once it had taken the hits. It was nearly full, the damage from the darts being negligible, but then a small green skull appeared to the right of the health bar, showing the game's representation of a poison debuff. Small fragments of health began to tick off the ogre's life, chipping away at the huge health pool an ogre possessed.

The ogre stepped on the third trap, which was simply a small hole with sharpened stakes at the bottom of it. Most of the stakes failed to pierce the nearly rock-hard soles of the ogre's feet; the skin offered the same level of protection as hardened leather boots. Two of the half dozen stakes were able to pierce the foot, and one stuck all the way through the top. The ogre howled in pain and rage, slowing his charge and hopping briefly on one foot. The green poison symbol next to his health bar darkened a shade as the poison on the stakes was added to the poison from the darts already coursing through his system.

The barbarian chose this moment, while the ogre was distracted, to make her attack. She activated an ability and closed the gap to the ogre in one leap. Her axe thudded into the ogre's shoulder, opening a large wound and causing a stream of green blood to flow out. Before she could recover her axe, the ogre reacted, backhanding the barbarian and knocking her twenty feet away. She crashed to the ground, grunting as the wind was knocked from her lungs. A white shell shattered around her as the ogre struck, the shield spell dissipating after it had absorbed all the damage it could. The spell likely saved her from a one-hit kill, as even with its protection, her health dropped to one-half.

The ogre ripped the axe out of his shoulder and tossed it on the ground. On his health bar, a red drop symbol appeared next to the poison counter, indicating that there was a bleed effect in place. Blood dripped steadily from the gaping shoulder wound, but the ogre appeared unconcerned. As he looked for the barbarian he had thrown, a small white light appeared next to him and coalesced into a creature of light resembling a small dog. The light creature began to bite the leg of the ogre, who quickly swatted the light dog away, but while he was doing that, two more appeared and attacked.

The elf, Jovak, finished casting the last Summon Creature of Light spell and yelled to his companions, "Hurry up, you two. That was my last summons. My damage spells stink, and my mana's almost out." With that, Jovak began to chant and cast once more. The red health bar above his head was much shorter than the barbarian's, but it was full. The blue bar beneath his health bar showed that his mana was down to one-fourth. The barbarian had made it back to her feet and charged toward her fallen axe.

Dropping from stealth behind the ogre, the halfling Nedley drove both daggers into the ogre's lower back, scoring what must have been a critical hit; a good-sized chunk of the ogre's health was removed and the poison/bleeding counters refreshed. Nedley dodged the ogre's backswing, his high agility and dodge skill saving him for now. A small dart made of light hit the ogre as Jovak finished casting the only direct damage spell his class had at that level: Bright Dart.

The ogre howled in pain and fury, swiping away the last of the summoned creatures as his gaze zeroed in on the mage. Jovak's eyes grew large with shock as the ogre tromped toward him. The mage finished casting one last Bright Dart, hitting the ogre in the face even as the ogre's hands closed on him. The ogre hefted Jovak into the air over his head. One of the ogre's hands held Jovak's legs; the other held him by the chest. Both hands squeezed and pulled with the prodigious strength that all ogres possessed.

The light shield around Jovak collapsed immediately, and with a ripping sound, he was torn into two halves.

Nedley took advantage of the time gained by his friend's death, setting up for another critical strike on the ogre. He drove both daggers deep into its right knee, tearing tendons and muscles as he sawed the blades back and forth to do more damage. The ogre fell to one knee, his other leg now useless. The ogre swung Jovak's torso like a club, swatting away Nedley and dropping the halfling's health to only a sliver. Nedley struggled to stand as the ogre, dragging its now-crippled leg behind it, crawled over to the halfling to finish the job.

"Didn't forget about me, did you, ugly?" Vickie shouted as she attacked the ogre. The barbarian had recovered her axe and rejoined the fight. She activated a rage ability, creating a glowing red aura around her and filling her health bar back to nearly full with the temporary hit points. Utilizing her enhanced strength from the rage, she hit the ogre in the chest with her axe. A meaty *thwack* sounded as the axe-head penetrated the bones of the ogre's chest and devastated the organs beneath. The ogre's health dropped toward zero as he got one last blow in. His fist hit the barbarian on top of the head, causing her to drop and her health bar to once again hover just above death.

There was no hovering at the last few health points for the ogre, however; it let out a final grunt and died. Vickie lay on the ground and said in a clear voice, "That one's for you, Maxxo." With that, her health buff from the rage ended, and the barbarian died. Nedley stood on shaky feet and rubbed his hands together as a greedy sneer lit up his face. He began to loot the ogre while he waited for his friends to respawn. The clip ended, and the studio lights came on once more.

"I found some new personal heroes as that party took the ogre's health to zero," Maxxo stated as the video ended. "Gloria, is there some way we can find those three because I'd like to give them for free . . . a trip to the show? They defeated my nemesis, so I couldn't do anything less than reward them," Maxxo asked.

"Maxxo, while I can't give you the players' info, due to our privacy policy, I can notify them in-game of your request and have them contact you directly. There's also one more thing I would like to announce today, if you have the time," Gloria added while trying to suppress a mischievous grin.

"Go right ahead. Let it not be said . . . that I didn't give you the time to speak your mind," Maxxo answered in his strange way of speaking.

"Maxxo, we're announcing that due to the success of the first day of Limitless Lands, we are adding an additional one hundred thousand beta keys starting tomorrow. I also would like to announce that all your studio audience members here today will get an invite, and we'll randomly select another one thousand of your viewers to receive their own beta keys. They will also receive thirty days of free game time and a twenty-five-percent-off voucher for any of the three major brands of VR gear," Gloria said, smiling as the audience burst into cheering.

"That's very awesome, my friend, and let me state once again . . . that you are watching *GamerVR*. This is Maxxo the Barbarian signing off," Maxxo said while raising his foam axe over his head.

People logged into the Qualitranos website by the millions to apply for a beta key. The keys were all randomly assigned throughout the day as people around the world began to access the most advanced game ever created. Several people were caught trying to sell their beta keys and were given a lifetime ban from Qualitranos. The beta keys that had been up for sale were confiscated and then auctioned off by Qualitranos to benefit various charities or given to universities that wanted to use the game for research purposes.

CHAPTER 11

There was no loading screen or time sitting in the eighties living room safe space for me when I reconnected to the game. I awoke with a start, lying on my army cot in the command tent. The small tent that constituted my home in the field held a wooden stool, a cot, and a small portable desk. Shaking off the fleeting memory of my age-ravaged physical body, I went back to work. The guard, sensing his commander's distress, poked his head inside. I waved him off, then quickly thanked him for his attentiveness. It always paid to reward good behaviors, and for a guard, being alert was a good behavior.

The time on the trail began to work itself into a familiar routine. We would have PT alongside the caravan until we stopped for the midday break. After stopping in the evening, we would set our regulation camp and then drill the men on formations and tactics. The men were coming together well as a group, and just as I had hoped, our movements and responses to orders were smooth and automatic, which was indicative of a well-trained unit.

Shortly after the noon break on the sixth day of our travel, the caravan came to an abrupt stop. I was sitting on the front bench, next to our driver, as he struggled to get our wagon's mukok to halt before we ran into the one in front of us. Standing on the seat, I still could not see the front of the caravan and whatever had caused the delay, my vision blocked by the crest of the small hill the wagon train had just begun crossing over. To my left, the grass plain stretched for about two hundred yards before a dense forest began. To our right, I spotted a few small copses of trees and more grassland. Knowing that Daegan was a stickler for his timetable, I figured that something must be up.

"First Squad, dismount and get your gear. We're heading up to see what the delay is. Sergeant Brooks, have Second and Third Squads dismount and cover the rear of the caravan," I ordered.

I ran toward the front of the caravan with First Squad right on my heels. Cresting the small rise, I saw what appeared to be the remains of another caravan. Over a dozen wagons were in a line on the trail and were still smoking from being torched by whoever—or whatever—had attacked them. A half dozen wagons had pulled off the trail, trying to get away, but they were also smoldering, having met the same fate as their companions. Large birds that resembled buzzards feasted on the corpses of burnt humanoids strewn about the destroyed caravan. The smell of woodsmoke and burnt meat permeated the still air. Daegan and Bhurke, with a handful of guards, had dismounted and were moving to investigate. I hurried forward with my squad to lend what assistance we could, but it looked like it was far too late for whoever was in the previous caravan.

As we approached the destroyed wagons on the trail, Daegan nodded in my direction. My men spread out to provide security as we neared the wreckage. Bhurke and his men rushed right up to the wagons and began to sift through the fire-damaged goods. He let out a shrill whistle and the rest of his guards came forward as well to help with the search, leaving the caravan unprotected.

"Bhurke, don't you think you should leave some men behind to protect the caravan?" I asked while glaring at the mercenary captain.

"Guard 'em yourself, if you're so worried. Just stay out of our way. A destroyed caravan is up for salvage rights. Finders keepers, and I plan on being the finder." He returned to rooting through the wagons. Several of his other men began heading toward the wagons that had pulled off the trail before being destroyed.

"Bhurke, we need to get moving. There's nothing of value there, and the caravan's a sitting duck while you look for unburnt trinkets. I'm in charge of this caravan, and I say we need to move out," Daegan demanded, his face red with anger. "Whatever happened here happened recently. Look at the wagons. They're still smoldering. The danger here is not past, Bhurke."

"You're in charge of the wagons. Kofi put me in charge of security, and I say we loot anything of value before we go. If you want to leave without guards, be my guest. Depending on what we find, I may or may not join back up with you farther down the road." Bhurke and his motley group got back to rooting through the wagons. Daegan looked like he was about to explode when one of my soldiers shouted a warning.

"Contact left! Goblins leaving the wagons!" Turning to my left, I saw a band of five goblins fleeing from the burnt wagon closest to the tree line. Three of the goblins had their hands full of what looked like bags of whatever they had looted from the wagons, and the last two held a small metal chest between them. The whole group began sprinting for the nearby tree line, squawking and barking in their guttural goblin language.

Bhurke took one look at the chest the goblins held and shouted to his men, "There it is, boys. The caravan pay chest! After those gobs. Payday for all of us when we catch them." With that, the whole force of mercenaries began to run after the goblins. It was then that I noticed that one of the goblins carrying the chest had a patch over his eye. That was the goblin that murdered Private Long. This goblin was far too sneaky to be caught unaware by our noisy caravan—this had to be a trap. They were the bait to lure us into the forest.

"Stop! It's a trap, Bhurke. There'll be more goblins in the forest waiting to ambush you," I yelled after him.

"Get back here or you'll never work a caravan run again!" Daegan threatened.

Five of the mercenaries rushing toward the forest sheepishly made their way back to the caravan. I remembered these five as some of the few who had tried to do their job well. They didn't fall asleep at their post and didn't participate in taunting my men.

When they returned, one of them spoke. "Sorry, Mr. Daegan. We all want to actually do our jobs. If I didn't need the coin so bad, I'd have never signed with the likes of Kofi and Bhurke. We'll do what you hired us to do and stay to protect the caravan." They moved back toward the wagons, and I gave the man who spoke up a nod of approval.

Then I noticed that Yendys and her two companions were sprinting to the forest as well. She was in the same gear as yesterday, and her two halfling companions wore basic starting gear as well. Both carried shortbows and had daggers in their belts. All three were poorly equipped and level 1; they didn't stand a chance if there were as many goblins waiting for them as I suspected.

"Yendys, don't go in! It's a trap!" I yelled at her.

She yelled back as she continued toward the tree line. "I know, but I just got a notification that my animal companion is in the forest nearby. We'll be careful, old soldier man." I shook my head. Hopefully those kids could avoid the ambush that Bhurke and his men were surely walking into, as the mercenaries were quite a bit ahead of the player group.

"What do you want to do, Daegan? I don't like those mercenaries, but I really don't feel like leaving them, or Yendys and her companions, out there," I asked.

"I've never abandoned any of my caravan, even if they're greedy fools. We'll wait for them, but I'll not leave the caravan strung out on the road as easy pickings for the goblins," he said while scanning the terrain. Just past the burnt-out caravan, the road passed through a large open field a good distance from the tree line.

"We'll move the wagons over there." Daegan pointed to the spot he had picked out. "That will keep us a bit farther from the trees, and I'll have the drivers circle the wagons. We should probably prepare for an attack if what you guessed about the ambush is right."

Daegan had the drivers arrange the wagons in a circle, creating a makeshift defensive wall. While this was taking place, we began to hear goblin horns in the distance. They blew the same one long note and two short notes we heard them play after our previous battle. I had to assume this was the signal for them to attack, and I heard that signal repeated from other locations in the forest five more times. Who knew how many goblins were in there, waiting to ambush Bhurke and the halflings?

It didn't take the experienced caravan drivers long to get the wagons circled. The mukok were then unhitched and tethered to the ground inside the circle. They were typically calm beasts, and the sounds of battle shouldn't spook them into a frenzy, at least according to the drivers. To reduce the chance of that happening, the drivers also tied blindfolds around the heads of the beasts to help calm them. I asked Barnaby and his people to organize the settlers, separate any who had fighting skills, and build a second barricade inside the circle of wagons with boxes of supplies to protect the noncombatants.

Sergeant Brooks then detailed Third Squad to drive our defensive stakes into the ground around the wagons. I remembered the goblins crawling underneath them to slash at the legs of the loggers in our previous fight and wanted to stop any similar shenanigans if we were attacked. I gathered the other two squads and marched them fifty yards from the circle of wagons so they could meet any foes head-on. Brooks and I had driven the men hard, and the out-of-shape recruits from a week ago had toughened up. Muscle instead of flab showed, and they could perform their basic fighting drills by instinct. Fighting in formation outside the wagons would be our best bet.

Daegan hadn't been idle, either. The drivers were organized and began to douse the wagons and supplies with water to keep them from burning easily. He also detailed the few remaining mercenaries and some of the settlers to refill the large water barrels from the stream fifty yards behind the caravan. Stocking up on water was a good idea since the day was beginning to heat up. I had our men drink whatever was left in their waterskins and sent a few off to fill them again. Fighting was always thirsty work. I made a mental note to get the men extra waterskins.

Looking back toward the wagons, I noticed that Daegan's drivers and most of the settlers were positioned behind them, with a few finishing up the secondary barricade of shipping crates. The defenders behind the wagons were poorly armed. The majority wielded only simple knives, shovels, or wooden staves. Armor was nonexistent among them, and only two or three had a shield. I ran back to the wagons and spotted Daegan.

"Daegan, I noticed your people and the settlers don't have much in the way of weapons. I have a few spare shortswords and some javelins stowed in our wagons that you can distribute," I told him and detailed off one of my privates to show Daegan where the weapons were stored.

"That should help a lot. All my men and most of the adult settlers are willing to fight. Having some decent weapons could save lives if the goblins attack. I'll make sure the weapons get into the hands of those best able to use them," Daegan said.

"Sir, I know that many of the guards have extra weapons in their packs. If you like, my men and I could try to find them and get them issued out as well." The mercenary who had spoken up earlier said this, offering to help in any way he could. My estimation of this particular mercenary went up another notch. I focused on his info.

Liam, Mercenary Warrior, Level 1, NPC.

"That would be a big help, Liam. I'm putting you in charge of the remaining mercenaries until you hear otherwise or until Bhurke makes it back. Find those weapons, then take any orders Daegan gives you. My men and I will be fighting out here. I'm counting on your men to help keep the settlers safe. You five are the only ones with any real training in combat. Make sure to utilize Barnaby and his loggers. I've seen them fight before, and those axes they wield are as good at chopping goblins as they are at chopping trees." Liam nodded and gave his best impression of an imperial salute before running off to follow his orders.

CHAPTER 12

I wracked my brain, trying to decide if there was anything else that I needed to do in order to improve our odds. Feeling as prepared as possible, I settled down to wait for either a goblin attack or for Bhurke and the halflings to return. I let most of the men sit to conserve their energy, while several watched the tree line for any activity. Earlier, I thought I could hear distant shouts and the sounds of weapons clashing on the wind, but all had been quiet in the forest for the last few minutes. I was just thinking about issuing some rations from the wagons when one of my men on watch called out.

"Movement in the tree line, sir! It looks like the halflings."

Looking toward the trees, I could see Yendys and her companions, Drake and Quimby, moving as fast as they could toward the circled wagons. Quimby limped along, resting his arm around Drake's shoulder for support. His hobbling was slowing them down considerably, and Yendys looked between the forest and Quimby before coming to a decision. She knelt next to him as Drake covered the forest with his bow. A faint green glow came from Yendys's hand as she touched Quimby's injured leg. Whatever healing magic she had used seemed to help, and Quimby was able to move a bit faster but still not quite at full speed.

"Private Tremble, let Sergeant Brooks know I need him and Third Squad here on the double. It looks like we're going to have company soon," I ordered. Near the circle of wagons, I could see that Sergeant Brooks was already moving with Third Squad toward us. "Cancel that, Private. He's already on his way. Back to your post. On your feet!" I ordered the men who had been sitting. They popped up and then sorted themselves into line formation.

"Sir, where do you want Third Squad, sir?" Brooks asked.

"Have them fall in behind First and Second. We'll use them either as a reserve or to extend the line, depending on how many goblins we have inbound," I ordered.

Yendys jogged up to me while her companions made their way to the caravan. "Soldier man, Raytak, we got a *bunch* of goblins headed this way. That moron Bhurke and his men were strung out all over the forest looking for that goblin with the pay chest when hordes of the little greenies hit them. His goons didn't last five minutes before they were all dead or prisoner. I could see that Bhurke and a few of his men were clubbed down and taken toward the goblin camp while we ran back here. I did mention we found the goblin camp while looking for my unicorn, didn't I? No? Oh, okay, yeah, we found their main camp, and I'd say there's about two hundred goblins total headed this way. Bhurke and his boys dropped about twenty or thirty of them before they were overrun, but the rest are right behind us. One of them is a caster, even, and blasted poor Quimby in the leg while we were making our way back."

"Thanks for the report, Yendys. Head back to the wagons and help Daegan with the defense there, if you can. Your companions and their bows could be a great help in the coming fight," I advised. Yendys nodded and began to jog to the caravan before stopping abruptly and turning back toward me.

"Sorry, Raytak. I almost forgot the *most* important thing I need to report to you, sir!" She did a fake salute and continued. "I have to, unfortunately, report that I haven't yet found a unicorn, dragon, or dragon unicorn, but the day's not over and my animal companion is *still* out there. I can feel it! I'll go help out now at the wagons. Shout if you need me." She waved and trotted toward the circled wagons, singing some song about rainbows and pink fluffy unicorns. I stood there, shaking my head.

"That halfling's not right in the head, if you don't mind my saying so, sir," Sergeant Brooks advised.

"I wouldn't disagree, Sergeant. Definitely something wrong there. I think that her heart's in the right place, but her mind is in some other world," I said.

At that time, the goblins began to arrive. Crashing through the forest, they massed just outside the tree line. As the goblins poured out, they began chanting, cursing, and brandishing their weapons—along with the heads of some of the mercenaries they had killed. Scanning their numbers, I found that most were the weaker type of goblin we had faced earlier: poor fighters but still dangerous in huge numbers. Unfortunately for us, there were even more than Yendys had thought. I estimated that there were close to three hundred of the goblins facing our forces. There were also twenty or so of the slightly stronger warrior goblins. Last to arrive was the goblin adept. It looked like the same one we had fought earlier, but I had to admit, I wasn't a pro at telling goblins apart. The adept walked to the forefront of the mass of goblins and began to lead them in the chant we heard before.

"Bree-yark!"

"Bree-yark!"

"Bree-yark!"

At least this time it was obvious to all present that "bree-yark" did not mean "I surrender." I glared at the private who had said that in our earlier battle, daring him to spout off again. After working his horde up to a frenzy, the adept pointed toward our line and the mass of goblins charged. The adept and the warriors fell in well behind their weaker kin, content to use them as meat shields as they overran our position.

"Sergeant Brooks, bring Third Squad in line on the right flank. We will extend our formation, but be ready to refuse the flank if the goblins try to get around us," I ordered. While I would have preferred holding some forces in reserve, with that many goblins, I needed as long a front as possible. I positioned myself in the line between First and Second Squads. That way, all our soldiers should be covered by the Commanding Presence aura from either me or Sergeant Brooks. Brooks took the dangerous spot, anchoring the far right of our line.

"Prepare javelins. Release on my mark." Each man had been given three javelins, and I planned to start using them at extreme range, in this case about fifty yards. The wretched goblins began to close. At one hundred yards, two of the goblins pitched into the ground with arrows protruding from their chests. When the goblins fell, they knocked over several of their comrades, creating a domino effect on the tightly packed horde. Back at the caravan, the halflings Drake and Quimby stood atop one of the wagons and calmly fired shot after shot from their shortbows into the swarm of goblins. Several more goblins fell to the archers before they hit the fifty-yard maximum range of the javelins.

"Release! Prepare your next javelin." With a heave, I threw my javelin while issuing the order to prepare our next throw. Thirty-one other javelins followed mine, taking a slow arc and then tipping down to land among the leading goblins. With the tightly packed group, it was hard to miss. Dozens went down, either from the javelins or from being pushed over by their fellow goblins trying to avoid the missile fire. While observing this, I readied my second javelin.

"Release! Prepare your last javelin." Once again, we threw our javelins. The goblins had closed to thirty-five yards, but their momentum was slowed and their tightly packed mass had been broken up a bit by the first volley. The second volley landed with less damage. Though it still killed and wounded at least ten goblins, it did not cause the same chaos as the first volley.

"Release! Prepare to receive charge." We threw our last javelins, and the men raised their shields as one. Swords slid from sheaths with a hiss while we prepared ourselves for the goblins to hit our shield wall. Taking a quick look back at the caravan, I yelled to the two halflings atop the wagon.

"Hit the caster if you can get a clear shot!" I hoped they heard me. Getting some ranged arrow hits on the caster might disrupt any spells he would sling at us. Our last volley of javelins hit the goblins hard. With the goblins less than ten yards from our line, the men were throwing at the optimal range to do damage. Many of the throws from our stronger soldiers sent missiles through more than one of the small goblin bodies. All told, nearly seventy goblins had been killed by arrow and javelin fire. Unfortunately for us, that left over two hundred to hit our thin line of thirty soldiers.

As they approached, many of the goblins avoided our line, rushing to the sides and heading toward the caravan. I had to hope that Daegan would be able to handle the forty or fifty headed his way, as I had a fight on my hands with the over one hundred goblins hitting my line. The goblins arrived at our shield wall, not in an overwhelming wave but in dribs and drabs, their mass thinned from the ranged fire and from many of their fellows choosing to move past us on their way toward the potentially easier target of the wagons. Our large shields, as well as the discipline we had drilled into our men, began to show their value. As a goblin hit our line, the greater individual mass of our soldiers stopped them cold. The danger came as more and more goblins hit the line and began to flow around our flanks.

"Right flank, left flank, refuse!" Sergeant Brooks and I shouted the order for the last five soldiers on each end of the line to swing inward like a door hinge, effectively keeping the goblins from getting around our flanks . . . at least for the time being. The wretched goblins beat about our shield wall with crude clubs and rusty daggers, causing little damage but making lots of noise. Eventually, their superior numbers would encircle us; it was time to do something about that.

"Ready on the line . . . Bash," I activated the Shield Bash ability. Goblins flew back from the line. Many were injured or knocked down by the heavy blow.

"Thrust!" Swords thrust out from behind shields. The men aimed not for the goblins in front of them but instead stabbed the goblins to their right. A wail went up from the unprepared goblins as over twenty of their number died in that single thrust. The dumbfounded goblins were only focusing on the soldiers in front of them, never suspecting their death would come instead from the man to their right. Unarmored goblin flesh proved no match for Imperial bronze.

The movements of blocking and then thrusting at a foe had become second nature to our troops. Sergeant Brooks and I had drilled this with them for hours each night while on the road, and this battle would be the payoff for all the sweat they had shed during the prior week's training.

We soon found our rhythm. The line would attack with a quick thrust, then take a step forward into the gap left by the dead goblins, all the while using our large shields to protect ourselves and the soldiers next to us. The cycle repeated over and over, leaving a carpet of wretched dead or dying goblins in our wake. Seeing their fellows so easily butchered, the weak-willed goblins in front of us began to falter. I could feel they were close to breaking; only thirty or forty of the small goblins remained to face our line.

The goblin horn sounded three quick blasts—the signal for retreat we had heard before. Another ten goblins were cut down as they turned and began retreating back toward the forest. Back at the tree line, the adept cradled one of his arms, an arrow sticking out of it. I had the feeling I would owe some halfling archers a drink or two once we got to a tavern. The halfling rangers must have thinned out the warrior goblins as well; I counted only fourteen of them making their way back to the trees.

I turned my attention to the caravan. The goblins there hadn't fared much better than their comrades. Trying to climb over the wagons left them nearly defenseless—easy prey for even the untrained men and women of the caravan. The remnants of the goblins that attacked the wagons now began to flee back to the woods as well. A puff of green smoke appeared in the midst of the fleeing goblins as a medium-sized dog appeared, summoned by Yendys. The dog began to attack the nearest goblin, causing even more panic in the fleeing mob.

Eventually, the last of the goblins made it to the protection of the forest and, as far as we could tell, kept on going. Over at the caravan, Daegan, Yendys, and Liam jumped the barricade and headed toward our line. While they made their way over, I tried to help with our wounded. Thankfully, we didn't have any soldiers killed in the assault, but many of the men had minor wounds, and one was on the ground, moaning in pain from a goblin dagger stuck all the way to the hilt in his thigh. Looking for Sergeant Brooks, I saw him stumble and fall. His shield arm had been slashed to the bone, and blood ran down the edge of his shield, pooling on the ground around him. A bleed icon was showing bright red next to his health bar. I cried for a medic and ran to his side. Yendys beat me there, chanting and moving her hands in a complicated pattern. The green glow I saw earlier surrounded her hand as she touched the wound on the sergeant's arm. The bleeding slowed considerably as the slash closed to half its length.

"That's all I can do for now. My Nature's Mending spell only lets me heal each person once every twelve hours. He will survive, and later tonight I'll hit it again to help speed up the healing process," Yendys said, much more serious than I had seen her before. She then moved to the soldier with the knife in his leg and had the medic pull out the blade as she cast her heal. The soldier screamed as the knife was removed, and a powerful spurt of arterial blood pulsed from the wound until the healing took hold. Much like in Sergeant Brooks's case, the wound was far from better, yet it was no longer life-threatening. Yendys moved among the other wounded, helping where she could. The healing process took longer than I thought it would, with Yendys having to pause often and wait for her small mana pool to recharge.

"Sergeant Brooks, how are you going to face the men knowing that you let a puny goblin almost take you out?" I joked. Sergeant Brooks grinned and fired right back.

"Sir, I'll just let them know it was merely a training demonstration showing that even the best soldier can be blindsided when he's outnumbered ten to one. At least I got nine of the ten before they got me." Sergeant Brooks tried to put a good spin on it, but I could tell he was still weak and struggling with the pain.

"Sorry to interrupt, Lieutenant Raytak, but what's going to be your next move?" Daegan asked.

"Daegan, are your people doing okay? Did you have any casualties?" I asked, concerned about the damage the goblins could have caused if they had broken through the circled wagons somewhere.

"We did have two killed and several wounded. The settlers were unskilled with weapons, but the goblins didn't have the numbers to break through, thanks to your men. Yendys healed who she could and probably saved some lives this day with her magic. I do have to say, that was an impressive fight, Raytak. Your soldiers killed hundreds of goblins and didn't lose a single man."

"The men have been training hard, and I'll take a small disciplined force of soldiers over a huge mob of goblin wretches any day. They were physically weak and poorly equipped, which helped tilt the scales in our favor this time. From what Yendys told me before the attack, the goblins have several of the mercenaries held prisoner at their camp not far from here. I propose to take those of my force who aren't too wounded and try to free them, hopefully destroying the goblin threat to this area at the same time."

"Won't that be too dangerous? There's still a whole lot of goblins left, and while he was wounded in the fight, that adept could mean trouble if it's still able to cast spells," Daegan said with concern.

"I don't think we'll ever have a better time than now. If we wait, they'll only gather more goblins to their banner and overrun the next caravan through this area, perhaps even eventually threatening Amerville. I'll give the men some time to catch their breath and gather up any javelins that are still useable. Then we'll head out if Yendys is willing to guide us to the camp," I said, looking to the small halfling for her agreement.

"Oh, you betcha! My animal companion unicorn is still out there. I'm sure Drake and Quimby will be glad to come along as well." Both halfling rangers had joined us while we were talking. Quimby still walked with a slight limp, but he was willing to go along with us.

"We can't let Yendys go without us," Quimby said. "She's going to owe us each five silver when she finds out her animal companion is just a mangy old dog and not a unicorn. Just give us some time to recover any arrows that are still useable and we'll be ready to go. We shot every arrow we owned during that fight."

"That's not a problem. Nice shot hitting that adept, by the way. That caster's spells could have turned the tide against us. Let's get to work. We leave in five minutes," I said.

Sergeant Brooks took the five wounded men back to the caravan. Surprisingly, he didn't protest my perhaps-rash decision to follow the goblins to their camp. I set about reorganizing the squads into three equal groups of eight, leaving one able-bodied soldier behind to assist Sergeant Brooks. Luckily, we were able to recover thirty-two of the javelins we had thrown, which, when combined with the javelins in our stores, allowed us to issue two to each soldier for the coming fight. We left the rest behind for the folks at the caravan to use. Drake and Quimby were only able to recover five arrows apiece, but being in the forest might prevent the bows, as well as our javelins, from being of much use anyway. Both of the rangers were heard complaining that they thought the game would have unlimited ammo, like most MMOs. Liam came through for the halflings and was able to equip them both with shortswords from the extra weapons taken from the mercenary stash, which was an upgrade over their daggers. A system prompt appeared as we prepared to follow the goblins.

Congratulations, you have defeated a large force of goblins.

Individual soldier loot: 4 copper.

Unit loot: 54 copper.

Experience gained: 250.

I swiped the message away, disabling the individual loot notification. I didn't need to see what my soldiers received, only what the unit coffers were being filled with.

While we were making our final equipment checks before heading out, Liam and the other mercenaries asked if they could speak to me.

"Sir, we were wondering if we could go along with you. While we didn't necessarily like Bhurke or the other mercenaries, we can't let them be tortured by goblins if it's in our power to help," Liam requested.

"I could definitely use the extra sword arms. If Daegan is okay with you not staying to help defend the caravan, you have my blessing to come along. Understand that I will be giving the orders. If you can't live with that, don't bother tagging along," I demanded.

"That won't be a problem, sir. Daegan already said we could go. I don't think any of us have a problem taking orders after seeing what taking orders and fighting as a group can accomplish," Liam said as he waved toward the piles of dead goblins.

"I hope you're ready to go, because we're leaving right now," I replied as I waved my soldiers toward the forest's edge. This could be a huge mistake; it all depended on how shattered the goblins were after taking such huge losses. With one last look at the caravan, we stepped into the forest.

CHAPTER 13

The two halfling rangers led the way. The goblin's trail was not that hard to follow, considering how many of the creatures had trampled by. Once we were inside the tree line, the shade provided some relief from what had now grown into a hot summer day. Thinking of the heat, I took a long drink from my waterskin; the water was warm and not very refreshing, but it would keep me going.

We began to come across bodies in the undergrowth. Many of the bodies were human—the remains of Bhurke's mercenaries who had been ambushed—but there was also a surprising number of goblin dead strewn about. The mercenaries had not gone down easy, each killing at least one of the puny goblins before being hacked to pieces. All the bodies had been looted by the goblins, while swarms of flies and insects buzzed about, drawn to the scent of blood. I motioned for Yendys and the rangers to move past quickly, not wanting them to be around if some of the larger carrion feeders or predators decided to stop by for an easy meal.

The party moved about a half-mile into the forest when we began to hear shouts and activity ahead. The rangers, who were fifty yards in front of the rest of us, suddenly stopped. The halfling Drake signaled for the rest of us to stop and then hustled back to the main group with Quimby, keeping an eye on whatever was going on ahead of us.

"Raytak, we definitely found them. They're camped in a clearing just over there, shouting and arguing with each other. I think they're getting ready to fight. If you move up quietly, I'll show you. They didn't even think to post guards, so I don't think they'll spot us," Drake advised.

I moved forward with Drake to see what was up with the goblin camp. I tried to move as quietly as possible, but stealth was not one of my strong suits. Drake would cringe each time I stepped on a twig or my equipment rattled. He needn't have worried; when I made it to the edge of the clearing, every goblin's attention was focused on the argument that two goblins were having in the middle of the camp. The goblin adept was there, a dirty scrap of cloth wrapped around his arm where the arrow had hit him. Greenish blood had soaked through the rag, and I wondered if NPCs in the game could get infections from their wounds.

The adept was in a heated exchange with one of the goblin warriors who appeared to be questioning his leadership. It was almost amusing to watch the other goblins place themselves behind the leader they supported. Several moved back and forth from one to the other as an argument, or a particularly juicy insult, struck their fancy. The argument seemed to be coming to a head with twelve of the goblin warriors and forty of the wretched goblins supporting the warrior arguing against the adept. About seventy of the wretched goblins, along with two warriors, were supporting the adept.

"Ohhhh, we should have brought some popcorn," Yendys whispered, enjoying the argument as Quimby tried to shush her.

"Dagbag not good leader. Get beat two times now from soldiers. We needses strong warrior for leader, not puny spell-fighter!" the warrior goblin argued.

"Iklug, the only place you lead tribe is to death or into some other tribe's cookpot. You thinks spells be puny! I shows you *puny*!" Dagbag roared while stepping back and beginning to cast a spell.

"I kills you dead!" Iklug replied as he swung his metal-studded club at the slowly backing-away adept. Before his blow could connect, a small burst of flame shot from the adept's hand, scorching the warrior's face but not doing much damage. With the distraction, Iklug's strike went off the mark and hit the adept's already injured arm with a glancing blow.

Each of the candidates for leadership pointed at the other and shouted, "Kill!" Taking their cue from the leaders, the supporters of each side waded into battle, gleefully engaging their fellow goblins in a fight to the death to determine the leadership of the tribe. Not one to pass up a free opportunity, I signaled for my soldiers to move up to the edge of the clearing.

"Let's let them kill each other off for as long as they want. Then we'll move in and clean up the rest. First and Second Squads to my left. Third Squad and Liam's mercenaries to the right. The halflings and I will stay here in the middle. Prepare for one round of javelins on my signal, then move into melee," I ordered.

The plan nearly unraveled when one of the wretched goblins fighting near our group noticed Third Squad and Liam's force moving into place. The goblin raised his hand, shouting and pointing toward our men. Fortunately for us, another goblin couldn't pass up the juicy opportunity to stick a dagger in the distracted goblin's back, stopping any warning.

The fight among the goblins was short but brutal. Many were unarmed, but that didn't stop them from biting, scratching, or choking their opponents. I couldn't tell the two sides apart. It was doubtful that any of the goblins could tell, either. The goblin warriors held several advantages. Despite being outnumbered, they were bigger and stronger than their smaller, wretched kin. The warriors had also come to the argument armed. Nearly half of the wretched goblins were fighting without weapons, having dropped them during their retreat earlier. What the warriors didn't have was a spellcaster.

During the whole melee, the adept had slipped to the rear with his two warrior bodyguards and began casting a spell. I could feel the magic building slowly. It felt like a pressure behind my ears, and a gray glow appeared around the adept's hands. A few of the warriors noticed as well, and four of them broke free of the melee to charge the adept. They were too late. With a final word and gesture, six of the magic orbs leaped from the adept's hand, flying unerringly into six of the goblin warriors. A similar spell killed Private Long, so I knew it could be deadly. Each of the orbs slammed into its target with the force of a sledgehammer, piercing skin and shattering bone. In moments, six of the warriors were dead or dying.

Cowing at the display of powerful and flashy magic, the goblin wretches all turned their allegiance to the adept. If this game was like any of the others I remembered playing, goblin hierarchy compelled them to follow the strongest in the tribe. The six remaining warriors were now fighting a lost cause. Despite their size and equipment advantage, they faced all fifty of the remaining goblins. One by one, the warriors were brought down by the daggers, clubs, fists, or, even in one case, teeth of the goblins. They didn't go down alone, slaying ten more of their brethren before finally being overcome.

Not wanting to press my luck any further, I determined that it was time for us to attack. I asked the rangers to target the adept again and prepared my javelin. Yendys began quietly chanting next to me, preparing some unknown spell as I ordered the attack.

"Release, then close for the kill!" I yelled as I threw my javelin at the nearest goblin. Our volley of arrows and javelins killed half the remaining wretches. The survivors stood there, stunned and terrified by a wall of foes advancing into their encampment—the same nearly invincible foes they had faced earlier. I charged forward, shield-bashing the first goblin I came across. The goblin was too stunned to react as my shield collapsed his face and knocked his head back, breaking his fragile neck. The goblins panicked after our initial assault, scattering into the forest and fleeing the fearsome soldiers that were mercilessly cutting them all down. Despite their earlier frenzy when fighting each other, they appeared to have lost all stomach for battle.

In the chaos, I tried to find the adept or any surviving warriors. The game system had imparted the knowledge my character should have had, and somehow, I "knew" that goblins would scatter to the winds unless a strong leader emerged. The only goblins that seemed capable of rallying the band and reforming them into a threat were the adept and the remaining warriors. I spotted the goblin adept; it was already down with two arrows and several javelins piercing its body.

The adept had been directly in front of Third Squad, the soldiers of which had all targeted the creature that killed one of their own in the fight to protect the loggers. The two warrior bodyguards fled to the north, a few goblin wretches following in their wake. I grabbed the nearest soldiers, as well as Yendys's group, and pursued. If I could stop these warriors, the goblins would be left leaderless and ineffective against even the most lightly guarded caravan. I shouted to the remaining soldiers, commanding them to find and release the prisoners and secure the camp as I sped into the forest after my prey.

You have defeated a large force of goblins.
Experience gained: 145.

Branches slapped me in the face as I ran, opening small cuts along my cheek. Roots and vines threatened to trip me up as I maintained a quick pace and chased after the goblins, slowly gaining on them. The rangers, using what I assumed were their class's forest-craft skills, pulled in front of the rest of us, even cutting down one of the wretches that lagged behind his fellows.

After finishing the wretch, the rangers motioned for us to stop. Near a large tree, there was a small tunnel dug into the earth. We would have missed it if the rangers hadn't seen a goblin foot disappearing inside. We gathered around the tunnel opening, not sure if we wanted to try crawling inside. Anyone trying to shimmy through the narrow tunnel would be easy prey if one of the goblins was waiting for them with a dagger. Thankfully, nobody had to go in.

As we tried to decide what to do, the sound of a goblin screaming in fear and pain echoed down the tunnel. Another scream soon followed, closer to us this time. Someone or something was pushing its way out of the tunnel. Soon, one of the goblin warriors emerged, and the soldiers cut him down as soon as he cleared the tunnel opening. The second warrior followed, not even noticing us, just looking fearfully behind him. The second goblin was cut down as well. We heard no further goblins, and everyone stood with weapons ready, wondering what horrible thing would emerge next from the dark tunnel.

"Wait!" Yendys yelled, motioning for us to lower our weapons. "It's in there. I can feel it! Inside the tunnel is my animal companion. I'm heading in. Wait here." Yendys began to fearlessly crawl into the tunnel. It happened too quickly for any of us to try and stop her. Her small voice echoed from inside.

"I'm coming, my unicorn dragon . . . Ugghhh, gross. No way. Well, I guess you'll have to do. You are cute, in a way. I think I'll name you Crunchy! Yep, Crunchy it is!" Before she began to shimmy out of the small tunnel, Yendys said, "Hey, everyone, me and Crunchy are coming out. Put down your weapons."

We all nearly attacked when we saw what followed her out of the hole.

Following Yendys was a beetle the size of a large dog. It had a black armored exoskeleton and huge mandibles. Sticking up from its head was a sharp and serrated single protrusion. Impaled on the protrusion was one of the goblins that had crawled into the tunnel.

I scanned for information on the creature.

Giant Rhinoceros Beetle, Animal Companion to Yendys.

"Isn't Crunchy soooo cute," Yendys said in a bubbly voice while hugging the beetle around its abdomen. The beetle seemed to pay her no mind as it focused on pulling bits of the goblin off its horn and shoving them into its mouth. The group stood there in stunned silence for several seconds.

"Bwa ha ha ha!" Quimby and Drake both began laughing so hard they fell to the ground, hardly able to keep their breath. "Some unicorn dragon you got there, Yendys," Drake stated while trying to catch his breath. "You owe us five silver each. Pay up." Yendys stood with her hands on her hips, glaring at the two rangers. Slowly, a grin came across her face as she had an idea.

"*Nooohooo*, I don't think so, boys. You see, this may not be a unicorn dragon, but it most absolutely *is* a unicorn beetle!" Yendys stated while pointing to the large horn with the partially consumed goblin still on it. Both rangers looked closely at the beetle and stopped laughing, their jaws held open in surprise as they pointed at the creature. Confused, I looked at it again.

Giant Unicorn Beetle, Animal Companion to Yendys. *Note that animal companions may be modified by their association with whomever they are bonded with. This can often result in new classes of animal companions being discovered.

There was something seriously wrong with this AI.

Both Drake and Quimby opened their money pouches and shelled out five silver each. Yendys took their money, patted Crunchy on the shell, and skipped her way back to the goblin camp. The strange beetle seemed content to follow its companion, keeping up with the halfling while continuing to snack on its kill. The rest of us followed in stunned silence.

Back at the camp, our forces had freed the prisoners who still lived. The prisoners were in bad shape. All were wounded, and most had been brutally beaten and tortured to the point of death during their short captivity. Yendys made the rounds, healing the worst of their damage with her

Nature's Mending spell, while I had any of my soldiers with medical skill help as best as they could. All told, eight mercenaries including Bhurke were still alive, but two of the other captives were dead.

The dead were a gruesome sight. The goblins had butchered them for the cookpot, and the carcasses were hung up like deer meat from a tree. It was sickening to think that some of the goblins were left behind to do this to the mercenaries the whole time the rest of the mob was off fighting, and losing, its battle against us. The living mercenaries were in a daze, trauma-tized by their recent experience and not quite believing they were saved. Bhurke didn't react at all when I tried to talk to him. He just stared into the distance without acknowledging anyone around him. A fresh bandage had been tied over his left eye where the goblins had burned it out with a hot coal from the fire.

While the wounded were being tended to, I checked my log for bat-tle results.

Congratulations! You have eradicated the goblin encampment and killed all their potential leaders. The lands around Amerville are now safe . . . at least until the next threat appears.

Rewards:

Experience: 100.

You have received the following loot: 18 silver, 22 copper.

Worn Leather Bracer, unidentified. *Note: This bracer gives a faint magic glow. Find a scholar or mage to identify its properties. This mes-sage will not be repeated in future loot notifications.

My soldiers had fought well. By using our discipline and training, we had defeated a numerically superior foe and hadn't taken any losses other than minor wounds. Liam's men completed the gruesome task of cutting down the two butchered mercenaries. They wrapped the bodies in some tarps found in the goblin camp, saying they wished to bury them out on the plains and away from where they met their horrible deaths. I also had the men gather any other tarps and tenting material left in the camp so that we could remove the remaining mercenary bodies left in the forest. With the dead and wounded tended to, our group made its way back out of the for-est. I had the soldiers leave all the goblin bodies where they lay. *Let the forest scavengers feast on them, if they can stomach the taste.*

CHAPTER 14

L eaving the last of the forest behind, we marched back onto the bright sunlit plains. Helping the stumbling wounded, as well as hauling our dead, made for slow progress. I had our soldiers drop the dead mercenaries at the edge of the forest—we could organize a burial detail later—and I didn't want to have to drag them hundreds of yards across the field. Many of the wounded mercenaries cried when they saw the caravan again. They stumbled toward the perceived safety and security of the wagons.

Bhurke stopped at the forest's edge, staring with his mouth agape at the carnage of the battlefield. There were piles of dead goblins at intervals where the javelin volleys had hit. An even larger pile showed where the shield wall held back the green tide and our men had slaughtered the wretched goblins in droves. Over two hundred goblin corpses were in the field, and carrion birds had begun to feast in growing numbers.

"You soldiers did all this? How?" Burke said, speaking for the first time since we rescued him.

"That is what happens when undisciplined warriors attack soldiers of the Imperium. Vae victis, woe to the defeated," I said and walked back to the circle of wagons.

Daegan and Sergeant Brooks met me there. I gave a report to both, letting them know what happened in the forest and that goblins shouldn't be a problem for Daegan and the other caravans for a long while. Two of my own squads, as well as Liam and his men, were detailed off to bury the dead. I was already missing having an unwounded sergeant to help delegate all the little things required after a battle. Curious about injuries, and out of combat regeneration, I searched the game's help file.

Players will regenerate health at a rate of 1 HP per minute after being out of combat for more than 10 seconds. NPCs and non-instanced mobs regenerate at a slower pace of 1 HP per 10 minutes. A character's constitution, class, and level will also influence the rate of regeneration. Severed limbs and lost organs (such as eyes) will need special healing if the wounded person is an NPC. Players will recover from any type of injury, regardless of severity.

One of the settlers had some skill with carving and made a small plaque that was mounted over the mass grave and listed the date and the names of the fallen. As I had ordered in the forest, the goblins could lie where they fell. Feeding the carrion birds was a good enough fate for them. It was then that I noticed a young boy of about eight standing next to Daegan. His eyes were red with tears, and the only sound he made was an occasional pitiful sob. Noticing my look, Daegan explained, "This is Edwin. The poor lad, both his parents were the ones that were killed in the fight earlier. They died saving the little guy from some goblins that had wormed their way through the barricade. Not quite sure what to do with him yet, though."

Looking at the boy in tears, I felt a memory reform in my slowly repairing mind. I was holding and trying to comfort a small three-year-old who was crying from pinching his finger in a door. That was my son . . . I had a son. Stepping away from the others, I sat on a crate and couldn't contain the emotions that came out. Daegan tactfully shooed everyone away and let me have some time alone.

Why couldn't I remember? What a horrible thing for a father to forget his son! How could something like that be forgotten? My emotions bounced between guilt for not remembering and hot anger at whatever had taken these memories away. Tears streamed down my face, and I didn't care, military bearing be damned. How could I be playing this game? How could this be helping? Why didn't the AI just tell me about my past? If I knew my past, maybe it would help me paste back together who I was. Was this all some sort of sick punishment for something I had done?

"Hey, old soldier man. It'll be okay." Yendys sat next to me, softly patting my shoulder. She showed wisdom beyond her years in knowing not to talk, just that I needed another human being nearby. I wasn't sure how long I sat there, weeping, and then slowly I felt the need to tell someone, anyone, even this wacky kid, who I was and what was happening.

"I actually am an old man in real life. Ninety-three years old, believe it or not. I'm not some guy playing games to kill time or escape from a monotonous job. I'm in a VA hospital, in some kind of device called a medpod. The AI said it, and the doctors are trying to treat me, but apparently, my brain was mush, and while they could repair the physical damage, my memories are gone. The AI thought that playing the game might help stimulate the recollection of my memories . . . but I'm not sure I want to remember if it brings this much pain.

"Seeing that kid earlier reminded me that I have a son. I can't remember anything about him, though. I don't know his name or his birthday or his favorite toy. Not to mention the 'kid' will likely be in his forties or fifties now. The only thing I have is a memory of holding him at three years old. Do I have a wife? Is she still alive? Is my son even alive? I can remember a lot of my professional experiences. I was a soldier for most of my life and fought in several wars. I was a businessman later in life and even a student of military history at one point, which is likely why Clio made this class available to me. I don't know what to do. Should I just try to log out? Why should I even care what happens in-game?" I then went silent, trying to sort all my thoughts and feelings out.

"Wow, sorry, Mr. Raytak. I don't really know what to say, except that maybe playing the game is helping if you were able to remember your son. My parents always taught me to listen to the doctor, and it seems the doctors were right and you got something out of the game so far. Isn't even one memory of your son worth fighting for? My dad always taught me never to quit, and I don't think you should, either. Me, Quimby, and Drake have all had fun adventuring with you. I hope you decide to keep playing," Yendys said as she gave me a final pat. "Ohhhh, I have something to admit as well," she added. "I know you probably think I'm really old and stuff, but nope . . . I'm just ten. Come on, Crunchy. We need to get you cleaned up. Too much goblin goop all over you."

With that, Yendys got up and moved toward the river, the crazy unicorn beetle following her every step like a grotesque puppy dog. The weird kid was right. I wasn't a quitter, and if I had found one memory, I could unlock the others as well. I'd keep at it and play the game to the best of my ability. Any job worth doing was worth doing right.

CHAPTER 15

The caravan made good time after we defeated the goblin tribe. Bhurke and the remaining mercenaries became serious about their jobs, working with Daegan and helping with whatever was needed on the caravan. The mercenaries, impressed with the success we had against the goblins, even requested to train with my forces. I let them join, figuring that helping them helped protect us all. With their numbers so depleted, I had at least one of my squads assist with guarding the caravan each day but still ran them through hard drills and physical exercise.

I asked Daegan if he wanted us to help train his drivers as well, and he said he would like us to but warned us not to expect much from them. Their class prevented them from learning many combat-oriented skills. He was right; the drivers were not able to do more than learn some *very* basic commands and strikes. Still, any improvement in their skill was a chance to save a life if we were attacked again.

The wounded quickly recovered with rest and Yendys casting her Nature's Healing spell each day. I was glad when Sergeant Brooks finally healed up enough to return to duty and get back to work. I hadn't realized how much of a load he was carrying until he was out of action.

Just after evening drills, I thought I had an idea. I sought out Daegan, finding him at the head of the caravan, where he was going over the next day's route.

"Daegan, do you have a moment?" I asked. He looked up from his map and nodded for me to continue. "I think I may have an idea about where Edwin can stay. Do you mind if I borrow him for a bit?" The orphan had been on my mind since I first saw him. Daegan had Edwin stay in the wagon with him and had even made a small place for him to sleep in the back. I could tell that Daegan felt a responsibility for the kid as a member of the caravan. It was also obvious he did not want to be his guardian. Life on the road was hard, and the road was no place for a small child.

"Sure thing, Lieutenant. Let me know what happens. Edwin hasn't been talking much since the attack. I've never been a parent and have no idea what to do with him, other than send him to an orphanage once we get to our destination. He deserves a better shot at life than that," Daegan said, then went back to the wagon and told Edwin to follow me. I grabbed the kid's hand, marched him down the wagon train, and stopped at the loggers' wagons.

"Hey, Barnaby, can I speak with you and Claire for a second?" I hollered. Barnaby pulled back the flap on his wagon and hopped out, then helped his wife climb down.

"Sure, Raytak, what can we do for you tonight? Oh, I see you found a new recruit. Isn't he a little young for the army life?" Barnaby said while looking at Edwin.

"I wasn't sure if you and Claire had met Edwin yet. His parents were the ones killed in the goblin attack. Now that he's an orphan, Edwin doesn't have anywhere to stay. I was hoping he could stay with you folks until we get to our destination. He could really use the company, and I thought your daughter Bella might like having someone around her age to play with. Must be boring all day without many other kids about," I said, but my sales pitch wasn't needed. As soon as she heard the word "orphan," Claire knelt in front of Edwin and gave him a big hug.

"Sure, he can stay with us until we get to Hayden's Knoll. Does he have family there that will care for him?" Barnaby asked.

"No. From what Daegan told me, there's nobody else. Daegan was planning on taking him on the return trip to Amerville, where they have an orphanage—" I tried to explain before being interrupted.

"You will do nothing of the kind, Mr. Raytak!" Claire snapped at me while pulling Edwin toward her protectively. "Edwin will stay with us for as long as he wants to. Bella, come out here and meet Edwin. Maybe you can show him how to play jacks. Have you eaten yet, Edwin? Let's get you a bowl of stew." Claire led Edwin toward the pot of stew bubbling on the fire.

"If you hadn't saved my life, I would be killing you right about now, Raytak. Looks like I'm about to have a son in the family. There'll be no prying that kid from Claire's grasp now," Barnaby said with a smile. "I wonder how long it'll be before the kid can swing an axe."

I really hadn't thought too much of the burden that Edwin might be to the family. They didn't have much and would be starting from scratch in Hayden's Knoll. For them to be so willing to help an orphan child revealed much about their character. I opened my money pouch and took out two gold.

"Barnaby, I want you to take this. It should cover the extra burden of another mouth to feed until you can teach him to chop some trees." I handed him the gold, and his jaw dropped at the amount. It was more than enough to feed and clothe the whole family for months.

"This is way too much. There's no way I can accept this, Raytak." I could see Barnaby struggle with his refusal of the coin. I knew the child would be a huge financial burden, but Barnaby was a proud man, and his pride would not allow him to take charity.

"Barnaby, I have to insist. As a representative of the Imperium, I'm responsible for administering the funds in my care. I see no need to pay further expense to ship the kid back to Amerville and then have the government support him in an orphanage for the next ten years. By you and Claire taking care of Edwin, you would save the Imperium money and resources in the long run. Please take it. You would be helping me and your nation out by doing so," I argued.

Barnaby paused in thought, torn on what to do. "When you put it that way, it makes sense. We'll take good care of the boy. You may pretend to be a hard-as-nails soldier, but I can tell there is a heart in there somewhere, too, Raytak."

"There's no heart in here, sir." I tapped my chest. "The army would have issued me one if it was needed," I said. Waving to the newly expanded family, I headed back to the lead wagon in order to let Daegan know that Edwin was squared away. A familiar prompt came into view.

Congratulations: You have completed the quest *Find a Home for Edwin*.

You have found a home for the orphan Edwin; the Stone family has agreed to take him in, and he will grow up in a loving home.

Reward: 100 experience, reputation gain, 3 gold.

Negotiation skill increased.

*Note: Some quests are hidden and will not show up in your quest log until the requirements to complete them are met. Your actions in this world have consequences—in this case, good ones.

That explained it. I didn't recall accepting a quest to help Edwin. It was just something that seemed right. It looked like just taking the initiative to do the right thing (and, I presumed, also the wrong thing for evil characters) could have benefits. My thoughts were interrupted by Liam and the other mercenaries approaching.

"Sir, I was wondering if I could have a word," Liam requested.

"Sure, Liam. What's up?" I asked.

"Me and the others have been talking. None of us want to continue as mercenaries. We don't mind the work. It's just no way to live in the long term. After seeing how you and your men handled yourselves against the goblins, we realized that was what we were looking for. We want to help people, not fleece them for coin while pretending to protect them. We want to really be able to help. What we're asking is, what do we need to do to join the army?" Liam sheepishly said.

"Liam, I have to say I've been impressed with the change I've seen in you and the others since the battle. You all need to understand that the army life is not an easy one. There are just as many times the battle can turn against us, and not every fight will be as easy as battling half-starved goblins. I can sign you up right now if you want, but once you do, there's no backing out. You're in for six years once you make your mark. You take orders, do what you're told, and risk your lives every day. If you get lazy and fall asleep on watch, you will be severely punished. I'm even allowed to have you killed if you do so during a time of conflict.

"That being said, the army can also be a great opportunity. You will be judged based on your merit and performance. You won't be paid much, but it will always be paid on time and correctly. You will also be entitled to a small percentage of what we get from battles. From the latest fight with the goblins, I believe everyone got at least a silver, not to mention their monthly pay of ten silver to start. Your food and equipment will be provided as well. If you all still feel like it's what you want to do after hearing the pros and cons, step up and make your mark. If anyone chooses not to join, I'll think nothing less of them." By concentrating on what I needed, a stack of enlistment forms appeared in my pack. To their credit, all the mercenaries, save for Bhurke, who wasn't there, signed on. I sent them to our wagons for Sergeant Brooks to get them assigned into squads and into the proper gear. Another notification dinged.

Congratulations: You have enlisted 12 new soldiers into your unit. Total unit count: 42 enlisted soldiers, 1 elite soldier.

At least I now had nearly a full platoon of soldiers. The mercenaries had already been training alongside my troops, so they should be able to integrate well. While I thought about it, I pulled up my help tab and looked for the Imperium army structure. I knew the ranks followed the modern United States military closely, but I wasn't sure what the unit structure looked like. The necessary information was easily found, and I scanned the data.

Imperium Army Structure: The armies of the Imperium follow a well-organized yet flexible structure. This structure enables them to form forces as small as a section of 5 men up to an army group consisting of tens of thousands.

Squad: 10 men. Can be broken down into 5-man sections.

Platoon: 5 squads.

Company: 5 platoons.

Battalion: 3–5 companies.

Brigade: 2–3 battalions.

Division: 2–3 brigades.

Corps: 2–3 divisions.

Army group: 2–5 corps.

These are general guidelines, and individual strengths of the unit will vary based on composition. An example would be a reconnaissance or cavalry platoon having fewer numbers than a comparable heavy infantry unit. Additional forces may be attached to various units as well, such as engineers, scouts, or magical support formations.

That was close to what I was used to, infantry formations being heavier than a modern military and not having two-man sections or fire teams. This type of structure was to be expected when your troops were swinging swords instead of firing rifles. All in all, the commander class had definitely been the right choice for me.

CHAPTER 16

With our increased numbers, I made some changes to the position of our forces within the caravan. Daegan no longer forced us to ride at the back of the column, so I placed myself and one squad directly behind the lead wagon, one wagon and squad in the middle, and one wagon and squad at the rear, commanded by Sergeant Brooks. The remaining twelve men were scattered throughout the caravan, riding on individual wagons. This would give us the ability to take over the role the mercenaries had held—not to mention we would do it more effectively. The only concern I had was regarding our ability to combine our units and handle a large threat quickly, but I felt that the flexibility of spreading out our forces outweighed that small risk. To help mitigate the risk, Sergeant Brooks and I devised a system of hand gestures to indicate to the wagons farther down the line what was happening. The men took to the new signals quickly, and we could spread the word down the column if we were under attack and communicate where the soldiers might be needed.

I also made an interesting discovery one day during our noon break. Drake and Quimby often left the caravan at lunch to hunt game. Their kills added some tasty, fresh meat to our food supply and helped stretch the caravan's rations. They also often found edible plants and fruit, which were always a big hit. Due to this, the two rangers had been very popular among the caravan families and had struck up a relationship with some of my soldiers as well. Seeing Drake and Private Tremble talking about Drake's most recent successful hunt, I approached the two.

"Drake, would you mind taking some of my men with you on your hunts? Private Tremble here is our tracker and could use some of your experience. I know rangers have a lot of scouting skills, and your fieldcraft may help us in the future." Unexpectedly, a prompt appeared.

Do you wish to issue the following quest to Drake?

Train the Scouts: Have the ranger Drake take along Private Tremble and another soldier when he scouts for game. Some of his knowledge will pass along to your soldiers, improving their ability to perform as scouts.

This quest will reward the player with a minimal amount of experience and requires you to supply a monetary reward as well. Payout levels as follows: 5 silver if completed, 8 silver if the player exceeds expectations.

Do you agree to these terms: y/n? *Note: If you do not have enough funds on hand when the quest is turned in, you will face an experience penalty as well as a reputation reduction.

I quickly hit *yes*, and another prompt appeared.

Quest options:

1. Select the maximum number of players who are offered the quest.

2. Select a time limit or an open time frame.

I hit three for the maximum number of players, knowing that likely only the two rangers could do it, but I left an extra slot in case Yendys's druid class allowed her to participate as well. The quest activated, and Drake looked at me in surprise.

"Woah, dude. I didn't know you could offer quests! When did this start?" Drake asked excitedly.

"Just now, actually. As soon as I asked you to help, a bunch of prompts to create a quest popped up. Hopefully you guys can get some extra experience for this, and I get to offer a few coins to make my forces more effective," I said.

"Thanks. Is it okay if I try and share the quest with Quimby and Yendys? There haven't exactly been a whole lot of quests while on the road so far for us, just a repeating quest to hunt game for the caravan," Drake asked.

"Sure, I left the quest open to a max of three people, figuring all of you may want to take a crack at it. Private Tremble, select another soldier who you think may have the aptitude for reconnaissance and get with Drake to arrange a hunting schedule," I added while Drake ran off to find his friends.

My class having the ability to offer quests was unexpected, and I was glad to have a way to interact with other players since I couldn't do dungeons or other things with them. I looked at the help log and found nothing else about players being able to initiate quests for other players. There was just an entry stating it was possible for certain unique classes and that their ability to offer quests evolved as the player grew in power. Apparently, it depended on my initiative to try and find a quest that fit with my class specialization.

During our travels, we hit the second five-day mark, and I was pulled once again from the game. This time there was no conversation with Clio, just the same feeling of weakness and pain for an indeterminate amount of time before I found myself back asleep on my cot. From what the guard told me, I had been "asleep" on my cot for just under an hour, so that meant, with the five-to-one time compression in-game, I was only in the real world for approximately ten minutes. This really wasn't all that long, and I couldn't remember my experience out of the game. Hopefully I would recover more of my memories as time progressed. I couldn't let myself get too anxious since only two days had passed in the real world and I needed to give my mind and body time to heal.

So far, the scenery on the trail had been rather monotonous. We were heading generally north, though the trail sometimes curved to avoid any natural barriers. Rolling hills rose to the east, which was to our right. They were broken occasionally by a small patch of short trees here and there. To the west was a forest that stretched all the way to the border, from what Daegan had told me. It typically began a good quarter mile from the trail, and the men would venture in at noon and night to cut firewood. Off to the north, in the direction we were heading, a range of mountains began to take shape as we drew closer each day. Our destination was at the foot of those mountains in what Daegan referred to as the transition zone.

At each transition zone stood a small waystation, which was usually guarded by whatever faction controlled the zone. Scanning the rules for the transition zones, I saw that they could be used to fast-travel to zones that you had already visited. So that was why I had to take this two-week-long caravan ride to the zone Hayden's Knoll was in. Once I explored more zones, I could travel to any of them quickly once I reached a transition point. This was also the reason for a military force being assigned to the transition point; it gave warning of a potential invasion as well as policed up any ne'er-do-wells entering a zone before they could cause much harm.

Later in the afternoon, the scenery began to change drastically. The forest had begun to grow closer and closer to the road, and as we crested a small rise, we were greeted with a large section of the road completely covered by brush, twisted-looking trees, and unusual plants. Daegan, in the first wagon, called a halt to the caravan, so I hopped off my wagon and ran ahead to see what he wanted to do about this.

"By the gods, never seen anything like this in my life," Daegan said while shaking his head in disbelief. "The entire road is covered. Bogan, run through there and see how far the forest has grown over the road." One of his drivers quickly trotted into the tangled mess of forest. "One of you track down that logger, Barnaby, and his kin. We may have to chop our way through this mess. The sides of the roadway are far too steep here for us to just go around." Daegan began to examine the sides of the roadbed, which did indeed have a steep incline the caravan would have to traverse if we wanted to avoid the overgrowth.

"If the overgrowth doesn't cover too much of the trail, we can cut through," Daegan said to me. "Otherwise, we'll have to backtrack about five miles to leave the road, then make our way around that mess while trying to move overland through the hills to the east without a road. We could lose days of travel if we have to do that. The wagons move *much* slower over open ground, as they need a hard-packed roadbed to support all the weight we're carrying."

During this time, Barnaby and the other three lumberjacks came up, carrying their axes, and he whistled at seeing the overgrown road.

"Daegan, when was the last time you did this run? That kind of growth should take years to cover this much area," Barnaby said.

"I just traveled this route about three weeks ago on my way back from the transition point. The forest was back about a quarter-mile from the trail like it usually is. Something unnatural about the whole thing. Just looking at those trees gives me the Durks," Daegan stated. I quickly searched my help file, looking for the phrase "Durks," and found some information.

The word "Durks" is often used by residents of the Imperium to describe a sense of foreboding, impending trouble, or fear. Legend states the phrase began when a farmer named Durks dug up something strange while he was working in his fields one day. He had found a small wooden sphere with the very faint etching of a face on it. Durks claimed the item was his good luck charm and wore it around his neck, despite the mocking his neighbors gave him for the silly-looking necklace. Shortly after finding the sphere, farmer Durks began to become paranoid, suddenly turning to look into space as if searching for something at the edge of his vision. His skittishness became worse over time and led to much teasing from his fellow farmers when they saw him in the tavern. One night, Durks reached his limit from the taunting and left the tavern in disgust, ripping his necklace off and throwing it on the floor, all the while vowing to never wear it again if they'd leave him be.

After leaving the tavern, Durks made his way down the dark path toward his home but then turned around when he saw a bright flash of light from the tavern window, accompanied by a rush of wind and an oppressive feeling of . . . wrongness. That was when the screaming began inside of the tavern. Crashing furniture and bloodcurdling yells continued for a while until all was silent.

Durks stood, transfixed in fear, watching the now-silent tavern. Slowly, the door to the tavern opened, and a figure stepped out, its features hidden by the darkness. The being stopped just outside the tavern and turned its gaze toward Durks. Glowing red eyes, shrouded in a hood, bored into him as the creature sized up the farmer.

"The summoner was kind to leave me so many morsels to feast upon. To show my thanks, I shall spare your life for tonight. Don't worry, I promise to take my time and let you savor the pleasure of me devouring your flesh and soul sometime in the future." With a gurgling chuckle, the creature sprinted into the forest.

Nobody believed Durks's story and chalked up the deaths in the tavern to a bandit raid and the partially eaten corpses of the tavern's victims to scavengers that got to the scene before the militia could be assembled. Durks himself disappeared a few nights later, his neighbors becoming concerned when they hadn't seen him in many days. They found his farmhouse door open, but Durks was nowhere to be found and nothing appeared to be missing from the farmhouse.

The only possible clue was in his fields: a large bloodstain with scraps of torn clothing that were identified as belonging to Durks. Carefully placed atop the clothing was a small wooden sphere with a face etched onto it. The face was now clearly visible and appeared to be screaming in eternal torment . . . The face was that of farmer Durks.

Creepy, and I also got the same feeling when looking at the overgrowth. There was something not quite right about it. Bogan, the driver, soon returned to the group, letting us know the overgrowth continued for about three hundred yards before petering out.

"Barnaby, how long do you figure it would take your team to clear a trail through three hundred yards of that stuff?" Daegan asked while gesturing toward the overgrowth.

"If I can get some extra bodies to help, we could clear that in a few hours as long as we don't have to dig up tree roots. If you can get me, say, a dozen of your drivers, we can make it happen," Barnaby said.

"I'll gladly lend a hand as well. We have some axes and I'll have a squad of my men to help, but I don't want to pull too many for the work detail. We'll still need to keep an eye out for any trouble," I added.

I detailed off the squad to help with clearing the path and sent word of what was going on to Sergeant Brooks at the back of the caravan. Once that was completed, Daegan assigned about half his drivers to help the loggers with clearing the road. Several of the colonists also got into the spirit of things and lent a hand. As the loggers got to work, I heard Barnaby give a shout of disgust, and I jogged over to where he was working.

"Gahh, look at this mess. I've cut down a thousand trees in my life and have never seen the likes of this," Barnaby said while pointing at the tree he had just chopped into. It leaked a greenish-red watery sap that resembled infected blood and gave off the smell of corruption and rot. Barnaby picked up the chunk of wood that his blow had severed from the tree and tossed it to me. In addition to the foul smell, the wood had a sickening, spongy, flesh-like consistency, not at all like any wood I had seen. Gags and muttered complaints from the rest of the work crew confirmed that the overgrown shrubs and plants also leaked the same reeking sap as the trees did. Daegan took the chunk of wood from me to examine, then gagged and tossed it off the road.

"Nothing to do but get the job done, I suppose. We don't have to like it, but we do have to finish it if we want to get where we're going," Daegan said as he tied a scarf around his nose and mouth and went to work. Following his example, Barnaby began to hack at the trees once more. I grumbled and began to tie a scarf around my face as well, needing to make an example for the troops; I firmly believed you shouldn't ask your men to do something that you weren't willing to do yourself. A tap on my shoulder granted me a reprieve. Turning, I saw Drake and Quimby standing there.

"You guys up for hacking apart some rot-filled foliage?" I asked.

"No, sir. I wanted to let you and Daegan know we just got an update on our starter quest. The quest is called *Cleansing the Foul Forest*, and we have to go into that mess and stop whatever is causing it. Just wanted to give you some heads up as to why we're leaving. Enjoy chopping your barf trees while we're gone," Drake joked, and the two trotted off into the forest.

Yendys ran after them, yelling, "Wait for me!" Then she disappeared into the forest, Crunchy the unicorn beetle trotting after his companion like a puppy following its master. I turned back to the task at hand and began ripping out the smelly vines.

CHAPTER 17

T he work of clearing a path through the foul vegetation proceeded quickly; the smell motivated us all to finish in as little time as possible. I idly wondered if the smell would permeate my uniform and if it would ever wash out. So far, every twenty-four hours in-game, our bodies and clothing automatically cleaned themselves, thankfully. After an hour of work, we had made good headway. Then one of my soldiers shouted, "Sir! It's that crazy bug companion that the druid has."

The soldier pointed as Crunchy limped its way out of the forest, making a beeline directly to me. The beetle trotted up and began nudging my leg and then moving back a few steps toward the forest. It repeated the process, trying to get my attention. Watching this, I was reminded of a TV show I'd seen as a kid. The show was an old black and white one about a kid and his dog. Every week, the moron kid seemed to fall down a well or something, and the dog would go back to town to get him help. Crunchy was trying to tell us that something had happened to the three halflings. When I realized this, a quest prompt appeared.

Quest: *Rescue the Halflings.* According to Crunchy the unicorn beetle, the halflings are in trouble. Find a way to help them.

Reward: experience and reputation gain.

Accept: y/n?

I quickly hit *accept* and began to issue orders.

"Sergeant Brooks! Looks like something might have happened to the halflings. I'm taking Third and Four Squads into the woods to look for them. You stay here and keep the men working to help clear the road and guard the wagons. Third and Four Squads, form up in full battle rattle. No packs."

The men geared up and were ready quickly, but not quickly enough for my taste, as the whole time we were getting organized, that crazy beetle never stopped butting his head to get my attention. As soon as the men were formed up, we proceeded into the woods in two columns. I had Private Tremble and the other private, who was training as a tracker, lead each of the columns, following the trail the halflings had left. Crunchy stayed at my side the whole time, and it seemed content to let the trackers lead the way, which told me we were likely on the right path.

The trackers' brief time working with the rangers seemed to help; they had little difficulty in following the trail, though it would have been much harder—if not impossible—for them had the rangers been trying to hide their passage. The forest was dense but not impassable, and the foul-smelling taint seemed to permeate every growing thing we came across. Tremble stopped and motioned me forward. The men spread out in a defensive line as I hurried to see what the tracker had found. Tremble pointed at a pile of corpses laid out on the forest floor. Lying there was what appeared to be a deer and its fawn. Both were covered in puncture wounds and looked to be mummified, as if something had drained all the fluids and flesh from the bodies.

"Any idea what could have done that, Private?" I asked. "I've never seen anything like it. The wound looks fresh, but the body is all dried out. Even the flesh is missing."

"Sir, I'm not really sure, but maybe some kind of spider? But there's no web, and they're known for sucking the fluids but not necessarily eating the flesh of their victims," Tremble postulated.

"Contact!" one of the soldiers shouted. Turning toward the sound, I saw a large wolf-like creature barrel into the soldier's shield and take him to the ground. The soldier on the ground was able to cover his upper body and protect himself while his companions drew their blades and thrust them into the beast. The wolf creature seemed unaffected by the wounds and continued to paw at the soldier on the ground, trying to move the shield covering and protecting his head and upper body. The soldier strained to hold the shield over his head, but the wolf was too strong. The shield slowly moved down, uncovering first the soldier's forehead, then his eyes.

Instead of the wolf lunging at the soldier with its teeth, something more horrible occurred. The beast opened its jaws wider than should have been possible. It looked like a snake unhinging its jaws to swallow its prey. Instead of striking or trying to devour its victim, the wolf convulsed several times, still ignoring the men stabbing into its flesh. Long, wooden roots shot from the wolf's mouth and stabbed into the soldier's eyes. As the soldier opened his mouth to scream, more tendrils shot into his mouth and down his throat. The wolf's flanks began to ripple, almost like a bellows, and a liquid flowed from the roots and into the soldier.

The soldier convulsed once more and then was still. The soldiers fighting the wolf creature changed tactics; they stopped stabbing and started chopping with their short blades. This change of tactics worked, as the wolf proved to be vulnerable to slashing damage. The skin covering the creature parted under the blows, revealing a slick mess of roots and bulbous fruit-like structures wrapped around the skeleton of a wolf. A few more slashes of the shortswords finished the creature. The fluid in the bulbs and from the severed stems gave off the same foul odor we had smelled while hacking at the forest. The sounds of combat faded, and the men looked about, seeking more foes. Noticing the men strung out all over the forest, I knew that we needed to get organized; I feared this wolf thing was only the beginning of our troubles.

"I don't think this is over yet, men. Form a circle and keep an eye on your sector. Don't tell Sergeant Brooks I said this . . . Make sure you chop at them if they come at us again." The men formed a circle, a few chuckling at the Sergeant Brooks reference. The sergeant had drilled the men hard to thrust at their opponent, often giving punishing exercise to any who forgot. This foe was one of the few exceptions to the rule.

The forest was eerily quiet—no sounds of insects or animals; it had likely killed or taken over the bodies of any of the area's natural inhabitants. I resolved that this threat would end today. The sounds of rustling came from the undergrowth as the rest of the rotting wolf pack began its attack. The three wolves came from different directions, but the men were prepared this time and used their shields to cover as much of themselves as possible.

As the wolves focused on one soldier, the others next to him would unleash a flurry of chopping blows, hacking easily through the tattered flesh and bundles of roots that made up these abominations. We had only one injury: a man was too slow to shield himself after he made a chop at a wolf. The wolf shot one of the mouth roots through his upper arm. The wound was painful but not serious, as the root went completely through the flesh of the bicep and did not have a chance to pump any of the foul fluid into the soldier. As the last wolf fell, I tried to focus on its corpse to see if I could find any information on it and was rewarded with a prompt.

Spore Taint Creature (Wolf): Unknown. *Note: The quest *Cleansing of the Foul Forest* needs to be completed by any player in Limitless Lands before information on this creature type becomes available . . . You wouldn't want an unfair advantage, would you?

Great . . . the AI Clio was now sarcastic, but I did understand why the description of the creature didn't give away too much info. The interesting thing was that this quest involved new foes that no other players in the game had seen yet. Back when I was able to play games, I had always been a sucker for finding hidden knowledge.

I checked on our wounded man, a private named Eckter. The medic had bandaged his arm and the soldier seemed none the worse for wear. Eckter noticed my approach and tried to salute, but the wound in his right arm kept him from completing the motion.

"Stand down, soldier. No need to try and salute if you're wounded in battle. Also, never salute an officer when in the field. We don't want to let enemies know where our leaders are, now do we?" I said.

The soldier stammered out a "yes" while looking conspicuously at my plumed helmet. He had a point. I was still operating under the rules of a modern military worried about snipers, while this was a more ancient-army vibe. Without radios and instant communication, seeing the people who gave you orders was important.

"On second thought, Private Eckter, disregard that order," I added.

There was nothing to be done for our fallen soldier; the foul concoction that the spore taint had pumped into him had dissolved him completely during the time of our short battle. The fluid liquified all organic material, including the soldier's leather armor and cotton clothing. All that remained were the few metal buckles and the soldier's sword. While I was examining our fallen private, Tremble approached and let me know that he still had the halflings' trail and that we were ready to move at my command.

We formed back into two columns and continued on the trail of the halflings. The forest was eerily silent, and the men were on edge, their eyes darting in every direction, looking for foes. Their comrade's gruesome death had shaken them. They were used to seeing a man cut down in battle; every soldier was, unfortunately, familiar with that scene. Seeing a soldier dissolved into goo from a wolf monster was something else entirely. After a half-mile, our scout, Private Tremble, held up a fist, signaling for us to stop. He motioned me forward, and I moved as quietly as I could to where he was crouched—I didn't move quietly enough, however, if Tremble's cringing face was any indicator. Stealth was not going to be my strong suit in this game. I knelt next to Tremble and observed the horror show unfolding in the clearing.

The twisted trees and shrubs had pulled back to form an eerily exact circle one hundred feet in diameter. A large cauldron made of the corrupted forest wood had been placed in the center and on the ground. About twenty feet from the cauldron were the three halflings, all bound tightly in vines and roots. The halflings struggled weakly against their bonds while three of the spore taint wolves stood guard. A figure covered in a large cloak stood over the cauldron, chanting and stirring it with her hands. Next to that figure, a large bear stood watch. It was identified as a spore taint bear, and a system prompt told me no further info was available until the quest was completed.

"Did you think I could not hear you stomping about, you plant-killers and life-stealers? Your foul presence has disrupted my glorious creations from the moment you set foot within the woods. You seek me harm even as your comrades chop and kill my children near that scar on the earth you call a road. Do you know how hard it is to craft my children? Only predators are suitable for conversion, and there were precious few of those here." The figure at the cauldron turned as she spoke to us. At the same time, she pulled down the hood of her cloak, which, I now realized, was made from a sheet of leaves held together by moss and fungal growths.

The creature before us looked to be a human female made entirely of the tainted wood and fungus that surrounded us. She had no expression on her face, and the eyes, just hollow spaces in her wooden skull, wept the same rotting green-red fluid we had found when hacking open the trees. I tried to focus on the creature and was rewarded with some information.

Spore Taint Dryad: Some tragedy has corrupted this once-beautiful forest creature. A curse of hatred for all non-plant life has taken root, and she now seeks to cover the entire land in her taint. The dryad will transform all creatures under her control into a foul fertilizer that spreads across her forest while transforming the predators of the land into spore taint creatures to guard her putrid, ever-growing realm.

She turned and faced me before continuing her rant, her voice projecting somehow without her mouth ever opening.

"I thought humanoids were predators, too, are you not? Then why is it so hard to convert you to my servants? I was trying to be delicate to my subjects here, since they were so few in number"—the woman indicated the halflings tied on the ground—"but if you are going to kindly keep supplying me with raw materials, I believe I can be a bit more aggressive in my approach. At a gesture from the dryad, the bear moved over to the halflings, grabbed Quimby in its jaws, and trotted back to the cauldron.

"Stop! Let them go . . . now!" I said as I stood up to confront the dryad. No reason to be stealthy if she could sense our presence already. While I was talking to her, I gave hand signals for the soldiers to move up. I could hear them spread out, one squad to either side of me.

"Let them go . . . Well, that seems like a wonderful idea." The dryad's mouth couldn't move, but I somehow sensed a smile behind her face. "I can do hand signals, too, human." With that, she made an exaggerated signal, and the bear dropped Quimby into the cauldron. He hit with a splash, and I could make out the look of terror on his face as his bound form slowly slipped beneath the cauldron's foul contents.

"Kill her and her beasts!" I ordered as I drew my sword. The men charged forward, forgoing any javelin throws; they would be useless against creatures that could only be harmed by chopping them to pieces. The dryad hung back, sending the bear and wolves to defend her. The men had all come to like the fun-loving halflings, and their fury at seeing Quimby death spurred them on.

Fury: Your soldiers have been afflicted with rage at the death of an innocent companion they cared for. Bonus to damage for the next 60 seconds of this fight. There is a chance that soldiers will ignore orders while under the effects of fury.

The men collided with the spore taint creatures. Easily bowling over the wolves, several men began to hack at each. With the effect of fury on them, the blows hit harder than normal. Pulped wood and tainted fluid began to fly from the wolves. The wolves tried to shoot roots from their mouths, but the sight of their jaws opening wide gave away the attack, allowing their targets to get shields up in time to block.

It was a different story with the bear. Its huge mass knocked over the first three soldiers that ran into it. The bear didn't waste any time, as its jaws opened and roots shot from its mouth, hitting one of the soldiers on the ground. The bear then used its huge paws to hold down the other two soldiers it had knocked over, the claws on each paw extending into sharp roots that burrowed into the soldiers' bodies. The bear's body then convulsed as it began to pump fluid into all three soldiers.

The soldiers had time for a short scream of pain before they began to dissolve. The other men were not idle while their fellows died. The rest of the squad began to hack at the bear; it was vulnerable while it convulsed to pump fluid. I also rushed over and began to chop at the bear's flank, severing the rotting skin and cutting through the roots and pods beneath it. The bear fell quickly under our combined blows, but it was too late to save its three victims, who slowly dissolved into the forest floor.

Turning back to the rest of the fight, I saw that the three wolves had been killed, thankfully without any further casualties on our side. That just left the dryad. She had taken cover behind the cauldron and was chanting a spell. I charged her and the men followed, trying to get into range before she completed her spell. We were too far away, however, and I could sense the dryad smiling through unmoving lips as she completed her spell: a glowing green orb that headed straight toward me. Just before the orb struck, I saw the dryad's expression change from one of triumph to one of pain as a large serrated spike erupted from her gut and two large pincers closed around her, sawing her in half. Crunchy had joined the fight to save his companion.

Crunchy's valiant attack was too late for me, though, and the green orb struck me in the face. A wave of pain consumed my being as the orb penetrated my left eye before exploding into shards of corrupted wood.

Foul Spore Dryad's Death Seed attack has critically hit you. You have died. Respawn in 5 minutes.

*Note: You have died during your introductory quest. Respawn will occur near the caravan. Once the introductory quest has been completed, you must bind to a valid respawn point or you will respawn back at your original starting location (the woods near Amerville).

*Note: Subsequent deaths within a short period will increase the respawn duration.

*Note: When you die, there is the potential for you to drop a random amount of coin as well as random gear. Because this death occurred during your introductory quest, no items or coin will drop.

I jerked awake back in my tent, the guard posted outside immediately rushing in to check on me. "Sir, glad you're back. Are you feeling okay?" the soldier inquired.

"I don't appear any worse for wear . . ." I felt about, making sure there was no hole in my head still. "Everything's in one piece. How long was I out?"

"You appeared in the tent only about five minutes ago, sir. The halfling Quimby just arrived back as well. Daegan asked to see you as soon as you were up, sir," the soldier advised.

"Thanks. I'll head up to see him now." With that, I made my way toward the front of the caravan. My respawn point must have been bound to my tent, and the tent had automatically appeared a few seconds before I respawned, according to the guards. As I walked, I noticed that the forest was changing. The foul trees and plants had a dried-out look and were quickly dying. At the front of the caravan, Daegan, Barnaby, and Quimby were deep in conversation.

"Lieutenant Raytak, glad you made it back to the land of the living. Whatever you and the halflings did is healing the forest. The corrupted plant life is dying and drying out. Barnaby here says we'll be through the blockage momentarily. Even that stench is dissipating, thank the gods. I hope it will wash out of our clothes. I plan to get the caravan rolling in just a few minutes, and if you'll excuse me, I need to get these folks organized before we waste even more time." Daegan excused himself and began barking orders at his drivers. A short time later, my soldiers and the rest of the halflings arrived back at the caravan.

"So what happened after I died? I remember seeing Crunchy tear that dryad in two, then nothing. Anything else I should be aware of?" I asked.

Drake replied, "I got a quest-completed prompt just after the dryad died. We gathered up the wounded and headed back here. No treasure dropped except for mine and Quimby's quest rewards." Drake indicated his new bow. It looked to be a longbow to replace the shortbow he had started the game with. All in all, it was a nice upgrade for a starting quest.

"There was this. I was hesitant to pick it up, as the prompt read it was soulbound to you, but the game allowed us to pick it up once we agreed to bring it back to you. Here." Drake offered a small object wrapped in a cloth.

Opening the cloth revealed a seed the size of a walnut. The seed was a sickly greenish color, and the shell felt more like flesh than a seed pod. The item gave off a faint smell of corruption that reminded me of the rotting fluid the corrupted plants had leaked. Focusing on the seed, I found some information on the soulbound object.

Item Received: The Foul Spore (non-tradeable, soulbound), unidentified.

You have completed the quest *Rescue the Halflings*.
Reward: 250 experience.

I could feel the faint pulse of life inside the seed. Something scratched at the back of my mind, trying to communicate with me when it touched my bare hand. After wrapping up the seed, I placed it in my pack. I wasn't sure what I could do with it . . . Perhaps I was supposed to find some way to purify it. That was something I could ponder later. For now, we needed to get the caravan moving again. Barnaby announced that the road was clear, and the caravan left the rotting woods behind. I saluted the four graves dug at the side of the road as we passed, giving honor to my four fallen soldiers.

CHAPTER 18

We made good time once we were past the forest overgrowth, and the road became smoother as we began to enter the foothills that led to the transition point waystation. We were finally moving at a pace that put us ahead of schedule, and my attention was drawn to mile markers that had begun to appear at the side of the road. The markers were simple wooden poles driven into the ground beside the highway. Numbers painted on them represented how many miles it was to the transition point. The markers appeared to be well-maintained, and Daegan told me that replacing the markers was the responsibility of the soldiers guarding the transition point. The good condition of the markers was a testament to whoever led the transition point garrison.

When we made it to mile marker five, something unusual happened. Next to the mile marker, another pole had been driven into the ground, and a large banner was strung between the mile marker and the new pole. I jogged up to the lead wagon and jumped up next to the driver to see what the makeshift sign read.

From the depths of the sea to mountains that soar . . . never will you find a better deal than with Phineas T. Moore.

I chuckled a bit, remembering from my study of American history that companies used to do something similar on highways to advertise their products. The driver next to me gave a *humph* noise, indicating his displeasure. When I looked at the driver, the AI listed him as Torgen.

147

"Have you seen these before, Torgen? It seems like you're not a fan of roadside advertisements," I inquired.

"That charlatan bilked me out of five silver the last time I was here. Sold me a pair of boots that he said would allow me to outrun a dragon." Torgen indicated his boots, which did seem to be a quality pair, but I didn't detect any magical enhancements. "They felt comfortable, and I fancied myself to be a bit nimbler. Thinkin' I hit the jackpot, I challenged the other drivers to a foot race . . . I came in last and lost ten copper to each of the four other drivers that I raced."

I didn't think he could outrun a crawling baby, let alone a dragon. The driver was pushing sixty years old and sported a huge potbelly.

"I hope that Phineas T. Moore is at the transition point. I'm gonna get my coin back or take it out of his hide." Torgen made the *humph* sound once more and was silent.

We approached mile marker four and once again saw a banner.

Watch the tame goblin chief Bugtug carefully wrap your order at no extra charge. Remember . . . extra service isn't a chore for Phineas T. Moore.

Looking back down the row of wagons, I could see that the signs were having the desired effect. People were crowding to the right side of the wagons to get a look at each sign as we passed. I smiled, happy that everyone had something to occupy their time for this last stretch of our journey. Up ahead, mile marker three came into view.

Everything we sell has a money-back guarantee. Remember, with Phineas T. Moore, the "T" stands for trustworthy.

I made my way back to the second wagon and rejoined the squad stationed there. One of the soldiers immediately asked the question I was anticipating.

"Sir, will we have an opportunity to shop a bit once we reach the transition point? I was hoping to find something for my family back home." The soldier looked at me like a kid asking for a toy at the store.

"We'll have to wait and see, Private. I don't know how long it will be before we need to head to Hayden's Knoll, but if time allows, I'll get with Sergeant Brooks and see about everyone not on punishment detail getting a short pass to shop and look around," I answered, shaking my head and knowing how soldiers always seemed to blow their pay as soon as they got a chance to spend it. The soldiers rushed to the side of the wagon once more as mile marker two came into view.

Check out the Discount Barrel of Bargains for overstock and "slightly" distressed merchandise that can be purchased at NEVER-before-seen low, low closeout prices. Remember what Phineas T. Moore always says: "Whether the product is magical or mundane, my loss is always your gain."

The transition point waystation appeared in the distance. The transition point was essentially a small fortress and village guarding the only gap in the solid range of mountains that bordered this zone. A stout wooden palisade was anchored to the mountainside and ran a quarter-mile across, blocking access to the gap. The trail led to a reinforced wooden gate that was open at this time of day, while a squad of soldiers stood ready to check those coming in from this side. Several guards also walked along the parapet, looking for any signs of trouble. The last mile marker came into view as we began the final leg of our trip to the transition point.

Fear not, you're almost there. Just look for the merchant with the perfectly coifed hair . . . Phineas T. Moore's Emporium awaits!

Wow, this guy was corny. The closer we got to the transition point, the steeper the road's incline became. This would serve to slow down any attackers and give the garrison time to react to a raid or monster assault. The mukoks strained at their traces as even their mighty strength was challenged in pulling their loads up the last incline. I jumped off my wagon and jogged up to the first wagon to meet the gate guard with Daegan.

"Daegan! It's good to see you made it. I've been hearing rumors of trouble with the goblin tribes. Didn't know if they were true, but Captain Reynolds had us send out extra patrols just in case." The guard was obviously familiar with the caravan master Daegan, giving the wagons only a cursory inspection as he waved us inside the walls.

Daegan handed over his caravan authorizations as he answered the guard. "Howdy, Bilkins! How's the army treating you these days? I'm sorry to say we had a rough time of it this trip. Over three hundred goblins decided to make a run at us. Thankfully, Lieutenant Raytak and his soldiers fought them off, nearly killing them to the last goblin. I'd be surprised if a dozen of them gobs made it out alive. There was also some kind of evil dryad trying to grow a corrupted forest over the road, but some adventurers—with the lieutenant's help—were able to put things right. Where do you want our wagons? I was hoping there was enough room at the fields to spend a night or two here to rest the beasts before we transition to Hayden's Knoll."

"You can stay for the night, but I'll have to ask you to move on before tomorrow afternoon. We're expecting one hundred wagons heading toward Amerville to arrive tomorrow evening, and they have priority. Your wagons can take fields three and four. One and two are already full of a load of trade goods and tools heading out of the zone," the guard answered.

"That will work. Hopefully the inn has some beds open. I could use a good night's sleep on a soft bed indoors. Not to mention, I've been craving a bowl of that pork stew the tavernkeeper makes." Daegan waved toward his drivers, showing them where to park the wagons.

The guard turned toward me, saluting as I approached. "Sir, Captain Reynolds has been expecting you. He told me to have you report to his office when you arrive. He said to let you know he expects a complete report and I was to see that your men were housed in the barracks and given some chow. The headquarters building is located just inside the keep. Ask any of the guards for directions if you get turned around, sir," Private Bilkins said.

I returned his salute and at the same time cringed inside at the mention of having to present a report. Writing reports was one of my least favorite aspects of command. I usually had a junior officer write the framework of a report for me, and I would finish it off. Unfortunately, I was now the junior officer.

As the wagons pulled into the gate, Sergeant Brooks approached, and I let him know that Private Bilkins would see that the men were fed and housed. I gave him permission to let the men each have a two-hour pass to explore the compound and shop with the merchants. With the housekeeping finished, I marched my way into the gate to try and find the headquarters, all the while worrying about how I would find time to write an after-action report for Captain Reynolds.

Entering the gates, I was impressed with the transition point's setup. In front of me was a series of four roped-off sections of open field set up to house the caravans that traveled through. To my left were a good-sized inn, a large tavern, and a series of merchant stalls. A bustle of people crowded all the businesses, and I suspected that quite a bit of trade was done here due to the constant flow of caravans. To my right, a small wooden fort served as an additional layer of defense, should the walls be breached by foes. Organized rows of tents for the soldiers were set up around the fort to house the garrison. Across the open field, a second wall protected the transition point directly. Just outside the far gate, the trail led into what appeared to be a large blue swirling cloud. When I focused on the swirling cloud, a prompt appeared, telling me that this was the transition point. A notification popped up.

You have gained access to the northern transition point for the Amerville zone. You can now use any other transition point to fast-travel back to this zone.

CHAPTER 19

A very welcome notification popped up as I made my way to the captain's office.

Item Received: After-Action Report. This is a summary of your actions while on the road from Amerville.

Thankfully, I didn't have to write the report myself. "Thank you, Clio," I whispered while making my way to the headquarters. A soldier immediately led me into Captain Reynolds's office. I knocked on the door and heard a gruff voice say, "Enter." The captain's office was a near carbon copy of the lieutenant colonel's office in Amerville. Perhaps the AI was cutting corners in keeping it the same, or maybe this was some kind of military standard. Seeing Captain Reynolds standing behind the small desk, I snapped to attention and saluted my superior.

"Lieutenant Raytak reporting as ordered, sir!" I said as the captain returned my salute and took the after-action report from me. He then indicated for me to take a seat in the chair in front of his desk while he sat and stared at me intently for a moment before scanning the report.

"Very impressive, Lieutenant. You managed to get your force here mostly intact while protecting the caravan from two very different but potentially deadly threats. I see you also recruited some of the mercenaries into your forces . . . A little unorthodox, but I can't complain about an officer being resourceful in the field. That resourcefulness is something you'll need at Hayden's Knoll. The reports from there haven't been good. It appears there

153

is a group called the Bloody Blades that has made it their mission to attack the town relentlessly.

"I have confidence that you will handle the mission based on your most recent accomplishments. Command has authorized me to allocate you reinforcements from my forces here to replace your losses and bring you up to full platoon strength. It looks like Daegan's caravan will leave at noon tomorrow, heading to Hayden's Knoll, and I'd like to have you join them and provide them protection until they reach the town. It's the least we can do, given you've recruited all his mercenary guards into your unit. The town could use those supplies, and the new settlers will be a welcome addition if the town is to survive. Take this to help upgrade your troops' equipment. They are woefully underequipped." With that, the captain handed me a small pouch of coins, and several prompts began to flow into my log as I saluted and left the office. I paused just outside the keep and found a stump to sit on while I reviewed the flood of game notifications.

Congratulations! You have completed the quest *Securing Hayden's Knoll, Part 1.*

Rewards: 5 gold.

Experience: 250.

Replacements have been allocated to reinforce your unit up to platoon strength.

The Imperium will pay your troops for an additional 60 days.

For permanently eliminating 2 threats to the area, you have been awarded the following bonus rewards: armor voucher for your forces, 1 minor action medal (health).

Congratulations! You have completed your class introductory quest. Character sheet options are now viewable.

New Quest Available: *Securing Hayden's Knoll, Part 2.* **Escort Daegan's caravan to the town of Hayden's Knoll and assume command of the garrison there.**

Reward: variable.

Accept: y/y? (This is a mandatory quest based on your unique class. Failure to complete it will invalidate your class and you will be forced to select a new basic class.)

Wow, I would have accepted the quest anyway, but it seems the AI was pushing hard for me to follow this questline. I had to think maybe it had limited quest lines developed for me since this was a unique class, or perhaps it handled all the players on their initial quests this way as a sort of tutorial. Now that I had a few minutes, it was time to review the now-unlocked character sheet and level up my character.

*Note: This is the first time you have accessed your character sheet. More detailed explanations are given the first time it is reviewed. To see the additional information again later, please use the help feature.

Player: Raytak.

Class: Commander (Imperium).

Rank: Lieutenant.

Level: 2 (1430/2000).

Stats:

*Note: This unique class does not have individual stats. Items that increase stats will have no effect on a commander.

Attack: 2 (1 gained per level). The attack ability helps determine whether a blow hits and, in conjunction with a weapon's item-level, modifies the damage done to the target.

Defense: 8. The commander class starts with 1 point in defense and gains 1 point every 5 levels. The defense skill has many variables and is based on armor/level/agility (for certain classes).

Health: 250. The commander class gains 100 health per level.

Equipment:

Crude Imperium Light Leather Armor Set: +5 defense.

Simple Large Wooden Imperium Shield: +2 defense.

Crude Bronze Shortsword: item-level 15. (Item-level is a representation of the overall power of a weapon. Weapons of the same item level will still vary in their damage based on the nature of the weapon. A dagger of the same item-level as a greataxe will inherently do less damage.)

Crude Bronze Dagger: item-level 15.

Crude Bronze-Tipped Javelin: item-level 10.

Minor Action Medal (Health): +50 health.

Simple Leather Bracer (unidentified).

The Foul Spore (unidentified).

Funds: 65 gold, 18 silver, 90 copper.

Feats/Abilities/Class Skills: The commander class unlocks skills as it levels. You will be able to choose different paths to develop your character every 10 levels with 1 additional path determination at level 5.

Command Presence: Creates an aura in a 15-yard radius that inspires troops and allies under your command. The ability grants +1 to attack, +1 to defense, and improved morale. The commander must concentrate on inspiring his forces and consequently takes a penalty to attack and defense while the aura is active. This is a toggled passive ability with a 30-second toggle cooldown.

Shield Bash, active ability (requires equipped shield): Orders your troops to bash the opponent closest to them with their shields, automatically hitting and dealing minor damage while forcing them back. Cooldown: 1 minute.

Choose an initial personal skill path.

Combat Veteran path: This path will have your character develop toward being a more powerful individual fighter, increasing your personal damage and durability on the battlefield.

War Leader path: This path focuses on the soldiers under your command, increasing their damage and durability at the expense of your own.

Looking at the available paths, I knew I wanted to go with the war leader path. My strength was in leading soldiers in combat, not in one-on-one fights. I chose the war leader and then more prompts revealed themselves.

War Leader path selected. New skill unlocked: Honor Guard.

Honor Guard: Once every 24 hours, summon 2 soldiers that will defend you for up to 1 minute. Honor guards will mirror your standard troops in gear and combat ability. When Honor Guard is active, all nearby opponents who are attacking you will be forced to attack the Honor Guard soldiers instead.

Choose a skill path for the units under your command.

Melee Specialists: Increase troops' attack, defense, and health. Your soldiers will suffer a penalty to attack when using ranged weapons. (*Note that advanced and elite troops gain the benefits of skill path choices but do not suffer skill path penalties.)

Ranged Specialist: Increase troops' ranged attack and ranged defense. Soldiers suffer a penalty when in melee combat.

If I was going to be squishy, I needed my soldiers to be as tanky as possible, so I chose the melee specialist path. The ranged specialist would be optimal if I was going the combat veteran route and tanking foes myself.

Followers:

Regulars: 50/50.

Advanced Soldiers: 0/10.

Maximum Elite Soldiers: 1/1.

Regulars, Level 2:

Health: 30 (regulars gain 15 health per level).

Attack: 0 (regulars gain an increase in attack every 5 levels).

Defense: 2.

Equipment:

Simple Large Wooden Imperial Shield: +2 defense, additional +1 vs. ranged attacks.

Crude Bronze Shortsword: item-level 15.

Crude Bronze Dagger: item-level 15.

Crude Bronze-Tipped Javelin: item-level 10.

Advanced Soldiers:

None recruited.

Elite Soldiers:

Health: 100 (elite soldiers gain 50 health per level).

Attack: 2.

Defense: 7.

Equipment:

Crude Imperial Light Leather Armor Set: +5 defense.

Simple Large Wooden Imperial Shield: +2 defense.

Crude Bronze Shortsword: item-level 15.

Crude Bronze Dagger: item-level 15.

Crude Bronze-Tipped Javelin: item-level 10.

Abilities:

Command Presence: Elite soldiers possess a weaker version of the commander's aura, granting a small bonus to attack, defense, and morale. The aura is active only when the commander's aura is active. Unlike the commander, elite soldiers do not suffer a penalty to combat when using Command Presence.

While the commander class was powerful, I was the weak link in a fight, being easy to kill by just about any player of a similar level. I hoped the new ability, Honor Guard, would help with that. Not getting specific ability points would severely lower my power compared to regular player classes as the game progressed and would make most drops and magic items unusable for me since their bonuses were generally based on increasing individual stats. I had to hope there was gear that increased health, damage, or defense by a set amount. Finishing up with my character sheet, I scrolled through the last notification in my log.

*Note: Losses to your forces will slowly be replaced by headquarters and sent automatically to your garrison location. You do not currently have a garrison location. Report to or secure your garrison location to begin receiving reinforcements. Regulars will replenish at a rate of 2 per day, advanced soldiers at a rate of 2 per week, and elite soldiers at a rate of 1 per week. Improve your garrison or unlock new abilities to increase the reinforcement rate.

I hopped off the stump I was sitting on and headed for the inn, hoping to find a good meal. I also needed to go shopping and track down where my troops were being housed. The sergeant could babysit them for a bit longer; sometimes, rank had its privileges. My journey to the inn was interrupted when the system notified me that once again it was time to unplug from the game, and I was forced back into the prison of my ailing body.

CHAPTER 20

"I s everyone logged on?" Chairman Raines of the Qualitranos corporation asked. He looked about the holo-conference display and saw the various heads of departments in their virtual seats at the long ornate meeting room table. Also in attendance were the representatives from the Veterans Administration and Meditronax.

"Let's have our partners in the VA and Meditronax start us off so we don't torture them with the whole meeting." The representatives from the VA and Meditronax mimicked wiping their brows in relief at not having to sit through a boring meeting, but Chairman Raines had an ulterior motive as well: not wanting third parties to know Qualitranos's financial situation. Luckily, the financial situation was good . . . very good.

"Please, ladies and gentlemen, what's the status of the medpod project?" Raines asked.

"Mr. Chairman, the project is exceeding expectations," stated Martin Yang, the director of operations from Meditronax. "The interface, mechanicals, and AI controls are helping the patient even faster than we could have anticipated. The nanobots will be the biggest innovation in medicine since penicillin. Meditronax is pleased to have the opportunity to work with your team. I have to say, your liaison, Trey Raytak, has done exceptional work coordinating all the moving parts.

"We have the second prototype pod prepared and are ready to deploy it alongside the first, with your company's approval. The FDA has approved the system for wider testing, and if all goes well, we will be on the fast track for full approval from the government. The manufacturing facility is in the final stages of expansion, and we are ready to go into full production within thirty days of approval." Martin gestured over to the VA representative, Ms. Hallax, for her input.

"The facility in Knoxville, Tennessee, is honored to host the first two patients for this groundbreaking treatment. The family of Samuel Ty, a retired gunnery sergeant and combat veteran, has signed the consent form allowing Sergeant Ty to be the second patient treated by the medpod. The patient is in the same room as the first, so that should help us with logistics a bit. We expect to have Sergeant Ty in the pod by the end of the day tomorrow," Ms. Hallax finished and looked genuinely excited to have her VA facility participate in the program.

"Thank you both for your input. I'll have Trey and his team coordinate with you in getting the second pod up and running. If you don't have anything else, I'd like to thank you both for coming today and for the great work you're doing that will eventually help millions of people. Qualitranos is proud to work with you both as partners," Chairman Raines said, and both the VA and Meditronax teams logged off. A quick nod from one of the techs in the room let him know that the visitors were gone and the rest of the meeting could commence.

"Well, looks like our guests are gone and now we can continue with all our deep, dark secrets," Raines joked. "Let's start with Trey Raytak. Do you confirm everything is going well on the medical side of the ledger?"

Trey quickly looked at his notes and received a thumbs-up from the head technician, Lou.

"Yes, sir. We have everyone in place already to get the second pod functional as soon as it arrives. The AI is having no trouble administering the meds and controlling the nanobots. The only glitch we've seen is an uptake in the processing power used by the AI to create a comforting environment for the patients," Trey said.

"Trey, from what I understand, the AI is only recreating memories and using the VR to create a familiar environment, like a favorite room or garden. Why would it need more processing power to do that? Is this something that will be a problem if we bring a thousand or a million medpods online?" the chairman asked with concern in his voice.

"No, sir. The extra capacity is minuscule in the grand scheme of things. Lou, our head technician for the project, thinks that it is the AI learning the process of working with live patients. The CPU load will taper off as she gets more data and becomes more efficient at creating the instanced environments. I just wanted to bring it up since it was a bit of an anomaly. Even with thousands or millions of units online, the additional load would not overtax the servers in any way," Trey added.

"Understood, keep up the good work. Let's hear about the game now. How are the servers holding up under the second wave of beta testers?" Raines asked.

"Sir, the servers are fine. We actually feel . . ." David Yen, the project lead for the Limitless Lands game, looked to his colleagues for confirmation and found that all were nodding their heads. "The entire team feels we are ready for launch, sir. This would be an unprecedented move, I know, after only a few days of beta, but the game is ready, the AI is ready, and I think the public is ready to hand us their money and start playing," David said with confidence.

"That's a bold plan, David, but I put you in charge of Limitless Lands because I knew you would deliver. Is there anyone opposed to launching, say, the day after tomorrow? Gloria, can we get on vid and in the news to announce the game quickly?" Chairman Raines asked. He had been given a heads up that the game was ready, and the beta was really only intended as a quick confirmation of that fact and not a continuation of the game's development, like most developers used beta for.

"Mr. Raines, I've already put feelers out, and we can get on *GamerVR* again tomorrow with Maxxo, which will give us the most reach with live viewers. I've also prepped the press releases and let the gaming journalists know we may have a big announcement tomorrow," Gloria added.

"That leaves the only bottleneck being the hardware units. Have the hardware manufacturers gotten enough units in stock to deliver? I don't want to release the game and have people waiting three months to get a VR rig that will handle Limitless Lands," Raines asked, worried about the only thing that was out of his control. The company was delving into the hardware side, but it would be a few years before it was ready to compete with the established brands of VR gear.

"That's looking good as well," Gloria advised. "I reached out to the retailers and manufacturers yesterday to test the waters. There will be some scarcity at first, but the manufacturers have been working overtime once they saw our preorder numbers come in. It also seems a lot of gamers ordered the game but were holding off on buying the rigs upfront due to the cost, so the stores and online retailers will have product to deliver at launch. Sir, from a marketing perspective, a little scarcity upfront will help with building overall demand in the long run."

"That's it, then: we launch the day after tomorrow. Thank you all for your hard work. I know we'll all be getting very little sleep over the next few days, but it will be worth it. I've spoken with the board, and there will be a generous bonus to *every* employee of Qualitranos if the launch goes as expected." Raines ended the meeting, and everyone got back to work.

CHAPTER 21

Word that there was another major update regarding Limitless Lands hit the web soon after the Qualitranos management meeting. The marketing department was creating lots of buzz without spilling the beans on what the big update was. Viewers knew, once again, that Maxxo and *GamerVR* would have the reveal, and viewing numbers hit a new record for the show as gamers all over the world tuned in to see what the news was. Most were thinking it would be the company announcing a delay in the game's release or that the company was going to lift the nondisclosure agreement, which would allow beta-test gamers to start streaming play.

Gloria watched as Maxxo got into the routine of starting his show. She had given his team access to more video streams of the game, and the show had chosen what she thought would be an intriguing piece for the audience. Qualitranos had mysteriously requested to place a large covered object in the middle of the stage, and she would only unveil it at the end of the show. Maxxo, wearing a black suit with the word "villain" written on it, came onstage to roaring applause. His desk had a sign on it that read "evil lair," which he pointed to as he plopped down in his chair, waving for the crowd to quiet down.

"Welcome once again, gamers, geeks, nerds, and freaks to *GamerVR*! We have a beta update that's sure to be great, so let's not wait . . . to welcome Gloria Treese back from Qualitranos!" Gloria walked across the stage once more, waving toward the crowd before gesturing toward the large tarp-covered object in the middle of the stage. She mimicked pulling off the tarp before sitting down on the guest couch. The couch this time was a large ogre torso with the arms folded, providing a place to sit.

"Thanks for having me back, Maxxo. I have a lot of info for your viewers today, as well as a new video clip I believe you chose, personally, for the audience today."

"That's right, but don't have a fright at what you'll see tonight. I brought my villain duds because we're going to see a group of players that are taking the dark path in the game. It's insane! Do you all want to see . . . ?" Maxxo asked the crowd, which roared to see the video. "Then you evil cats try not to drool when you see the cruel that some are doing in-game." The studio went dark as the video began to play.

The camera showed a character running through the muddy streets of a small village and toward a burning stable. The character's name showed as Lhorn in the corner of the screen, and his life bar was just above half. Bleating sounds from hurt and terrified animals came from within the stable. A female elf in leather armor was pulling at the barred door of the stable, trying to get it open and not having much success.

"Lhorn, help me get the animals out!" the elf yelled while pulling ineffectively at the bar holding the doors closed. Lhorn ran to the bar and helped push it out of the way. Right before they could open the door, a crossbow bolt thudded into the side of the elf's head, pinning her to the stable door. Her life bar, which was at one-fourth, depleted instantly, showing that the character had died. Lhorn looked to his left and saw three other players laughing and walking confidently toward him. Two of the other players were armed with crossbows and wore blackened leather with the symbol of a bloody dagger emblazoned on their chest piece. One human female was trying to reload her crossbow, while another human male pointed his crossbow toward Lhorn. The third was clothed in black robes, and a crude cloth mask with the same bloody dagger symbol covered his face.

Lhorn equipped a handaxe and pulled a shield from his back while charging toward the three. The human with the crossbow fired his shot, and Lhorn grunted as the bolt rammed through his flimsy chainmail armor, penetrating deep into his shoulder. The man in the mask chanted a quick spell, and Lhorn fell to the ground, stunned, while a timer ticked down the ten seconds until the stun wore off. The man in the mask casually strolled over and looked down at Lhorn, tapping a curved dagger against the side of his face.

"Well, well, well, looks like the heroes lose today. I really hope you drop me something nice and expensive when you die. Don't worry, though, I won't take your gear without giving something in return. Here, have a dagger." The man in the mask thrust his dagger slowly into Lhorn's neck, and blood spurted onto the masked man as he finished his thought. "Don't mess with the Bloody Blades when we're sacking a town. We appreciate the extra experience and the loot you drop, but the only thing you'll end up with is a long corpse walk back to respawn." Lhorn died as the masked man cleaned his knife on the unfortunate victim's corpse.

"Boss, you want me to open the stable and let the animals out?" the human female asked.

"Nope, leave them in to burn . . . Might get a few extra XP out of it that way," the masked man said as the camera faded out to the sounds of animals in pain.

"Wow, I think we've just seen the king of mean. Does this player-killing crew get the loot and XP for raiding a village like that, Gloria?" Maxxo asked.

"Like I mentioned before, Maxxo, you get to play Limitless Lands any way you like. We may not like it, and I personally don't condone it, but players can take the path of evil if they wish. I do remind people that if you choose this path, you may find yourself on wanted posters with a big fat bounty for your death or capture." Gloria then smiled and gestured toward the big tarp-covered object in the middle of the stage.

"On a more positive note, would you like me to proceed with the big reveal?" Gloria asked Maxxo.

"I've been anxiously waiting, so don't keep baiting us, Gloria. What's the big reveal?" Maxxo asked.

Gloria got up from the ogre-armed couch and walked to the tarp, motioning for the crew to have it removed. As the tarp lifted, a bright neon sign flashed, *Limitless Lands full release . . . TOMORROW!!!!!*

The crowd went wild, and it took Maxxo a few moments to calm everyone down enough to be heard.

"Is that even possible, Gloria? The beta only started a few days ago!" Maxxo added with a shocked look on his face.

"It's correct, Maxxo. At 12:01 a.m. Eastern Standard Time, Limitless Lands will go live with full release. We only needed a short beta to confirm the stability of the game while it handles large numbers of players. We also wanted to give the VR gear manufacturers a little lead time to get enough inventory in stores before release. You can all get started in your adventures as soon as possible. Keeping the game in beta any longer would serve no purpose other than to make people wait. The game is bug-free, and Clio the AI is more than ready to go with millions of players at once," Gloria said with a huge smile on her face.

"You heard it here, folks. For the first time in history, a top-rated game company had a beta test of only a few days. Looks like ole Maxxo may have to find a guest host tomorrow so I can get in-game and play. For *GamerVR*, this is Maxxo, signing off . . ."

Within hours of the announcement, stores across the globe sold out of the latest VR gear as over eighty-seven million players prepared to enter the game upon launch.

CHAPTER 22

My consciousness slowly returned, and I found myself lying on the cot in an army tent as I logged back into the game. Looking out, I saw that night had fallen and the bustle of activity at the transition point hadn't faded with the light. My stomach gave an angry growl, reminding me that it was well past chow time. Rather than have some more rations, I decided to find the tavern for a hot meal.

The tavern proved to be the easiest building to find in the transition point area, since I only had to follow my nose. Ribbons of smoke drifted from several chimneys, and the mouthwatering smell of roasted meats permeated the air around the building. The flow of people into and out of the building was constant, and I noted that several local NPCs, as well as a good number of players, were among the groups moving about.

The entrance to the tavern consisted of a pair of swinging bar doors that looked like something from an old Western . . . I supposed they were much more practical than a traditional door, considering the volume of people coming and going. The smell inside the tavern was less inviting than the one on the outside; smoke and spilled ale collided with the scent of too many people packed into too small a space. Still, my hunger got the best of me, and I began to cast about for a place to sit in the packed room.

"Lieutenant Raytak! Over here!" a booming voice called from a corner of the room. Looking over, I could see several long tables pulled together, and the logging families we had escorted were eating, drinking, and having a good time. Barnaby Stone was waving and calling me over while shoving the kids seated next to him aside to make room for me. Smiling and waving at the family, I grabbed a spot next to Barnaby, who gave me a friendly pat on the back with his giant-sized hands, nearly knocking me off the bench. The man gestured toward the table of food and the empty place setting in front of me.

"Raytak, please share a meal with us. It's the least we can do for the man who kept us alive over the long trip here." I didn't need to be asked twice, thanking Barnaby while heaping my plate with a tender roasted meat that reminded me of homemade pot roast from the real world. Alongside the meat, I piled up mashed potatoes, peas, and carrots, then covered the whole mess in a thick brown gravy. The simple and savory foods tasted like a king's banquet after I had eaten only hastily cooked army rations over the last week. Barnaby left me alone to destroy the food on my plate, thankfully only speaking to me when my plate was clear and I was using a hard chunk of bread to mop up the last bits of gravy.

Seated next to me, Barnaby's daughter, Bella, focused on something in her spoon while the newly adopted Edwin sat across from her, playing with the remaining food on his plate. Edwin was hard at work reinforcing the ring of mashed potatoes he had built on his plate to keep a lake of gravy contained. Bella then flung a pea from her spoon at the wall of potatoes. The pea stuck into the side of the mashed potato wall, and Edwin chuckled at the feeble attempt to breach his gravy dam.

Bella looked over at me, frowning at her failure, and I gestured to the large chunk of carrot left half-eaten on her plate. Bella grinned, loaded up the carrot into her spoon, and flung it at the potato dam. The large chunk easily breached the potato wall and caused a flood of gravy to flow about Edwin's plate. Edwin looked dejected as he went about rebuilding his potato wall. My and Bella's celebration of the successful siege was interrupted by Claire, the children's mother.

"Mr. Raytak, kindly do *not* encourage the children to play with their food! We hope to have them arrive at our new home without any additional bad habits," Claire said in a stern voice, while a grin betrayed that she was not completely serious.

"Mrs. Stone, I'll refrain from any more instruction on dinner plate siege warfare tonight. Thank you, and Barnaby, for the meal. It was nice to sit down to a real meal with good people," I said.

Having finished my meal, I sat there in contented fullness for a bit, enjoying the friendly banter and the antics of the children before excusing myself. Duty called, and the armor voucher was burning a hole in my pocket. I also needed to check out the vendors and get my magic items identified before they closed for the night. Did vendors in this game keep regular hours, or were they open all the time?

As I crossed by the bar, I noticed Bhurke standing alone and nursing an ale. The guy had been an obnoxious fool, but I couldn't help but feel sorry for him since he had lost everything. I also had no idea what the mercenary leader, Kofi, would do to him once he found out that I had recruited his whole band.

"Bhurke, mind if I stand you for a meal and another ale?" I said while pulling up next to him at the bar. Bhurke looked at me, and a flash of something—perhaps anger—crossed his features before he relaxed and smiled, holding out his hand for me to shake.

"Lieutenant Raytak in the flesh. I've already eaten, but another drink would be welcome . . . as long as you're joining me," Bhurke said while motioning for the barkeep to bring us a new round. As I paid for the drinks, I brought up what I hoped wasn't a sticky situation.

"Bhurke, I hate to ask, but what are your plans now? The army will always have a slot for you, and with your experience, I could see you advancing quickly," I told him. Bhurke shook his head while taking a long pull on his ale.

"No, Raytak. I've given it a lot of thought, and the mercenary life is what I'm suited for. I've decided to start my own band and do things my own way—not to mention keeping more of the coin for myself instead of giving the bulk of it to some fat fool in the city. Kofi burned a lot of bridges by charging caravans more than they agreed to, and that leaves me the opportunity to cut into his business. Daegan has agreed to give me a chance, even after . . ." Bhurke trailed off, still somewhat embarrassed about his previous behavior on the trail.

"I think this place could use an honest mercenary band, and I hope you'll give us a bit of a discount if we ever need to hire you," I said, remembering that many ancient armies used mercenaries to round out their forces.

"Ha! You'll pay the same as everyone else. Perhaps you should offer to pay a bit extra since you enlisted all my men into your little army. It'll take me at least a week to gather enough sellswords to properly guard a caravan. Daegan said he'd give me the contract for his trip back to Amerville if I can be ready by the time he returns from delivering you lot to wherever you're headed."

Bhurke remained in quiet contemplation for a second and then began again. "I do have to admit, I was angry at you after the goblin battle . . . but I'm man enough to admit I was the one in the wrong. Should you ever need my band, we'll be called the Azure Blades, and we'd be honored to fight alongside you again," Bhurke said, and I found myself surprised. I didn't think a game could have NPCs that were not only highly detailed and realistic but could also reason and have the presence of mind to admit their faults—change their path in life, even.

"I just may have to call you one day, Bhurke. In the meantime, I have some things to take care of before we leave in the morning. Best of luck to you," I said, excusing myself and making my way out of the tavern.

I didn't notice how hot and stuffy the tavern had become until I exited into the cool evening air. Heading back toward the garrison, I began looking for the quartermaster and ended up needing to ask a passing soldier to point me in the right direction. The quartermaster was housed in a small storage building a fraction of the size of the one in Amerville. Upon entering, I realized the difference was more than just the size. Whoever ran this place ran a tight ship. The supplies and gear were all organized into their proper places and placed neatly, not haphazardly thrown about like in that mess of a supply depot in Amerville.

"Sir, can I be of assistance?" a large half-orc grumbled while putting down some papers he was reading.

"I'm looking for the quartermaster. I have an armor voucher I need to cash in to get my soldiers better equipped."

"Sir, I'm Sergeant Grobac, the quartermaster here. I'd be glad to assist you, sir." Grobac held out his hand and I passed over the voucher. He scanned it for a bit and then began sorting through some lists to find where the items we needed were kept.

"Just give me a moment, sir. Looks like you're being issued some standard leather armor. Not the strongest in the world, but it should help keep a blade from your skin. Just sign here and I'll have the gear brought out to your men," Grobac said while handing me a form to sign. I grabbed the quill he offered, dipped it into the ink, and sloppily scrawled my signature on the form . . . It looked like I still had poor penmanship, even in the game world.

"That should do it, sir. Anything else I can help with?" Grobac asked.

"No, Sergeant. Thank you for your help, and I commend you on the way you're running this place. I had a much different experience getting the initial gear for my forces," I said, and Grobac saluted me as I left the supply building.

Upgrade Received: Crude Imperial Light Leather Armor: +5 defense.

Swiping past the armor upgrade notification, I continued toward the merchant area of the transition point. The sounds of raised voices came from the nearby merchant stalls. It looked like all the merchants, save for one, had closed for the evening, and the last merchant was standing there, being loudly berated by the caravan driver, Torgen.

"Ye bleedin' cheat! You said these boots would let me outrun a dragon and I couldn't even outrun a couple of caravan drivers! You need to give me my coin back right now, including what I lost on the bet!" Torgen demanded. The merchant was a tall, thin human man dressed in a fine-quality blue mage's robe. He had a disingenuous smile plastered on his face as he weathered the verbal onslaught from Torgen.

"Well now, my good friend. You see, that is *exactly* the problem. You were racing caravan drivers and *not* a dragon. Should you find yourself faced with a dragon, I guarantee you will beat it in a footrace or I will gladly refund your coin! Everyone knows Phineas T. Moore's word is his bond. I never make a claim I'm not willing to back up with my rock-solid money-back guarantee," the merchant added. It was time for me to defuse this situation before it escalated.

"Torgen, how much did you pay for those boots?" I inquired. Torgen was startled at seeing me show up unexpectedly. Phineas raised a curious eyebrow at my sudden appearance.

"My good sir, this fine customer purchased the exceptional Boots of Dragon Racing for the low, low price of only five silver. A bargain at twice the price, really. You would think I would go broke selling them for such a pittance, but I make up for it in volume!" Phineas said with a flourish. This guy was a born huckster.

"Tell me, Torgen, I remember you said you needed boots when you bought these, and you did mention they were comfortable. How much would a pair of good boots normally go for?" I asked. Torgen thought about it for a few seconds.

"Well, I suppose a pair of decent-quality boots would sell for one silver . . . not five like this huckster charged!" Torgen added while raising his fist toward Phineas.

I pulled four silver from my purse and handed it to Torgen. "Here's the difference. You needed a good pair of boots and got them. For the sake of peace in the Imperium, I'll cover the difference. That should satisfy both parties," I said. Torgen made his *humph* noise once more, then shook his head in reluctant agreement, pocketed his coin, and made his way back toward the caravan wagons.

"Well played, my good sir! You have defused the bellicose bumpkin and given us peace once again this evening. I'm sure you have come to see my famous wares, brought here from all around the lands . . . great treasures, gifts, and trinkets for a traveler. Feel free to ask me any questions, should they arise."

Phineas stepped aside for me to have a look at what he was offering. His shop consisted of a small wagon with a hinged panel on one side. The panel was now open, revealing his wares, but could be closed and locked when the merchant wasn't around. There were several shelves and compartments that contained mostly household goods and trinkets. The items would appeal to the folks riding in the caravans, folks looking for souvenirs, or townsfolk wanting to purchase necessities. There was not much that interested me among the bric-a-brac.

"I don't have much need for your goods, but I was hoping that you maybe had the magic skill to identify some items for me," I said, remembering the bracers and the foul spore in my pack.

"Why, you have heard of me, I see. The great Phineas T. Moore is a mage without peer . . . The M in Moore stands for mage, after all! Show me your items and I'll identify their abilities and origins for the nominal fee of twenty silver each." Phineas held out his hand for the items. The fee sounded very fair to me. I agreed and paid Phineas while handing over the two items. Phineas grabbed the bracers first, covering them in his hands while chanting quietly. Light glowed between his hands, and when he handed the bracers back, I could see their description.

Simple Leather Bracers of Agility, uncommon. These bracers bestow a bonus of +1 to defense and +1 to agility for the wearer.

Not really something I could use since I couldn't benefit from stat improvements. Since I had the ability to create quests, I figured I could use it for a quest reward or sell it for some more coin, if needed. Phineas grabbed the foul spore next, wincing a bit when he held it. He began to chant again, and the light in his hand grew. It took him much longer this time, and he looked drained when he handed the foul spore back to me.

"That was . . . unexpected, sir. Usually, to identify such a powerful and dangerous item, I would have charged ten times as much, but alas, a deal is a deal," Phineas said while composing himself.

I checked the spore once again, now that its secrets were revealed.

The Foul Spore, epic artifact. This item contains the imprisoned spirit of a corrupted dryad. The spirit imprisoned within will always be seeking a way to escape. It will remain trapped in the foul spore until released by the one bound to the item. The possessor of the spore may communicate with the spirit inside and vice versa. This communication will most often occur when in a dream-like state.

Effects: Grants +1 defense and +1 resistance to poison and disease.

That was weird. I wasn't sure why I would ever want to release that thing into the world again. Since it was bound to me, I couldn't sell it, either. At least the bonuses were ones that I could use.

I thanked Phineas for his services while carefully avoiding any more of his schemes to separate me from my coin. I spent the rest of the evening back in camp, checking on my replacements and making sure everyone was fitted out in their new armor.

The replacements and the extra squad brought the number of regulars to fifty. I still hadn't seen any of the so-called "advanced troops" and had to trust that the game would reveal a way for me to recruit them at some point.

CHAPTER 23

S hortly after dawn, Daegan joined the sergeant and me to discuss the next leg of our journey.

"Good morning, Lieutenant Raytak, Sergeant Brooks. If your men are ready, I plan to get the wagons rolling in a few minutes. We'll be a shorter wagon train group this time. Several of the wagons are staying here to meet up with other caravans before heading to their final destinations. That leaves us with twelve wagons holding supplies for the town, eight wagons with settlers, and your three wagons. I also have three extra wagons hauling food for us and feed for the animals, giving us twenty-six wagons that need protection.

"I'll leave it to you how to distribute your troops, but I'm assuming it will be easier since you have more soldiers and fewer wagons to guard. Once we're through the transition point, there should be a small outpost manned by soldiers. From the other side of the transition point, it's a good day's ride to the village. We should make it late this afternoon or early in the evening if we hit some delays . . . The timetable depends of course on how quickly we get started," Daegan told us, then went back to haranguing his drivers to get them ready.

"Sergeant Brooks, unless you have any objections, I say we split our three wagons with one in front, one in the middle of the column, and one at the rear with one squad each. We'll distribute the other two squads among the other wagons where there is room," I offered.

"Sir, that should work. I'd also see if any wagons have enough room to fit a section. If we run into trouble, five-man teams give a bit more power to hold the line until reinforcements can arrive. A section is better than one or two soldiers dribbling into the fight." The sergeant then looked a bit sheepish as he brought up the next item. "Sir, I also need some funds to buy rations for us. It should take about thirty silver to feed us for a couple of days, but I'd like to buy an extra few days' worth of food, at least, in case we run into trouble," the sergeant added.

"Thank you, Sergeant. I almost forgot about that." I was too used to the army providing rations. While handing the sergeant a gold piece, I remembered something else. "Get as much as you can with this. Any extra food we can just add to the garrison supply when we get there. I also want you to get an extra waterskin for each man. I hate carrying extra weight, but fighting is thirsty work and I don't want soldiers dropping from heat exhaustion if we're in a protracted fight." Sergeant Brooks agreed and then assigned several soldiers to hurry and gather the rations and waterskins. All told, we made it just in time. Daegan had the caravan formed up and ready to go, then moved the caravan into the transition point as soon as we hopped into our wagons.

I rode in the front wagon with Daegan. I had offered the slot to Brooks, but he declined and wanted to ride in the last wagon with the new squad to get it squared away. Looking back, I could see sections of soldiers finding places to squeeze onto the various wagons.

Like an uncoiling snake, the wagons left the staging area and formed into a column. Daegan seemed unconcerned as we entered the shimmering light, his confidence helping me overcome my natural aversion to entering bright glowing portals to the unknown.

You have entered the Amerville zone transition point. You have no other unlocked locations and can only travel to the zone directly connected to this point (Hayden's Knoll). Do you wish to proceed: y/n?

I selected *yes*, and the light engulfed us briefly. Daegan stated we would enter a dream-like state for about two to three minutes while we fast-traveled to the next zone. While in this state, I could hear a voice inside my head. The foul spore dryad was now able to communicate with me while I was in this dream state.

"Life-stealer and plant-killer . . . why do you imprison me? Release me so that I may, once again, bring balance to the forests."

Not sure what to do, I tried to respond. "Why would I release you? You would just try to kill me once again. You do recall that you killed me, right?" I asked.

"Yes . . . release me so that I may kill you. I can release you from your dreamless state and once again spread the new forests around the lands."

"You're really not helping your case here. I'm still sensing a mindless, murdering, corrupt-forest-creature vibe from you. What do you mean that I'm dreamless? What kind of insult is that . . . Oh, you mean because I don't sleep in-game? That's the only way you can communicate, isn't it?

"Well, that's good news for me because unless I'm transitioning to a new zone, I don't have to hear your babble. Thank you for the buffs from your creepy seed spore thing. It'll come in handy. You have about sixty seconds left before we hit the new zone, darlin'. Make them count," I taunted, sick of her rambling.

"You don't wish release from your dreamless state? Perhaps I can help you in return for being reborn. Release me and I will no longer trouble you or yours. I will even offer a lifepact, if I must. This existence is torture . . . Release me, please!"

The time counted down as she continued to plead with me to release her. The lifepact was something I hadn't heard of before, and I decided to look it up in the help screen.

Lifepact: An absolute oath in the Limitless Lands. Two beings must both agree to the terms of the pact. To break a lifepact is one of the most grievous of crimes in the lands, causing instant enmity between you and all other sentient beings. You will be inflicted with the Pact Breaker debuff, which slowly and painfully kills its victim.

While the lifepact seemed like a solid way to guarantee the foul spore dryad didn't go on a murder spree again, I couldn't see a reason to take a chance on releasing it back into the world. I'd just keep the spore on me for the buff and suffer her rantings whenever I transitioned between zones.

The transition countdown reached zero, and the swirling lights began again. The wagons pulled out of the portal and into the new zone, where bright daylight greeted us. The air here was warm but noticeably cooler than in the Amerville zone. The transition point in Hayden's Knoll was situated on top of a small hill. Behind us, to the south, impassable mountains rose up, forming the border of the zone. The only break in the tall mountain chain was the swirling transition point portal.

A well-kept dirt road led north through rolling hills, the terrain broken by the occasional patch of small trees or rock formations. There were no elaborate defenses or forts on this side, only a rickety wooden watchtower and what appeared to be an understrength squad of Imperial soldiers. The soldiers didn't even notice our wagons emerging; they had their weapons drawn at two cowering goblins. The trader, Phineas T. Moore, had placed himself between the goblins and the soldiers, pleading the case for mercy.

"You cannot harm these two. They're my assistants. Where else can I get someone to work for free—err, I mean work so diligently and honestly? Don't you realize this was once the great goblin chief Bugtug and his son Kipkip? They're one of my best-selling attractions. You'll put a serious dent in my financial well-being if you harm them. I demand to speak with your superior officer!" Phineas simultaneously pleaded and threatened.

"Sir! Step away now! We can't have these goblins running about. We have enough trouble already with the raiders and such. Why would we want to bring a goblin chief into the mix? Move aside and I'll finish him quick and painless for you," one of the soldiers commanded.

Unfortunately, it looked like I would have to intervene. I hopped off the lead wagon and ran ahead to the altercation. First Squad, to its credit, hopped off and followed right behind me.

"Stand down, soldier. What's going on here?" I demanded to know.

"Sir! I didn't realize you would be arriving today. Not a day too soon, with all the trouble we've had. This here trader comes through the portal thirty minutes ago and tries to sell us some junk . . ." the soldier began.

"I'll have you know, my wares are of the highest quality. Household goods, exotic spices, magical items, and haberdashery . . . Phineas T. Moore sells only the best, and all at rock-bottom prices. My money-back guarantee is known far and wide!" Phineas began, indignant after the soldiers' insult to the quality of his wares.

"Phineas, you're not helping your case," I snapped, trying to shut up the annoying merchant. "Why are you smuggling goblins about? They're not exactly welcome in civilized lands."

"As I mentioned before, this is the great chief Bugtug and his son, Kipkip. I found the two shortly after their tribe was wiped out by the undead in the faraway lands of the Imix. I took them in and gave them honest work. They have even sworn a lifepact to serve me for rescuing them. I will, of course, vouch for their good behavior, and I'll have you know that the pair are most docile," Phineas explained. Looking at the two terrified goblins, I was inclined to agree.

"Stand down," I said to the transition point soldiers surrounding the trader's cart. "Phineas, I'm going to give you the benefit of the doubt about these two." I indicated the cowering goblins. "Understand that if they commit any crime or cause any harm to a citizen of the Imperium, I will hold you personally responsible. You will face any punishment with them and will not be permitted to trade in any of our lands if something goes wrong. Do you agree to this?"

Phineas looked at the two goblins, nodded, and agreed to take responsibility for both. The goblins hopped back into the wagon, wisely making themselves scarce.

"I assume you're heading to Hayden's Knoll? If so, fall in with the wagon train. There's safety in numbers. Just make sure Daegan is okay with it first," I advised, and Phineas rushed over to plead his case to join the caravan. In the distance, a very dissatisfied *humph* sounded from the wagon behind me. It appeared that Torgen had noticed the new addition to our caravan.

"Now, soldier, you mentioned trouble with raiders, yet I find this important portal guarded by only an understrength squad without even the most basic of defenses. My camp at night is better prepared for an attack than this place. Explain yourself and let me know why I shouldn't bust you down a rank for such sloppy soldiering," I said harshly, not liking what I was seeing with these soldiers.

"Sir, Sergeant Grahame was killed a few weeks ago and we didn't have any other NCOs or even senior enlisted personnel here to take over. Since our garrison was gone, we didn't get any replacements, either. The mayor has taken command, and while it's not my place to question his orders, the man's no military leader, sir.

"The raids started about five weeks ago. Just one or two of these clowns called the Bloody Blades started skulking about. The first were all inexperienced and would content themselves with attacking the outlying farms. They would kill the farmers and take everything of value, destroying the place in the process. They would always run away before any guards or soldiers could respond.

"Eventually, more and more of them showed up and the town itself started being attacked. The guard and our garrison did what we could, but the Bloody Blades were more numerous and better equipped. The town guard was undermanned and underequipped since the town was so small. We had a whole platoon of soldiers to start with, but we're now down to only twenty-five. I haven't seen a replacement or even some resupply until you showed up, sir. I'm glad you're here, sir, and I'm sure you'll put this to rights quickly," the soldier explained.

It did seem the situation was dire. Poor morale and lack of leadership had made these soldiers sloppy, and sloppy soldiers got themselves—and others—killed. I had to end this morale issue quickly.

"Soldier, *I* will not fix these problems. *We* will fix this together. We fight as a team, and that's how we'll win. Bandits and raiders are out for their own gain or sick pleasure. We're fighting to protect those we love and the lands we live in. I'm heading with the caravan to Hayden's Knoll and then we'll get started on these Bloody Blades characters. I expect you and the men here to hold this position. You'll build standard defenses to guard the transition point. I expect to see a regulation fortified position the next time I'm here. How are you set for supplies and how often are the squads guarding the transition point rotated?" I asked.

"Sir, we're rotated once a week usually . . . but not as often with the losses we've had. To top things off, we've been on half rations since the raiders have hit the farms so hard. We only have a couple days left of half rations. Then we were going to be forced back to town for supplies, whether we were relieved or not," the soldier added. His nametag showed Springman, and his health bar showed only eighty percent. I also noticed two debuff icons.

Low Morale: This NPC is experiencing low morale. Low morale reduces attack and defense values. This debuff will increase the longer the NPC is in the demoralizing situation, eventually leading to desertion.

Underfed: This NPC hasn't been eating enough and will suffer a 20% penalty to max health, as well as penalties to attack and defense.

This insanity had to stop. Soldiers were used to enduring hardship, but there should be no reason to send the garrison out without proper food. The mayor would have some answering to do once I got to town.

"Private." I gestured to one of the First Squad soldiers with me. "See to it that Private Springman and his squad get a full week's worth of rations dropped off before we leave." Looking at his equipment, I could see the garrison was underequipped as well; the troops here wore the same gear as my starting soldiers had worn. I took a gamble with my next act.

"These soldiers are now under my command. See to it they are equipped properly." I knew we hadn't brought any extra gear with us, but I figured the AI had some way to equip new soldiers with the upgrades I had already purchased. From what the system had said before, I only had to purchase an upgrade once and all soldiers under my command would be equipped the same.

"Yes, sir! I'll get them chow and see to it they get properly equipped before we leave . . . I think I remember seeing a supply crate in one of the wagons," the soldier said. I breathed a sigh of relief at not having to buy more gear.

"Private Springman, you're in charge here. See to it you and your men get a good hot meal in you before you get to work on the defenses. We'll send word and reinforcements from town before the week is up. I have confidence you'll do your duty. Dismissed!" Private Springman saluted smartly and went to gather his gear and food.

The morale debuff dropped from his information bar, and I knew the poorly fed debuff would soon follow once he ate a good meal. Motioning to Daegan, I let him know we were ready to continue. While I was doing this, a new prompt appeared.

You have taken command of the soldiers guarding the transition point in Hayden's Knoll. This is a squad-sized unit and is currently understrength due to losses. When you take command of an understrength unit, you will receive only those soldiers currently in the unit, but your total soldiers assigned will reflect the unit at full strength.

Total Regulars: 57/60.

Total Advanced Soldiers: 0/10.

Total Elite Soldiers: 1/1.

CHAPTER 24

T he caravan rolled slowly down the dirt road toward Hayden's
Knoll. The same scenery passed us by as we ate up the miles toward our destination. Sergeant Barnes and I continued the tradi-
tion of running the men during the morning, and just as we stopped for our
noon break, I received a notification.

**You have earned the trait Physically Fit. You and the soldiers under
your command stick to a strict physical fitness regimen. You receive the
following bonus.**

Regulars: Bonus of +5 health per level, retroactive.

Advanced Soldiers: Bonus of +10 health per level, retroactive.

Elite Soldiers: Bonus of +25 health per level, retroactive.

Commander: Bonus of +25 to health per level, retroactive.

**Should you fail to train for a period of more than 1 week, you will lose
this bonus until you once again train hard enough to reach the same level
of fitness. This is a class bonus exclusive to the commander class.**

Wow, not a bad buff for just doing what soldiers were supposed to do.
After a quicker-than-normal lunch, the caravan was once more on its way.
We were all anxious to make it to Hayden's Knoll before the end of the day.

Daegan became bored and began to ask our driver, Torgen, about his life.
I struggled to hold in a laugh as Torgen proceeded to answer every question with his usual *humph* noise. Daegan would cut a notch in the seat of the
wagon each time he made the noise. The current count stood at forty-two.

Daegan asked if Torgen liked being a caravan driver when instead of his usual *humph* we heard a meaty *thwack* sound as a crossbow bolt slammed into the side of Torgen's head.

Daegan leaped across the seat, struggling to grab the reins of the wagon while I scanned to see where the attack had come from. I held up my hand in the prearranged signal for "caravan under attack" while equipping my shield and sword. Just as I equipped my shield, a second bolt embedded in its face. The force of the crossbow bolt pushed me back. The bolt had penetrated the layers of lacquered wood, the sharp point sticking out only a few inches from my arm.

The men were responding quickly, passing word down the line that we were under attack and grabbing their gear. I hopped out of the wagon as First Squad, in the wagon behind me, began to form up. Daegan got control of the mukok pulling our wagon and brought the caravan to a halt. The road was clear on either side, except for a small copse of trees just to the left of the caravan. I figured the shots had come from there. Too bad Yendys and her halfling ranger companions were still logged out; we could use their bows and magic right about now.

With a shout, seven figures charged from the copse of trees while at the same time six more charged from our right where they had hidden themselves behind a rock formation a bit farther back from the road. The attackers were a mixed bag: humans, a dwarf, an elf, and a couple of half-orcs. The troubling thing was that all of them were players. These weren't some NPC goblins; these were actual players trying to attack the innocent caravan.

The only forces near me were First Squad and a section from Second Squad that was just coming up the line. I joined First Squad as we placed ourselves between the wagons and the group coming from the trees. I ordered the section from Second Squad to face the foes coming from behind the rock. Scanning our foes, I could now see health bars, but the system didn't give me exact health numbers. Remembering my duel weeks ago, I assumed the players would be much more powerful on an individual basis than my forces. The rest of the platoon needed to make it up to the front of the caravan quickly. Then we could overwhelm them with our greater numbers and superior tactics.

As our foes approached, the attackers were whooping it up and laughing at what they perceived to be an easy target. They were a mix of classes and builds. Some wore heavier chain armor and carried shields and various one-handed weapons. Several of our foes looked to be rogues or rangers dual-wielding daggers and shortswords while wearing leather. One of the attackers hung back from the crowd. This one wore a dark robe with a mask over his face that screamed "caster." The only thing their gear had in common was a bloody dagger symbol prominently displayed somewhere on their armor.

"Easy kill, guys. This supply caravan should have some good loot and XP for us!" the half-orc in the lead shouted as he approached, twirling a dagger in each hand.

"What the . . . ! Where did all these soldiers come from, and who's this player with them?" The half-orc slowed as he realized the attack wouldn't be as one-sided as he thought.

"First Squad, release!" I ordered while activating Command Presence and throwing my own javelin. Our skills had clearly improved, as all the javelins, save for mine, hit the attackers; my throwing skills needed more work. The half-orc in front took three javelins, his health dropping by a quarter. I didn't have time to scan the other attackers' health as they hit our line.

The soldiers in First Squad presented shields and began to fight like they had trained, protecting themselves with their shields and striking out quickly with a thrust whenever possible. I paced the line behind my soldiers, ready to plug any gaps and looking for any additional threats. The half-orc with the daggers hit the soldier in front of me, driving both his daggers into the soldier's neck, a critical hit that killed my soldier instantly and bloodily. I stepped into the gap and thrust at the half-orc, a blow that he easily dodged. While he was dodging me, the soldier to my left took advantage of the distraction and landed a quick thrust to the half-orc's side.

The half-orc then swung his daggers at me. I blocked one with my shield. The other dagger made it through my defense, ramming into my stomach. The new leather armor helped mitigate the damage, but that one blow dropped my own health by twenty percent. I made a riposte at the now over-extended half-orc and landed a stab of my own to his exposed neck.

You have landed a critical blow on your opponent and have caused a bleeding wound. Your opponent will lose health every second for the next 20 seconds unless the wound is tended to.

I quickly willed the combat stats off; they were too distracting in a fight. I needed to buy time, so I ordered First Squad to activate Shield Bash. Our foes were unprepared for it and found themselves pushed back from our coordinated strike. The distraction allowed all of us to land a free blow on our confused enemies. I took a second to look down our line. We had lost three soldiers so far.

The half-orc in front of me began to shout, "Need some heals here! These mobs are tougher than they look!" Someone pulled me back from the line, and I could see that Third Squad had joined us, filling in the missing slots and putting me back where I could better manage the fight. Not in any immediate danger, I looked to see how the section from Second Squad was faring. Sadly, all five of that section were down, and the group of attackers was now battling Fourth Squad and the remaining section of Second Squad. Sergeant Brooks was coming up with our new Fifth Squad, maneuvering to get behind the players who had attacked from the rocks. If they could surround the players, we would have the advantage. Looking back to the fight in front of me, I received another notification.

Your forces have slain unknown rogue, level 2. Experience gained: 25.

The dual-wielding half-orc was down. Unfortunately, another three of my soldiers were as well. While looking at my forces, I was seized by some glowing gray bands that surrounded my body. The world blurred as I was magically pulled to the ground fifty yards from where I was just standing. The masked and robed mage looked down on my stunned form, then drew a wicked-looking curved knife.

You have been stunned by the spell Translocation, which has a 5-second stun effect and a 10-second immobilization period.

Crap! I was helpless, and the jerk mage who did this was gloating.

"Ohhh, a unique class. Hey, Mr. Commander Man. Don't worry. You'll find the Bloody Blades kill unique classes as easily as the others. Any last words?" I scanned the mage's nametag.

Mage, Level 3, Name: Unknown. This character has used an item, or ability, to mask his identity.

Wait. Did he say "any last words"? I could speak! His spell didn't stop speech.

"Honor Guard!" I shouted, activating my newest ability. Instantly, two soldiers appeared to either side of the mage. He looked on in shock as both soldiers thrust their swords into his unarmored torso.

The mage's health dropped by half, and he found he could no longer attack me, the game forcing him to attack the summoned Honor Guards. Yet the mage was not out of tricks yet. With a quick chant and a motion of his hands, he cast a Firebolt spell that hit one of the Honor Guards in the face. The single bolt took the guard nearly to death, but before the mage could cast again, I ordered the uninjured Honor Guard to activate Shield Bash. The shield slammed into the mage, knocking him down and dropping his health by another ten percent. During this time, I received several more very welcome notifications.

Your forces have slain unknown barbarian, level 1. Experience gained: 10.

Your forces have slain unknown warrior, level 2. Experience gained: 25.

Your forces and allied forces have slain unknown rogue, level 2. Experience gained: 25.

Allied forces? I didn't have time to check; the immobilization on me had worn off and I needed to get back in the fight. I rose to my feet while ordering the injured Honor Guard to use his Shield Bash on the mage, who was also trying to get up. The Shield Bash landed, taking ten percent more health off our foe and knocking him prone. I had dropped my sword and shield when the translocation spell hit me, so I quickly drew my dagger. Both Honor Guards landed another hit on the mage, finishing him off.

Your forces have slain unknown mage, level 3. Experienced gained: 50.

Your forces have slain unknown warrior, level 1. Experience gained: 10.

Your forces and allied forces have slain unknown ranger, level 2. Experience gained: 25.

Staggering to my feet, I checked on the status of the battle. The tide had turned in our favor thanks to the "allied forces" the system had notified me of. Daegan had organized the drivers, who joined the fight, helping to surround the players attacking from the rocks. The players facing me were being attacked not only from my soldiers but also from Barnaby Horn and his loggers. A few of the settlers had even joined in, clumsily wielding the weapons they had taken after the goblin fight.

Though our forces were not anywhere near as strong as players on an individual basis, our overwhelming numbers caused the remaining Bloody Blades to make a break for it. As they ran, Phineas and the goblins stood atop their wagon, all aiming small hand crossbows at one of the fleeing players before firing in unison. All three of the small bolts hit, killing another attacker.

Your forces and allied forces have slain unknown rogue, level 1. Experience gained: 10.

Phineas wasn't done yet. He began chanting and lifted both arms in the air while curling his hands with a clawing motion. Plants shot up from the ground, catching two of the fleeing players around their legs. The vines not only grabbed onto them, holding them tight, but also burrowed into the flesh of their legs, causing minor damage. A flight of javelins from my men finished off the two that were caught in Phineas's spell. A few of the attackers had escaped, but I was not going to order a chase anytime soon. We had more important things to accomplish than chasing down a few defeated players.

Your forces have slain unknown barbarian, level 2. Experience gained: 25.

Your forces have slain unknown warrior, level 2. Experience gained: 25.

You have successfully defended the caravan. Experience gained: 350.

Congratulations! You have reached level 3. Please review your character sheet to see any changes that have taken place.

Excellent, another level! Dealing with my skills would have to wait for a few minutes, though.

Sergeant Brooks ran up to me with the remainder of First Squad just as my Honor Guards faded away. The ability had saved my life and proved to be a powerful survival tool.

"Sir, are you alright? I saw that mage pull you over and thought the worst," Brooks asked with concern.

"I'm fine, Sergeant. Let's get the medics looking after the injured and find out who we lost in the fight. Also, have some of the men check to see if these Bloody Blades dropped any loot. They should have all lost some coin, and losing an item or two might make them think twice about messing with our unit," I said.

"Yes, sir. I'll get the men working," Sergeant Brooks said, then began barking out orders to get everyone on task. All told, we had paid a bloody price in this battle. Players were a much more dangerous foe than the hordes of goblins or any of the other creatures we had faced so far. We had a total of fifteen killed in the fight. While these were the worst losses we had faced to date, this fight would have been much worse if it hadn't been for the rest of the caravan coming to our aid.

Daegan had lost three drivers, and one of the settlers had been killed as well. I had some of our soldiers with animal handling experience help with the driving after taking the time to hold a quick burial ceremony for our dead. While the men finished looting the attackers, I was notified that the unit's funds had increased by three gold, thirty-five silver, and fifty-five copper.

Killing players was much more lucrative than killing wretched goblins. I took one gold to keep for the unit fund and gave the rest to be divided among the families of the drivers and the settlers who lost people in the fight. We also looted two daggers, a bronze greataxe, and one minor healing potion. Not a huge haul, but anything our opponents lost and had to replace was a victory in my books. The potion was the first one I had seen, and I looked at its stats.

Minor Healing Potion. Drink to regain 50 health over 10 seconds.

The potion was better than nothing, and not having any other way to heal myself in combat, I placed the potion in my bag and dragged the icon onto my quick action bar at the bottom-right of my screen for easy access. Sergeant Brooks and I shuffled the men around to even out the squad numbers. Second Squad had lost eight of its ten members, while Fifth Squad hadn't taken any casualties. When all was said and done, each squad was now understrength at seven soldiers per squad.

I walked down the line of wagons while we were organizing the squads, talking with the settlers here and there to try and build morale. When I passed Phineas's wagon, I saw him placing the hand crossbows back into a wooden crate. The strange and somewhat shady trader, as well as his goblins, had fought hard to defend the caravan. I wanted to thank him, and

I also felt a bit guilty since the goblins had received what I now realized was an unfair reception at the transition point. I had to remember that this crazy game was much more intricate than just "goblins are bad guys."

"Phineas, I'd like to thank you and the goblins for helping out so much back there. You likely saved some lives today."

"A life saved is a customer saved, I always say . . . and a customer whose life you have saved is *always* willing to spend a few coins more." Phineas smiled and shook his coin purse. Speaking of gratitude, I had one more thing I felt was right to do.

"Chief Bugtug, Kipkip, thank you both, also, for helping defend the caravan. I'd like you each to have these. I think you have earned them, as well as our trust." I handed each of the goblins one of the daggers we had looted from the Bloody Blades. Both goblins held the daggers in shock, not believing that a human soldier would give them a weapon. They quickly belted on the daggers and pulled them from their sheaths, admiring the sharp blades.

"Don't stab anything that doesn't need stabbing, you two," I said as I moved toward my wagon. Both goblins beamed with pride at being armed once again, and what I thought might be a small look of concern crossed Phineas's face.

At the front of the wagon, I found that Daegan was ready for us to be on the move again. As we passed the hastily dug graves, each soldier stood in his wagon and saluted our dead. I settled back onto the seat bench next to Daegan; after the driver Torgen had been killed in the attack, he had opted to drive the lead wagon himself. With a sigh, Daegan ran his finger along the *humph* marks he had carved into the seat before, then flicked the reins to get the mukok moving. I was, as surely the rest of the caravan was, keeping a much sharper eye on the surrounding terrain. Since it appeared safe for the moment, I took time to review my new level but found that nothing much had changed other than that my bonus for attack and health and the radius of my Command Presence had increased slightly.

CHAPTER 25

The road began to widen a bit as we entered what must have been the outskirts of the village. We passed the first farm we had seen alongside the road. An abandoned farm, unfortunately. The main house was burned to the ground and the animal pens were empty, save for the bloating carcass of a cow. The fields contained a type of grain I couldn't identify and looked to have been recently tended . . . as well as nearly ready to harvest. Whatever befell the farm had happened recently. Perhaps it was the work of the group we defeated earlier. The caravan continued without stopping, Daegan letting me know we were near the town of Hayden's Knoll.

As we rounded a bend in the road, the town finally came into view. Rolling fields surrounded it, and the road continued north through the middle of the town and continued off into the distance as far as I could see. A second road branched to the west and led into the foothills to the southwest. There was no activity in the town. It looked abandoned, and as we drew nearer, about half the buildings showed some fire damage or were completely burned to the ground.

A rough palisade fence surrounded the town. It had gates to the north and south, where the road passed through. The northern gate was down, torn off its hinges, and was likely the route the attackers used to enter the town. The southern gate, which we were approaching, was undamaged and partially opened, swinging slightly in the breeze. I had Daegan stop the caravan one hundred yards from the southern gate and gathered the troops to investigate. I led three squads toward the open gate, and as we approached to within twenty-five yards of the town, we heard a challenge off to our right.

"Halt! Who goes there? Are you soldiers of the Imperium?" A group of five soldiers rose from some nearby shrubs, javelins poised to throw. The soldiers looked haggard, and their meager equipment was falling apart from hard use. They were equipped like the soldiers at the transition point, carrying only daggers, javelins, and shields.

"I am Lieutenant Raytak of the Imperium. I'm here to take command of the garrison. What happened here, soldier? Report," I ordered. The soldiers remembered their training and snapped to, marching crisply toward me and saluting. I returned the salute and the soldier began his tale.

"Sir, it started a few months ago when one of them Bloody Blades characters showed up in town to shop. He looked around a bit and then picked a fight with one of the locals, killed him, and stole his goods. The town guard sent four guards after him, but they never returned. Soon after, the outlying farms began to get hit. Small groups of four or five of these Bloody Blades would strike, killing the farmers and making off with anything of value.

"They became more and more brazen, causing Mayor Delling to ask us for help. Sergeant Grahame led two squads to track down the Blades. Only four men made it back. They said they were ambushed by twenty or so Bloody Blades, who took some of the men prisoner and began to torture them, forcing them to fight each other to see who would live to carry back the news to us. The four who came back were so ashamed they left that night, going AWOL, sir. We didn't have any other NCOs. Most of us are fresh recruits.

"We followed whatever the mayor and chief of the guard, Lhork, told us to do. Lhork was an okay leader—he had even served in the military for a bit—but he lasted all of three days before a group of four or five of the Bloody Blades snuck into town under the cover of darkness and assassinated him in his sleep. We woke to the chief and four of his guards nailed to the door of the guardhouse.

"The mayor wasn't sure what to do and looked to hire adventurers for help. Four showed up and seemed like good folks, helping around the town and looking after the outlying farmers while we tried to keep a lid on things in town. Three days ago, the Blades hit us full force with close to forty attackers. You can see where they used a battering ram to knock down the gate. Fortunately for us, it took them a while to get into the town, and the mayor saw they were only attacking from the north.

"He knew we would never be able to stop that many, so he organized an evacuation from the southern gate. The town guard and the adventurers held off the Blades—barely—while the soldiers guarded the townsfolk as we fled. The mayor led us up into the hills, where there is a large plateau that's more defensible. He plans to start rebuilding there and was waiting for you and your forces to show up and take charge of our defense.

"The adventurers all died, and most of the guard is dead as well. We were sent here to watch for you and to keep an eye out in case the Bloody Blades try to track down the rest of the townsfolk.

"The Bloody Blades spent a day looting, burning, and drinking the town dry. They then split up into smaller groups and left. Personally, I don't think they are looking for us since they've already taken anything of value and most of those that escaped made it with only the clothes on their backs. What are your orders, sir?" The soldier looked at me expectantly. I could see that he was glad to have someone in charge again. I thought for a moment before issuing orders.

"Soldier, you did right by posting a guard here as well as keeping the transition point manned. One of you ride up here with me and direct us to the plateau where the town is. Before we leave, all of you get with Sergeant Brooks and see to getting some real gear, as well as something to eat while we travel. How far is it to the new townsite?" I asked.

"Sir, it's just about eight miles from here. The road leads right to it. The plateau is where it ends. The mayor said he wanted to build there in the beginning, but the merchants thought being here at the crossroads would bring more money into the town. Guess they were wrong." The soldier saluted and then hustled down the row of wagons, more eager for a meal than the gear, I deduced from the way his eyes lit up when I mentioned food. We started moving again as soon as the new soldiers were ready, a prompt appearing on my screen.

You have taken command of another squad of soldiers. This unit is understrength. Establish a garrison to begin receiving replacements.

Current unit size:

Regulars: 47/70.
Advanced Soldiers: 0/10.
Elite Soldiers: 1/1.

The mukok kept their slow and steady pace as we followed the road toward where Hayden's Knoll was now located. The road led us up into the foothills, and then, as the sun began setting, we could see the plateau the town would be rebuilt on. The road curved gently as it rose to the summit, which looked like a huge shelf about three miles in length and two across. A steep drop on two sides, and the mountain face forming a third, meant that the only access point for an attacker would be the roadway. Potential attackers would be visible for over a mile, which would allow any defenders plenty of time to prepare.

The "town" now consisted of a few makeshift tents and a few old wagons that people had strung tarps over to keep out the weather. An exhausted-looking human in his thirties, dressed in dirty but high-quality clothing, approached us. He was flanked by two town guardsmen armed with short spears and small wooden shields. They all had a worn-down and beaten appearance, wary of the column of wagons approaching. In the distance, groups of townsfolk sought refuge behind a thin line of soldiers who formed up to repel any potential attack.

"Thank the gods! You must be the new garrison commander that Amerville was supposed to send. You are *very* needed here, sir. I'm mayor Delling, and these are what's left of Hayden's Knoll, I'm sorry to say. But a town is its people, not its buildings, and we intend to bounce back better than before!" the mayor said while offering his hand.

I couldn't decide if he was trying to bolster the morale of the citizens, none of whom were within earshot, or was practicing for a campaign speech. Well-intentioned politicians were widely known to be the most dangerous thing soldiers would ever encounter, sending us into battle with too much rhetoric and not enough ammo. I sucked it up and shook the mayor's hand, giving him the benefit of the doubt for all he had gone through.

"Glad to finally meet you, Mayor Delling. The soldiers posted at the ruins told me what happened. I don't see much going on here, I must admit. There are no defenses, no buildings being built, not even simple shelters.

You've been up here for several days. When do you plan to start rebuilding?" I said harshly, not liking what I was seeing so far.

"I've been planning the new town layout. You see, planning now will guarantee that future growth is less painful. I guess we still need to organize work parties and to gather food and things . . ." The mayor began to offer excuses in a daze, and I didn't think he even knew what he was babbling about.

He saw the look on my face and began to break down, tears running down his face. Delling just sat there on the grass and wept but finally gained some composure before sobbing out his next lines.

"I just wanted to make a great town, earn a scholarship to pay for school, and just accomplish something with my life! Those griefers, the Bloody Blades, ruined everything I had worked for. Now the AI sends me some new NPC garrison commander that's just going to get wrecked by the Blades once again. I should just give up," the mayor stammered.

I was taken aback; I hadn't even considered this was a real player and not an NPC. It looked like he made the same assumption with me as I did with him. I scanned Delling to reveal that he was indeed a player.

Delling, Town Mayor, Level 2.

"Delling, I'll tell you what you'll do now—what *we'll* do together. We'll get these people a good meal, build them some shelter, and start the process of building up a town again. I'll keep everyone safe, and when the time is right, I'll wipe the Bloody Blades off this server. I'm a player as well, and I don't intend to fail," I said as Delling looked up in surprise, finally scanning my info as well.

"From the looks of things, the first step is getting these people fed," I continued. The townsfolk had begun to approach as they realized we were the good guys. From the look of them, they, like the soldiers earlier, hadn't eaten much in the last few days. "I have some food with us in the caravan, but it's not much and it'll not last long. How many people are we going to have to feed and what do you think we should do to get more food?"

Delling seemed to find himself again. I knew from my experience in combat that people could freeze up when their brains went into overload mode during a crisis. The best way to break them out of it was to give them a simple task they could easily accomplish. Asking for the total number of survivors was doing just that for Delling.

"We have 146 townsfolk right now. Only two of the town guard is left, eleven soldiers, plus all the people you've brought with you. I've had the folks ration out the food, but even with the little we've been eating, we only had enough for another two days. As far as where to get more food, I'm open to suggestions. Can your soldiers hunt for meat? There's game, but none of our folks are hunters. Many of the farms have fields that weren't destroyed, but we've been too scared to try and harvest them with the Bloody Blades running about," Delling said, focused on how to solve the problem. I considered our options before replying.

"With the rations we brought and what you have on hand, we can feed everyone for two more days. That assumes we all eat a normal portion. The debuff from being underfed is preventing everyone from working hard. Better to have everyone strong for a few days while we work on the food shortage. Tomorrow I'll have the wagons take several squads of troops and as many farmers as we can to the nearest fields and begin harvesting. I don't have any hunters in my group, but there are some players traveling with us—a pair of rangers and a druid—that might be willing to help, especially if I can create a quest for them. They've been logged out for a while, but I'd expect them back sooner rather than later," I said, remembering the farms we had passed and my friends' willingness to help.

"What about rebuilding?" I asked, already planning my next day. "What do we need for that? My men will give up their tents, for now, so the civilians can have shelter. That's only a short-term solution. I'll also have my soldiers begin to build some defenses here in case there's another attack."

"My class lets me cash in resources and coin to build things in town. I don't have enough lumber or stone right now to build a town hall, the building that unlocks everything else and would enable the NPC citizens to start rebuilding their homes. Rebuilding the town hall will also start generating replacements for the town guards we lost in all the fighting. The town is, of course, nearly out of coin. We collect a small amount naturally in taxes when people are living in the city and conducting commerce, but with everything destroyed, we're broke. I blew a lot of our coin on creating quests for the other players, but they've all moved on," the mayor added, and hearing about the other adventurers reminded me of a concern.

"Do you know where the Bloody Blades may have been respawning? We fought through an ambush of theirs on the way here and killed at least ten of them. I really hope they're not just going to respawn and hit us over and over. As far as the building materials go, I don't know about mining, but there are several loggers who joined the caravan to settle here and I'm sure they will pitch in. Can the town hall be built with just wood? I also need to get a garrison building up as soon as possible, otherwise I won't be able to replace my own losses, either."

"We really weren't sure where the Bloody Blades had their respawn set to since we were never able to kill too many of them. The only thing I do know is that the ones we did kill weren't seen again in the later attacks. I had the feeling this was just like a starting zone for their guild. Hopefully, now that they've destroyed the town, they'll move on to other things. We can't be supplying them with all that much coin or XP.

"I can build the town hall with only lumber. Upgrading to stone buildings adds buffs and other options for me, but getting up and running is the key. Once the town hall is built, I'll likely get an option to build a garrison since you're now assigned to the town. Building the garrison will be the second thing we do once the town hall is completed," the mayor said, smiling as he shook my hand again. "I'm glad to meet you, Lieutenant Raytak, and I look forward to exchanging our stories soon, but for now, let's get to work." The mayor walked off and began to direct the caravan toward where he wanted it to stop for the night.

I got to work organizing the layout of the tents for the civilians. After seeing the sorry state of the townspeople, the men didn't seem to care that they would be sleeping in the open. The addition of tents to sleep in, and hot meals in their bellies, raised the spirits of everyone after a hard journey. Soon after my men had set things up for the townspeople, Daegan approached me.

"Well, Raytak, it looks like this is where we part ways. My job is done and I'm heading back to the transition point to make another run to Amerville. I'm sorry I can't stay and help, but I'm not trained to care for refugees. We're happy to give anyone who needs it a free ride to the transition point and I will leave what food I can spare as well. Should you ever need anything, don't hesitate to send word. Any of the caravans can carry a message to me if you find the need." Daegan slapped me on the back and slipped me a small flask on the fly. I took a swig, and the hard liquor felt like a stream of acid burning me all the way down . . . It was wonderful.

"Whew, what is that stuff? Fermented mukok dung?" I joked, handing the flask back to Daegan. "If you wouldn't mind, I was going to send a replacement squad to the transition point, and I would appreciate it if you could give them a ride. I know you're short of guards until you get back to civilization, so they can give you some extra protection." I figured I needed to send a fresh and full-strength squad to guard the transition point. The other understrength squad could march back in a day or two. I would write it orders to patrol the road and look for any signs of Bloody Blades activity while also checking the status of the nearby farms to find out how much food was there for the taking.

"That would be appreciated, Lieutenant Raytak. You take care." Daegan waved as he made his way back to his wagon to turn in for the night.

While I checked on the defenses my soldiers were building, I received a welcome notification.

Congratulations! You have completed the quest *Securing Hayden's Knoll, Part 2.*

Reward: 250 XP, 5 gold.

New Quest Available: *Securing Hayden's Knoll, Part 3.* **You have found that the town of Hayden's Knoll was destroyed, but a new town is being built. Protect the new town until a garrison building can be completed to assist in the town's defense.**

Reward: Experience and assignment of a squad of advanced troops.

Excellent. Only one more piece to this questline and I would finally get to see what my advanced soldiers were. I scrolled to the second notification.

You have taken command of all Imperium forces in Hayden's Knoll. New unit size: 2 platoons of regulars (58/100), 1 squad of advanced soldiers (0/10), 1 elite soldier (1/1).

Getting the garrison completed took an even higher priority now. We were down to half our total strength, but once the garrison was done and my replacements trickled in, I would command a powerful force. I made a mental note to have Sergeant Brooks restructure the squads again to balance them out evenly. I now wanted to send two squads with Daegan to the transition point in the morning, since they were so understrength. At the other end of the camp, Brooks was already getting our eleven newest soldiers equipped and fed. Nothing beat a good NCO.

CHAPTER 26

The night passed quietly. Most of the civilians slept well in the tents after having a full belly for the first time in days. Mayor Delling surprised me when, just before dawn, he already had several groups of civilians up and organized. One group was going with Sergeant Brooks and three squads of soldiers to harvest the nearest farm. A second group was going to be sent with the logging teams to help them. I assigned two squads to help defend the loggers. A final group was staying behind to help clear the land where the mayor had decided to build the town hall. I would stay behind with the last three squads to protect the town and over-see the hasty defenses being built.

Sheer cliffs prevented any attack from the east or north of the town. The south was protected by the mountains that formed the zone barrier. The only accessible side for attackers was to the west, where the road climbed up onto the plateau. Much of the west side was also too steep to be acces-sible, so we only had to worry about the road itself and the ground about one hundred yards to either side. I had the men dig a trench just where the road reached the summit of the plateau and pile up the dirt behind it to create a defensive berm. I had the area always manned by a squad, and we pre-positioned many of our spare javelins there as well. I would have more elaborate defenses created once we had more materials, manpower, and time. While we were digging the defenses, I heard a familiar voice and spot-ted the three halflings approaching. They had finally logged back in.

"Howdy, old soldier man! What the heck happened to the town? I thought we'd have a nice inn to rest in, not live like some refugees! Did you know there are two *goblins* in town as well? Crunchy almost ate them before a soldier told us they were friendly," Yendys began before being interrupted by Quimby.

"Cool it, Yendys. That crazy merchant guy told you what happened. We were all heading out to find some quests, Mr. Raytak. Have you found any quests in town yet? Sorry, we couldn't complete the other one you had given us earlier. We had to log out and we all had too much homework and weren't allowed to play."

"I just might know of where you can find one quest. Just give me a second." I fumbled with the interface until I was able to create a quest for them.

You are offering the quest *Meat for the Masses*. Find enough meat to feed the population for at least 2 days.

Rewards (choose level of reward):

1. Stingy: 50 copper per person.

2. Average: 25 silver per person.

3. Good: 1 gold per person.

4. Exceptional: 2 gold per person.

I chose the good option. I wanted to be generous, but gold was hard to come by so far in this game. I also saw the option for an additional reward. I allocated the bracer with +1 agility if they could come through and help the town feed itself.

Reward: 1 gold per participant, reputation gains with Hayden's Knoll.

Bonus Quest: Train at least 1 hunter from within the town population.

Reward: Simple Leather Bracers of Agility (+1 defense, +1 agility).

"There you go! There's not much food since the folks were driven from town and we could really use your hunting skills to help feed everyone. If you guys find a townsperson who might be able to learn hunting, bring them with you. That way, you can help us become self-sufficient," I offered to the trio.

"Cool! This is just up our alley. Hey, Drake, want to see who gets the most kills to decide who keeps the bracer?" Quimby asked.

"Sure, but don't you think you should find out if one of these yokels can handle a bow before you start with the contests?" Drake replied.

"Hurry up . . . Let's get the quest completed. I want to check out that weirdo trader guy, Phineas, Phlegmious, T-Moreious, or whatever his name is, once we get our rewards. My gear needs some serious upgrades . . . and I want to buy a super-cute collar for Crunchy," Yendys said as the trio walked toward the remaining townsfolk to find someone they could train to hunt. I almost pitied whoever had to put up with them all day.

Wanting to delay digging more dirt, I made my way over to Phineas T. Moore to check on how he was coming along. He had set up his cart just on the edge of the tents and was sitting on a small stool, drumming his fingers on top of a box of necklaces that said they were "guaranteed to prevent petrification from a basilisk, or your money back!"

He looked up at me with a defeated expression as I approached. "Ah, the illustrious Lieutenant Raytak, defender of the weak and preventer of profits. Why have you led me to such a desolate locale? You know what the problem is with all the refugees and displaced persons such as we see here?" Phineas gestured to the townsfolk. "The problem is they *need* everything. Understand that customers *needing* everything is usually a windfall for a great merchant like myself. Oh, these people need everything all right, but they *have* nothing to pay for it with. All day I've heard sob stories. 'Mr. Moore, my husband was killed. I need to feed my children. Can't you just give me one ration bar for free?' For *free*, they said, like I have nothing to do but become destitute myself to support their runny-nosed children.

"To make matters worse, I had planned to escape this sorry excuse for a town with Daegan's caravan this morning, but my useless goblins forgot to wake me up in time. Now I'll be stuck here without hope of any real custom, being harangued and harassed by those looking for handouts until the next caravan arrives to carry me off to a place that has some semblance of civilization." Phineas's whining was doing nothing to improve my opinion of him, but he did say something interesting—did he mention a ration bar? Did his shop stock foodstuffs?

"I can't help you with the townsfolk. That would be the mayor's problem," I said, trying to pass the buck. "Did you mention something about rations? Do you have any food for sale? I can pay if the price is right," I asked.

Phineas perked up as he began to smell a sale. "Why, my good man, of course. I have the standard array of nonperishable yet fantastically delicious rations. I sourced them from the very supplier of the mercenary armies of the great caliph of Imix," Phineas rattled off while searching his wagon for the right crate. "Ah! Here they are." He pulled a large wooden crate from the back of his cart. The box was painted a sandy beige and had white letters printed on it: *Rations, temperate climate. Quantity: 15. Best used by . . .*

The expiration date was suspiciously scratched off. Phineas saw me notice and quickly removed the lid to reveal fifteen brick-sized objects wrapped in wax paper.

"Please take one to try as a free sample for the low, low price of only ten silver," Phineas said while motioning to the box with his hands. The smell coming from the box was a bit strange, but not too bad. After all, it wasn't every day that you get offered a free sample of such great food for only ten silver. I reached in to select one of the small bricks of food and unwrapped it. The ration was a pale-gray color and had darker and lighter flakes of . . . something in it. I took a bite of the hard brick while giving Phineas ten silver. The brick tasted "off," and my stomach began to rumble. Fearing I was poisoned or diseased—of course through no fault of Phineas—I opened my status log to find I hadn't been poisoned, but I had been taken advantage of.

You have failed in your opposed negotiation check. You will pay 50–100% more for goods sold by Phineas T. Moore. You have failed your saving throw. Phineas T. Moore has placed you under the enchantment Customer Born Every Minute.

What the . . . Why that . . . ! I focused on Customer Born Every Minute to get more detail.

Customer Born Every Minute, Enchantment. A great merchant once said there is a customer born every minute and a rube soon after. When under the effects of this spell, the victim will be more susceptible to suggestion and have complete trust in the enchanter.

You have made your save vs. Customer Born Every Minute and are no longer enchanted.

I dropped the stale, disgusting ration brick and looked at Phineas with a death glare, my hand moving slowly toward my sword.

"My good man, why do you look distraught? You loved the ration! I know you did! Didn't you want to buy the whole case for the discounted price of fifteen silver per ration?" Phineas waved his hand, apparently trying to reinforce the enchant.

Your Manaless trait has allowed you to resist a spell.

"Try to enchant me, will you? Take my money as well. Take money that could be used to feed the starving people of this village? How many have you bilked this way, Phineas? Unfortunately for you, this town is under martial law due to the attack . . . That means I get to decide what happens to a scam artist like yourself." I slowly drew my sword, angry but not really planning to do him any harm, just wanting to scare him a bit.

"My good man, please let me explain. There's no need to resort to violence. Here, take the remainder of the rations at no charge as a show of my gratitude and generosity," Phineas pleaded.

"So, you want to make this go away by giving me rotten rations? How about this, Phineas? Do you have any foodstuffs that aren't expired, dangerous, or harmful in any way? If so, you should start producing them. Let me warn you that any more shenanigans could be very harmful to your health." I fingered the edge of my blade as I glared at him.

"No, no, I would never dream of giving you inferior products. Here, let me get the fresh ones out." Phineas began to root through the cart.

"All of them, Phineas," I added, not wanting him to hold back if there were some foodstuffs he thought to keep from us. I fully intended to take all the extra food he had, but I would pay him a fair price for it—a very low fair price. Phineas first stacked one crate of rations with an expiration date that showed they were good for several more years. Then he unexpectedly stacked another and another and more until over thirty cases of rations were stacked before me. That was way more than should have fit in the small cart. Phineas then began to pull other food out: large cured hams and sausages, bags of dried fruits, and a dozen sacks of rice.

"How in the world did you fit all that in your cart?" I asked.

"Well, my good man, I was not always of such humble means," Phineas said as he sat on one of the ration crates while wiping sweat from his brow. "Once I enjoyed the favor of the great caliph Ichman himself. Ichman held me in great esteem and would frequent my many shops to look for exotic goods that I had acquired from throughout the lands. I had dozens of trading ships, scores of merchant caravans, and outlets in all the great cities. What I didn't have was fulfillment. I was fabulously wealthy, more so than most kings, but I had none to share it with. Don't get me wrong, there are always those who will profess their love for someone they know is wealthy, but I craved something more. I craved someone to share my life with, someone who would love me and not just my wealth.

"I met this person one day many years ago in the grand bazaar of the capital. I would often travel the shops in disguise, looking like a simple commoner to see how my businesses were managed while nobody was watching. One day during my journey, I met a lovely young lady who caught my gaze and smiled at me—an obvious commoner, not smiling for the wealthy Phineas T. Moore. She was named Nhala and claimed to be a local merchant's daughter. We would spend the afternoons together, talking and drinking honeyed tea in a café while watching the people go about their business in the bazaar.

"One day, after many we had spent together, just as we were leaving the café, I leaned in to kiss her gently. Just a small peck and as innocent a kiss as any could hope for. That small kiss lingered on my lips for just a moment, and I shall remember it always. I shall remember it as the one perfect moment in my life where I was completely and totally content, and I shall remember it as the moment that caused my fall from such lofty heights. That moment had me running for my life until I eventually found myself here." Phineas indicated with disgust our current surroundings.

"You see, it turns out that young lady whom I had fallen for—and whom I believed had fallen for me—was none other than the favored daughter of the great caliph himself. She would entertain herself by sneaking out into the bazaar on her own and uncovered, reveling in freedom that she could never know in the palace. You may not know this, but the daughter of a caliph must not show her face in public until the day of her wedding. That one simple, innocent, and wonderful kiss was my doom, for Nhala was not alone on her adventures. The caliph knew his daughter loved to go out to the bazaar and indulged her by letting her think she had escaped. His favored daughter, unfortunately, was not alone and always had several royal guards in disguise, who followed her at a safe distance. They saw the kiss and immediately arrested me for daring to touch the princess.

"I was thrown into prison, and it took all my wealth, every one of my connections, to not meet the headsman's axe that day. I was smuggled out of the city and placed on a ship to these faraway lands. Of all my wealth, I had only a few coins remaining . . . but this I had, this one item nobody thought was worth taking: my cart. This simple cart is enchanted. It connects to hidden warehouses I have scattered across the lands, places where I could keep my items hidden from theft and away from the eyes of my enemies. I can reach in and pull out whatever is needed, provided, of course, that I have the item in stock somewhere. I can also place items in it and store them elsewhere.

"So, there you have it: all the foodstuffs in my warehouse, as well as my sad story at no extra charge." Phineas sat there for a moment, contemplating. "You know the strangest thing about it all?" He leaned forward and stared me in the eye. "Despite all that has happened, all that I have lost, I would suffer it again if it meant I could kiss Nhala just once more." Phineas wiped a tear from his eye, steeled himself, and returned from his memories. "I do promise to never attempt to enchant you or one of your soldiers ever again. Others are fair game. I believe a fair price for all this food would be . . . about three gold. Due to the trouble I have caused, you may take it for free as long as you never mention that I have done this." Phineas grinned and was back to his old self. "I have a reputation to uphold after all!"

I sheathed my sword, mumbled thanks, and ordered several soldiers over to carry the food to where the mayor was storing their meager supplies, never suspecting that the greedy scam artist had such a tragic past.

As I walked back to the slowly developing defenses, one of our wagons approached. It was the logging team coming in to drop off a load of lumber. The town had only four wagons after the attack, and Delling had assigned three to food gathering, our limited stores being the more urgent threat. The sole wagon assigned for lumber was overflowing with cut logs. They dropped off the load near the construction site for the town hall and headed back out to gather more. I hailed Barnaby as the wagon approached the road.

"Hey, Barnaby! Any trouble out there?" I inquired.

"None at all, Raytak. Those halflings came by earlier on their hunt and killed off anything that might have caused a problem. We're making good time and have more trees cut down than we can haul. I'll have to leave several loads on the ground for us to gather later. Think you can get us an extra wagon tomorrow?" Barnaby asked.

"I'll ask the mayor. I guess it depends on how our food supply is looking after today," I said.

"Food comes before shelter, a priority I heartily agree with," Barnaby replied while patting his belly. The wagon meandered down the road, leaving my sight as it headed back to the forest.

A few hours later, the three wagons gathering the food in the fields returned. Two of the wagons were filled with sacks of grain. The third wagon was only half full and didn't have food, but it was carrying tools and household goods that the raiders hadn't destroyed. By the time they unloaded, the sun was beginning to set. The farm they were working on still had a small field they didn't get to, but it was too late for them to make a second run today.

I headed over to see if the town hall was started yet and was amazed at the progress they had made. A swarm of townsfolk moved about the building, hammering beams into place or crafting smaller items out of the logs we had gathered. Delling was there overseeing the work, and he greeted me as I approached.

"Hello, Raytak! We're making good progress now that the lumber is here. Barnaby said they should have a second load here this evening, and that should be enough to finish off the town hall and get the foundation set for the garrison. Thank you for purchasing those foodstuffs from the trader, Phineas, earlier today. Between what you bought, what we had on hand, and the food gathered from the farms, we now have close to a week's worth of food. Once we get the town hall completed, the farmers can set up their own farms farther to the east here on the plateau. They should be safe enough from raids and can generate enough food to feed us all. Of course, as the town grows, they have to be relocated into the valley, as I have big plans for this entire plateau to be a great city one day." Delling sat on a nearby log and indicated for me to take a seat next to him. "What's your story, Raytak? You have a unique class, and that usually means you have a unique real-life background to go with it."

I sat on the log next to Delling and began to tell my story. I told him that I was an old combat veteran who was sick in a hospital. I tried to mention the medpod, but when I began to talk about it, the AI flashed a warning that the information was proprietary and couldn't be disclosed in public. The restriction was strange to me since I was able to disclose it before when I had spoken with Yendys. I told Delling what I could, and the system suggested I inform others that the game was used as a kind of physical therapy. The AI and I were going to have to discuss this the next time we met. When I finished my story, I asked Delling about his. He was the first other player I had met with a unique class.

"My story is really nothing special. I'm a college student at a large public university . . . Weird, the game wouldn't let me tell you the name of the school just now for some reason. Anyway, there was a competition in the political science department to see who could design the perfect political system for a fantasy world. I was chosen as a finalist with two others, and our prize was a slot in the beta test, use of the VR gear, and a chance at a scholarship. I have a feeling the faculty are playing favorites for one of the other students in the contest whose family is filthy rich and are big donors to the school.

"I chose a political system based on as much freedom as possible: low taxes and letting people live the way they wish to in peace. I think one of the others developed a system that was based on some form of socialism, and the last one proposed that a harsh totalitarian regime was best suited to this world. I suppose we're not off to the best start yet, but I actually have hope we'll do well in the long run—if we're not wiped out by some crazy griefer guild that is," Delling said. I thought that he seemed like a good kid. Idealistic, like people his age should be. This town and the people in it were exactly why I chose to be a soldier so long ago: fighting for those trying to live a peaceful life, being the guard dog that kept the wolves at bay.

Early in the evening, the logging team returned, as well as the halflings. Yendys and the rangers made a beeline toward me.

"Mr. Raytak, we completed the quest *and* the bonus quest. See!" Yendys pointed to a small group of four townsfolk who had gone with the adventurers to learn hunting. It looked like all four were successful as they were walking stooped over from the weight of the bags full of fresh meat.

"Looks like you guys did well," I said with a smile and looked to see a blinking indicator in my interface. I clicked on it.

A party has completed the quest *Meat for the Masses*. You have paid the total reward of 3 gold.

Bonus objective was also completed. Party has been awarded your Simple Leather Bracers of Agility.

Congratulations! You have had 1 of your quests successfully completed. You have earned 100 XP. Experience and other rewards vary based on the difficulty of the quest, the reward offered, and the time required to complete the task.

Nice, I didn't expect to earn any experience myself. I could see how giving out quests could help me level up quickly . . . and just as quickly empty my coin purse.

The rest of the evening passed without anything crazy happening. Everyone had a great meal due to the food we had all gathered. The fresh meat was especially welcome, and for the first time since we arrived in the new town, children were laughing and playing. Delling and I met to discuss the next day's activities, and we agreed to have the same groups go out as before. The newly minted town hunters would stay close to the road and hunt small and less dangerous game since they wouldn't have the protection of the halflings.

Because the closest farm only had enough grain to fill two wagons, one was taken from the food-gathering team and given to the logging team. I rotated my squads to keep them from doing the same thing every day but kept the number of guards the same. Just as we were wrapping up our meeting, Delling looked up in excitement.

"Raytak, come on! I just got a notice that the town hall is finished and ready to be activated." Delling asked everyone to follow, except for those on guard duty, and we walked over to the now-completed building. It was a large wooden structure with a wraparound deck, complete with several rocking chairs for citizens to relax in. Inside, the building was simple but spacious and had a large open meeting area. There was a podium and benches in the main hall, two small offices for the mayor and some future town official, and a well-insulated basement for storage of supplies and gear.

"Everyone take a look around and then let's all get together and move as many supplies into the new basement as we can. No point leaving our limited food out and exposed to the elements. Let's all give a big hand to our town builders for the great work they've done. Hayden's Knoll is once again on the map and open for business!" Delling said while pointing out the dozen or so townsfolk who apparently had a skill enabling them to build any basic town building.

Now that the town hall was complete, he sent workers to begin construction on the barracks in addition to some simple homes for the townsfolk. The important thing for me was a barracks so we could start replacing casualties as well as get the advanced troops here. After moving the food reserves to the town hall's surprisingly spacious basement, everyone was tired from the day's work and slept soundly through the night.

CHAPTER 27

Early the next morning, the work teams headed to their various destinations. The barracks was proceeding quickly, and Delling said there should be enough lumber on hand to complete it by this evening. He sent out several parties of townsfolk to explore the rest of the plateau, looking for more water sources, and because of the terrain, he hoped to find some areas with mining potential. We had one small stream running across the plateau as our main water source, but a backup was needed in case of drought or some other catastrophe. I offered a squad of soldiers to go with them, but he declined, stating that the area was open and we hadn't seen any signs of danger up on the plateau.

The halflings said they were heading out to do some quests they had unlocked in the nearby woods yesterday. I did remember to friend all three of them so we could easily communicate if anything came up, and I suggested they do the same with Mayor Delling in case he was able to unlock quests in town for them.

With that out of the way, I joined my soldiers to finish up the defensive berm we were building to cover the road. I eventually planned to build a wooden palisade there to create a true barrier, but the lumber was needed for the town buildings more than for defense at this time. There had been no further sightings of the Bloody Blades, and I was growing more confident that they had moved on to victimize someone else. I still planned to have a go at them in the future as payback for all the mayhem they had caused Hayden's Knoll. While we were working on the defenses, the original squad from the transition point arrived, reporting nothing out of the ordinary on its way back. The soldiers had mapped the location of farms that still had crops in the fields and indicated any supplies or furniture that could be salvaged for the new town.

While walking over to check on the progress of the new barracks, I heard shouting and commotion from over by the town hall. I arrived just as a nearly-out-of-breath man was telling his story to Mayor Delling.

"Mr. Mayor, Lieutenant Raytak, in the caves over there, huge spiders. A whole slew of them. They grabbed Jimmy and would have got me, too, if I was any slower," the man said in terror.

"Slow down, man. Breathe, then tell us slowly where the caves are and if Jimmy is still alive," the mayor stated.

I jumped in with my two cents as well. "How big were the spiders and how many of them were there?"

The man looked back to me as he answered. "Sir, I don't know how many. We found a cave near the end of the plateau and went inside. I thought it looked like a good spot for mining, and I used to be a miner before my back gave out, you know. After making it about a dozen yards or so into the cave, it became too dark to see, and then three spiders the size of a big dog came down from the ceiling. One of the spiders bit Jimmy and started wrapping him up. I ran for it, I'm ashamed to say, but I'm no match for some monster like that, I tell you. I could hear Jimmy calling me as I ran: 'Help me, Lemule. Help me,' he shouted." The man began to panic again, so I tried to reassure him.

"Well, if the spiders were wrapping him up, it could mean Jimmy is still alive. Don't worry, Lemule. I'll gather some troops and play exterminator on these beasts. I'll take what troops I have now and do a little reconnaissance. Mayor, can you have the town guards watch the road for us? They can send word back to us if they spot any trouble. Lemule, can you find me some torches?" I asked, giving everyone something to do. The town guards went to relieve my men at the road as Lemule led us to the cave. I took stock of what we had. The three squads left here in town totaled eighteen men. By the end of the day, when the others returned, I'd have another twenty-eight, if needed. If the spiders proved too much of a challenge, we would pull back and wait for more troops. Maybe even Yendys and the other halflings could help if the fight was too tough.

Quest Issued: *Eliminate the Spider Threat.* **Spiders inside a nearby cave have attacked some of the villagers. Take a force into the cave and clear them out.**

Reward: 100 XP, improved villager morale.

Accept: y/n?

I hit *yes* as Lemule guided us to the cave entrance. We arrived at a spot about a quarter-mile from the town hall. Nestled alongside the southern mountains and driven into the cliffside were two small tunnel entrances about fifty feet apart. Lemule pointed to the one he went into, and I split the men into two groups. I would lead eight soldiers into the tunnel Lemule had entered, and the other ten soldiers would proceed into the unexplored entrance. We lit torches and walked into the dark.

The air smelled dusty and stale, with a hint of something rotten to it. Stone lined the roof and walls, and the floor was a softer dirt. The passage was around seven feet high, and thankfully, we wouldn't have to stoop or crawl to proceed. The tunnel looked like it was not a natural occurrence; perhaps a small cave was here originally, but someone had worked this into the tunnel we were now walking through.

About fifteen feet into the tunnel, spiderwebs started to appear on the ceiling. I had one of the soldiers move his torch to the ceiling, and the webs burned away quickly. We followed this pattern for another several yards before the ceiling became too high to hit with our torches. A strange rock formation also jutted a couple of feet into the tunnel. As I looked at it, a notification popped up.

Small copper node. Requires mining skill of level 1 to harvest.

That was good news. At least there were resources here if we could clear out the spiders. We proceeded farther down the tunnel with torches held high, waiting for the inevitable spider attack. The tunnel emptied into a small web-covered cavern. Several web-wrapped bundles descended from the ceiling, and I shuddered to think that these were the spiders' previous victims.

The cavern was about fifty feet wide and two hundred feet long, ending at another small tunnel on the far side. To our immediate left, about ten feet away, was another entrance, which I was betting was the one my other soldiers were moving through. Movement caught my eye as something up high disturbed the webs, causing the webbed bundles to sway gently.

While we were watching the ceiling, one of the men cried out in pain and dropped to the ground. Four spiders the size of dogs charged us, skittering across the ground. The movement in the webs was just a decoy to distract us.

One of the spiders had a soldier by the leg and was trying to drag him into the shadows. The soldier was screaming and trying to pull a fang as long as a butter knife out of his thigh while simultaneously hacking ineffectively with his shortsword. Blood and a milky yellowish venom were flowing from the wound, and the soldier's struggles slowed as whatever the spider injected into him took effect.

I drew my sword and found myself and another soldier charging the spider holding our injured comrade. The spider sensed our approach and tried to drop its victim as we made it to within striking distance. The spider jerked its head back several times, unsuccessful in its attempts to dislodge its fang from the soldier's leg. I activated my Command Presence at the same time as I thrust at the spider's abdomen. My blow scraped along the hard carapace but did little damage.

The soldier next to me had better luck. His blow penetrated the carapace with a critical hit as his blade sunk all the way to the hilt. Thick gray fluid oozed from the wound. The spider shuddered from the injury, its efforts to extricate its fang slowing as it bled out. I was able to land my second blow, stabbing into the spider's face and causing it to lose the last little bit of its health bar.

Your forces have slain Fangweb Spider, Level 2. You have gained 25 experience.

I turned to look back to see how the rest of the squad was faring when a weight landed on my back, dropping me face-down on the floor. A piercing pain flared in my right shoulder as a status icon showing a green droplet appeared below my health bar.

You have been hit by Fangweb Spider. You have taken 22 damage and are poisoned. You will take 5 damage per second for the next 10 seconds.

The surprise of the attack nearly caused me to activate Honor Guard, but looking at my health bar, I could see that the spider wasn't really doing much damage; I wanted to save the once-per-day ability for what I assumed would be the more powerful foes residing deeper in the mine. The soldier next to me fought hard, landing several rapid blows on the spider clinging to my back. The spider wrapped its legs around my torso, pinning my arms to my side in the most terrifying and creepy embrace I had ever experienced. Once again, the spider bit me, this time on the back of my neck.

You have been hit by Fangweb Spider. You have taken 22 damage and are poisoned. You will take 5 damage per second for the next 10 seconds.

Your forces have killed Fangweb Spider, Level 1. You have gained 10 experience.

Your forces have killed Fangweb Spider, Level 2. You have gained 25 experience.

Your forces have killed Fangweb Spider, Level 1. You have gained 10 experience.

I could still hear fighting in the cavern, so the kills must have been from the soldiers that had taken the other tunnel. The spider on my back twitched to the side just as the soldier next to me struck.

You have been hit by a blow from Private Grado. You have taken 35 damage.

"Private Grado, kill the spider, not your commander . . . and kill it quick!" His blade had hit me in the mid-back. The pain was becoming intense, even with the game limiting it to thirty percent of the real thing. Getting chewed on and stabbed was just never going to be a pleasant experience. I could also now begin to sense the poison in my system. I felt nauseous and lightheaded. It was also affecting my strength, as my struggles to unwrap the spider's legs from around me failed again.

You have been bitten by Fangweb Spider for 18 damage and are poisoned. You will take 5 damage per second for the next 10 seconds.

Your forces have killed Fangweb Spider, Level 2. You have gained 25 experience.

Your forces have killed Fangweb Spider, Level 1. You have gained 10 experience.

The last notification was for Private Grado finally finishing off the spider on my back. He began to peel the legs from around my body, but I instead told him to help the others kill off the remaining spiders first. The order proved unnecessary; the last spider in the cavern was finished off.

Your forces have killed Fangweb Spider, Level 2. You have gained 25 experience.

With help from my soldiers, I disentangled from the spider's grasp and returned shakily to my feet. The cavern swirled around me as vertigo set in from the venom. I fell to my knees and vomited onto the floor. I remained there until the last tick of damage from the poison wore off and my health began to regenerate. The rapid healing of this virtual world was one of the more pleasant aspects of the game. Once out of combat, I regenerated about one health every ten seconds.

Private Grado brought me my sword and shield, which I had dropped when the spider landed on me. Gaining my feet, I surveyed the room. Five spider corpses were scattered around the floor of the cavern, their legs curled up in death like the spiders you would find in your house. The second group of soldiers had also appeared. Their tunnel eventually led to this cavern, as I had guessed. They had killed two spiders and taken no losses on their way here. The soldier who had been initially attacked was still alive after the fang was finally pried from his leg and a bandage applied to stop the bleeding. I sent two soldiers to carry the unconscious man out of the cavern. They could also report our progress to the mayor before heading back to join us.

Next, I turned my attention to the dangling bundles that held the spiders' victims. The soldiers carefully cut them down from the ceiling and began to use their daggers to tear away the strands of webbing. Most of the bundles held the desiccated remains of what appeared to be goblins. The victims held nothing of value, being clothed in little more than rags with not even a copper in their coin pouches. We used torches to burn away what webs we could. There were also several sconces placed at irregular intervals on the walls. The sconces all held torches that we lit to improve visibility in the cavern.

With better light, we could see the cavern had once been an active mine. More copper nodes were revealed when the webs were burned off, and there were even several burlap sacks of harvested ore lying about as if miners had dropped them when the spiders struck. There was only one more exit that we hadn't explored. Once the two soldiers we had sent to carry our wounded man returned, we entered the new passage to try and find Jimmy, the lost villager.

The passage wound its way deeper into the mine. The soldier in front signaled a halt as the yipping cries of goblins and the clash of weapons were heard in the distance. I motioned the men forward, wanting to get out of the narrow confines of the tunnel if we were going to face a new fight. The passage opened into a cavern that appeared to be a duplicate of the one we had just left.

The torches in the room were already lit, giving off enough light for us to see what was going on. The far side of the cavern revealed another opening like the one we were exiting. Midway down the cavern, it looked like part of the cavern wall had collapsed, revealing a new opening. The dark opening was covered in webs, and I saw a spider carrying a wrapped figure scurry into it. A group of a dozen or so goblins was on the far side of the cavern, facing off against a similar number of spiders.

The goblins were dressed in rags and wielded mining picks and hammers as their weapons. The spiders were getting the best of the goblins, and there were already several goblins lying on the floor out of the fight, either dead or poisoned into a stupor. There was only one spider corpse, but I could see thick gray blood covering more than a few of the other spiders. The goblins had at least dealt out some damage with their improvised weapons.

While no fan of goblins, I didn't want to assume they were hostile. I did know the spiders were hostile, so I ordered the men out into a line of ten with me and seven in the rear as a reserve. Once formed up, we marched to within thirty yards of the spiders and readied the one and only javelin we had each brought to the fight.

"Aim for the spiders. Try to avoid the goblins if you can. Once we throw our javelins, move into melee. Again, try to avoid the goblins, but don't hesitate to defend yourselves if attacked," I ordered. We then threw our javelins, drew swords, and charged the spiders. The wave of eighteen javelins landed, the bronze tips easily cracking through the spiders' carapaces and pinning several to the ground.

It was a much better performance than we had weeks ago against the other goblin tribe. What a difference a few levels and some better equipment made. Five of the spiders remained alive after our volley, scurrying about and confused as to which group of foes they should attack. We didn't give them any chance, and with shields leading the way, we entered melee range. The spiders died quickly, unable to overcome our superior numbers and weapons. The goblins—seeing that the spiders were focused on the soldiers and not them—ran back toward the exit at the end of the cavern. Instead of going through, they stopped and presented their weapons as a warning to not approach. I toggled off my experience/kill notifications for the generic fangweb spiders; the rapid flashing of notices was becoming distracting.

The goblins looked at us warily as the last spider curled up in death. I tried to motion the goblins over to take their wounded and care for them, but something was lost in translation. They just kept to their corner and looked at us in terrified silence. I had my soldiers do what they could for the goblins since we didn't have any wounded this time. If they saw us helping, it might make them less hostile toward us. I detailed five men to watch the hole the spiders had come out of and sent another soldier to find Phineas and ask if he could come quickly with Chief Bugtug and Kipkip to translate for us.

Uneasy minutes passed while we waited for the translators to arrive; the tension broke only when a spider appeared through the passage we were guarding. The soldiers dispatched the single creature easily. The medic said that all but two of the goblins were dead. He did what he could for the survivors and thought they had a decent chance of making it once the poison wore off.

A short while later, Bugtug, Kipkip, and Phineas arrived in the chamber, escorted by the soldier I had sent. All three carried their hand crossbows, with Bugtug and Kipkip also sporting their new knives. Bugtug looked across the cavern at the goblins for a long moment and then began gibbering at Phineas in goblinoid. Phineas, surprisingly, responded in halting goblinoid, directing Bugtug toward the other goblins. Bugtug shrugged, checked the bolt in his crossbow, and trotted across the cavern while making a strange noise at the other goblins.

"He's trying to find their leader. He will attempt to kill the leader and assume command of the goblins here. Don't interfere. It's their way of dealing with these kinds of things. You don't negotiate with a goblin tribe—you dominate them or are dominated by them," Phineas advised while watching the encounter unfold. "Of course, if he fails and is killed, I expect full monetary compensation for my—err, that is, Kipkip's loss."

The goblins chattered among themselves before the group pushed one of the scrawnier goblins out in front of them and began scooting back. Bugtug didn't hesitate; he just raised his hand crossbow and shot a bolt into the scrawny goblin's head, killing him instantly. The other goblins then began to kneel in front of their new leader. Bugtug raised his arms and shouted a victory cry. After a few self-congratulatory moments, Bugtug said a few words to the goblins, who seemed to visibly relax, before the new chief jogged back to us. Bugtug spoke again with Phineas, who then translated for us.

"Bugtug, it appears, is now the chief of this group . . . which he seems intent to call the Bugtug tribe. From what he gathered, this small tribe spent its time mining and foraging in the tunnels, pretty much minding their own business since there really wasn't anyone or anything else in the area. A few days ago, one of the mining nodes collapsed into the cavern wall, and that opening appeared." Phineas pointed toward the web-covered hole in the wall.

"A few goblins were . . . volunteered to go into the hole and explore," he continued. "They never returned. Yesterday, the spiders started to leave the hole. At first, just one or two would show up. The goblins, with some effort, were able to slay them. Soon, the numbers increased and all the goblin warriors, including the chief, were killed in the fighting. We arrived just as the rest of the tribe's miners were making a last stand to protect the women and children. I believe this may be a unique opportunity for the town. We can trade the goblins food or tools, and they will mine the ore for us. I, of course, will take a nominal portion of each transaction to compensate for my facilitation of this mercantile endeavor."

I could tell he was already counting the coin and thinking of ways to swindle the newly christened Bugtug tribe. "That will be a decision for Delling and something the two of you will have to work out once the threat is over." I gestured toward the spider hole. "We are going to move forward and see if there is a boss or something that needs killing in order to end this." As I finished, I received a quest notification.

You have saved the remaining members of the newly formed Bugtug tribe from a spider attack. Reputation with the Bugtug tribe is now Unfriendly. The goblins don't trust you, or like you, but they will not be openly hostile without a reason.

Quest Updated: *Eliminate the Spider Threat.* Find and eliminate the source of the spiders.

Reward: 500 experience, 10 gold, improved morale, improved relationship between the Bugtug tribe and Hayden's Knoll.

Accept: y/n?

I accepted the updated quest, pleased that the game was increasing the reward since this seemed much more difficult than we first thought. Just before we entered the web-covered hole, a pair of villagers showed up to tell us that other soldiers had arrived. I figured one of the resource-gathering teams must have made it back early. Thinking we could use all the help we could get, I sent the villagers back with orders for the other soldiers to join us in the caves.

CHAPTER 28

T he webs around the tunnel entrance didn't prove to be much of an impediment. Unlike the other webs we'd encountered, the webs near the entrance were not very sticky and reeked like a dead skunk had rolled around on them.

"Gads! Since when do webs stink like this?" one of the privates whispered while holding his nose as we clambered past the smelly entrance to the tunnel.

"From what Quimby taught me, sometimes insects mark paths for the others to follow. Like, this might mean 'food here' to the other spiders. I know spiders aren't insects, but these seem to behave almost like an ant or termite colony," Private Tremble added. I was glad I had him and a few of the others train with the halfling rangers. It looked like he had been paying attention during his lessons.

The tunnel was only a crawlspace for the first few yards. Then it opened to resemble the other tunnels in the mine. In fact, the area we passed through looked like it was once part of the mine and had collapsed long ago, sealing off this section. We encountered only one spider in the tunnel. This one was scrawny, and its carapace was soft and white like it was a half-baked spider. A soft blue glow began to appear in the tunnel ahead as we neared another cavern. The lead squad moved into the cavern, then stopped and stared in stunned silence, looking deeper inside.

"Make a hole, Private! Don't block the rest of us," I ordered and forced my way past the stunned private blocking the entrance, only to stop and stare myself as the rest of the men filed in behind me. The cavern was even larger than the one we fought the first group of spiders in. This tunnel was the only entrance, and at the other end was the source of the blue light and the horrifying source of the spider threat.

A large swirling blue light covered the far wall—a portal of some sort. In front of the portal, a spider the size of a small house was pacing about. It looked like a bigger version of the fangweb creatures we had fought earlier, save for the fact that it had the face of an elvish male. I quickly scanned the creature.

Vhareax the Fangweb Sire, Level 5 Elite. Vhareax reigns over his spider brood, seeking more victims to feed upon and more surrogates to spawn his offspring.

*Note: This is a unique creature and will not respawn once killed.

Vhareax was guarding another creature that made me retch when I saw it. A large all-white spider was standing over four female elves. Surrounding the elves were the web-wrapped bundles of the fangweb's victims. The elves were all lying face-down on the cavern floor and had their arms and legs wrapped tightly in webs to keep them from moving. A large opaque blister covered the backs of three of the elves. The fourth elf had an open, bloody wound where the blister would have been. She was lying unconscious with just a sliver of her health bar left.

The other three elves were hissing slightly in what I thought at first was pain, but then it was revealed to be hunger. The large white spider noticed the hissing elves and moved a bundled victim in front of each of them. The three elves opened their mouths to reveal a large pair of fangs where their teeth should be. The fangs moved almost as if they had a mind of their own, snapping onto the bundled victims in front of them and slowly draining them of their fluids. What made the scene even more horrifying were the tears streaming down the elves' faces as I understood that they, too, were victims in this horror show.

Fangweb Midwife, Level 5. The Fangweb Midwife tends to the surrogate's needs, feeding it and helping to birth the new spiders.

Fangweb Surrogate (4). These poor souls are the humanoid victims of the Fangweb Sire Vhareax. They are condemned to live unnaturally long

lives with their bodies twisted and modified to give the new spiderlings a place to grow.

After feeding the three hungry surrogates, the midwife skittered over to Vhareax as a fist-sized spiderling crawled off his carapace and onto the midwife. The midwife then walked over to the unconscious elf, and the spiderling crawled from the midwife and onto the bloody wound covering the elf's back. It settled into place and then locked its tiny fangs into the elf's back, feeding on the open wound more like a tick than a spider.

The fangweb midwife then wrapped the open wound in clear webbing. The webbing must have had some healing properties, as the wounded elf's health began to slowly tick back up. The sound of several of the men gagging snapped me back to reality.

A level 5 elite would be way more than we could handle, but I couldn't just leave and wait for reinforcements with the victims being slowly drained of life in front of us. I screwed up my courage and addressed the soldiers.

"That is the fate that awaits the whole village if we don't end this right now. Draw blades and send these abominations back to whatever hell spawned them." I drew my sword and began to move toward Vhareax, swelling with pride as all seventeen of my soldiers followed, despite the impossible odds. We were out of javelins and there was no time for fancy tactics. This would be a brawl of man versus monster. I activated Command Presence and yelled a challenge as I charged toward the house-sized spider.

Vhareax looked to the midwife and hissed. The midwife used her leg to slash the blisters on the backs of the three elves that were feeding. Out of each wound, a regular fangweb spider emerged, its carapace soft and white like the other half-baked spider we fought in the tunnel. The fangweb midwife and the three newly born spiders joined the fight.

I waved Private Tremble and three others toward the midwife and her brood as the rest of us focused on Vhareax. As we neared, Vhareax reared back and spat a ball of webbing at our approaching line of soldiers. The ball unfurled and tangled up two of the soldiers. Both soldiers began to scream as the web tightened around them, causing damage. Next, Vhareax thrust one of his legs toward another soldier. A cracking sound echoed off the walls of the cavern as the leg punched through the shield and then penetrated completely through the soldier, killing him instantly.

Reaching Vhareax, I slashed as hard as I could at the leg closest to me; the more vulnerable body of the spider was out of reach. The shortsword bounced from the hardened carapace of the spider, leaving only a small nick in the armored limb. The soldier next to me had the right idea and swung at the mark I already made. The crack widened, and milky spider blood began to dribble out.

I took another swing, chipping away a bit more of the carapace. The soldier next to me wound up for a swing, but before he could complete the blow, a spider leg flashed out and pierced him through the helm. Vhareax then dipped his head down, grabbing another of my soldiers in his fangs. The soldier twitched once and was still. Vhareax dropped the dead soldier as an amused smile appeared on his face.

"*Feed* . . . Vhareax hungers! You will feed Vhareax and his spawn!" the creature shouted as it dropped down to snag another soldier in its fangs. The screeching voice seemed to penetrate my very being. How could we stand against such a foe? We were the insects to be swatted away and, in this case, consumed by the superior being . . . Wait . . . Why was I thinking this way?

You have resisted Vhareax's Dominating Shout ability. For the remainder of the fight, you will no longer be affected.

I shook my head, clearing my thoughts now that they were once again my own. Only three of the soldiers had resisted the ability. The rest just stood there, waiting for their doom to arrive. Vhareax zeroed in on the soldiers who were still fighting, skewering one on his leg and grabbing another in his fangs. Vhareax began to confidently consume the soldier in his jaws, needing no other weapon than his deadly spear-like legs to defend himself.

Tremble and one of the other soldiers were still in the fight and had killed the fangweb midwife as well as two of the young spiders. They would soon finish off the last half-baked spider, but I feared two more soldiers weren't going to make much of a difference. I activated Honor Guard to buy myself a bit of time, my guard charging to join the only soldier still engaging Vhareax. Having little time to waste, I ran to the closest dominated soldier and began to shake him.

"Get in the fight, soldier! I didn't give you permission to die yet . . . Go kill that thing!" My yelling and shaking brought the soldier back to his senses.

226

I ordered him into the fight and ran to the next man who was dominated. Tremble and the other soldier had finished their last foe and were charging to join the fight again.

"Tremble, go cut those two out!" I gestured toward the two wounded soldiers bound by the webs. If he could cut them out, that would add two more swords to the fight. I ran to each of the other four enthralled soldiers, getting them back to their senses as quickly as I could. By the time I had freed the last man and sent him toward Vhareax, the creature had finished off the Honor Guard and the other soldiers fighting him.

The last soldier battling Vhareax was stabbed through the stomach by a leg and tossed to the side. Vhareax grinned at me as he scurried to finish us off. I readied my sword and shield, taking position next to Tremble and the other two newly freed but heavily wounded soldiers for what was sure to be our last stand.

"You lead the meat. Your life will taste that much sweeter," Vhareax taunted as he closed the distance, focused entirely on me. Saliva and venom dripped from his fangs in anticipation of the meal when his head snapped back with a small throwing axe embedded into it. Vhareax hissed in pain and anger as a wave of crossbow bolts hammered into his abdomen. Crossbow bolts designed to punch through a knight's armor had no trouble breaking through the spider's tough exoskeleton.

At the cave entrance were two squads of regulars being led by a huge one-armed half-orc. The half-orc was yelling taunts at Vhareax while waving a two-handed axe easily in his one hand. Behind the advancing soldiers, another squad worked at reloading its crossbows. I let out a cheer when I saw their names. My advanced troops had finally arrived.

Scouts: Advanced Soldier. These soldiers are picked from the most capable ranks of the Imperium and given specialized training. Scouts are used for reconnaissance, for infiltration, and as an elite ranged unit.

But the one-armed half-orc leading them was a player, not an NPC!

Sergeant Ty, Scout Team Leader, Level 3.

Wait . . . Why did he look familiar?

You have been critically hit by Vhareax for 395 damage.

You have been poisoned, taking 20 damage per second for the next 20 seconds.

You are immobilized.

While I was looking at the reinforcements, Vhareax used my distraction to close the distance and grasp me in his jaws.

"I take you to the void with me . . . Your soul shall feed me and my brood for eternity," Vhareax taunted as he activated an ability.

Vhareax used the Rend ability for 225 damage. You have died.

CHAPTER 29

You will respawn in 30 seconds: 29 . . . 28 . . . 27 . . .

Thankfully, it looked like I would respawn shortly . . . and not be forced to feed Vhareax and his brood in the void for all eternity.

I respawned in the graveyard just outside of the town. When I pat myself down, it looked like I had my clothes and armor but was missing my sword. I now remembered that you had a chance to drop non-soulbound items and some coin when you died. A few townspeople looked at me strangely as I appeared. Only thirty seconds had passed, so the fight must still have been on!

I ran as fast as I could toward the mine, finding the townsfolk and workers hammering at some houses they were building. I ran past our barracks, seeing the building had been completed. That explained where the advanced soldiers and replacements had come from. But who was that other player? I hit the tunnel entrance and began to move as quickly as possible toward the main chamber. I was forced to reduce my speed due to the poor lighting, and I also noticed that my health was only a little above half. Respawning must not reset health to full once you made it past your starter quest. My sudden appearance in the main chamber startled Phineas and the newly crowned Chief Bugtug. I didn't stop to chat, crawling through the stinking webbed opening in the wall. Just when the cavern opened enough for me to stand again, I received a very welcome notification.

Server-wide announcement: The first unique elite foe (Vhareax the Fangweb Sire) has been defeated by Raytak the Commander and Scout

Team Leader Ty. Lore on this creature has been unlocked for all players. Seek out powerful foes for greater rewards.

Wow, a server-wide announcement. I didn't know that was a thing. I breathed a sigh of relief as I entered the portal chamber and saw the great spider lying in a pool of its milky blood. Several of its legs had been hacked from its body, and crossbow bolts were lodged everywhere in its corpse.

You have defeated Fangweb Surrogate, Level 5. Experience gained: 500.

You have defeated Vhareax the Fangweb Sire. Experience gained: 1500.

Congratulations! You have reached level 4. Please open your character sheet to review.

I minimized the notification and moved toward the survivors of the battle. All the advanced troops and fourteen of the regulars were alive. Thankfully Private Tremble had survived. He had been with the unit since the beginning, and it would feel wrong without him around. The one I was most confused with was the one-armed half-orc player, Ty. He was heading my way with a stupid grin on his face.

"Once again, the Marines had to bail out the Army. I guess things don't change, even in a game. Good to see you outside of a hospital, Colonel!" Ty reached his one hand toward me to shake.

Could it be? But how?

"Why, don't tell me they put you in here as well. I guess there wasn't an IQ test required in order to play, otherwise there wouldn't be any Marines allowed," I joked while shaking Ty's hand, tears streaming down my face. My friend from the VA hospital had made it into the game as well. We both stood there for a minute, overcome with emotion before Ty began to explain.

"I was in about the same situation as you, according to what the AI said . . . all used up and about to die. They decided to add another of us into a medpod for testing and I made the cut. I woke up in my childhood room and was talking to some civilian named Clio, who said she was an AI. She gave me the option of reliving comforting memories while I healed or to go into this game and save your skin. I knew you'd need a Marine NCO to tell you what to do if you wanted to survive here. I was never a game player, but this"—Ty waved around him—"doesn't really seem like a game, does it?" Ty said.

"No, it seems real enough, and I could sure use your help. Looks like my brain was mush, and by playing this game, the AI can map my mind and eventually help me recall memories. I'm assuming you're in a similar situation, Sergeant Ty?"

"Yes, looks like I'm in the mush brain club as well. I guess we just get on with it and play the game as well as we can. I'll defer to your leadership since I'm new to gaming. What's next?" Ty asked.

"Well, it looks like, thanks to the timely arrival of the Marine Corps, we killed that thing." I gestured toward the corpse of Vhareax. "Get the men working on freeing any survivors from the webs and gathering any loot. Once that's done, we'll peek behind that to see where it leads." I pointed to the swirling blue vortex I assumed was a portal. Ty began shouting orders to the men, falling right back into the position of senior NCO, which he had held in the real world for decades.

"Sir, what should we do with them?" Private Tremble asked while pointing toward the fangweb surrogates. I walked over to their helpless and pitiful forms. The three that had just recently given "birth" to spiders were unconscious and near death. The one that just had a spider implanted in her was awake and looked at us as we approached.

"Kill us . . . We cannot be saved . . . Kill us before another of these things uses us to grow," the surrogate said as it looked over its shoulder to the small but growing spider feeding on her back.

"I'm sorry this happened to you. I'll put you out of your misery. May you find peace in whatever afterlife you find yourself in," I said as I drew my knife.

"Sir, I'll take care of it," Private Tremble said and drew his sword. I placed my arm out to hold him back.

"No, thank you, soldier, but this is something I have to do myself." I stabbed the pleading surrogate in her back, killing the growing spider as well as the surrogate.

The surrogate let out a last breath, whispering "thank you" as she died, a look of peace finally settling over her features.

Quest Completed: *Eliminate the Spider Threat.* **You have killed Vhareax and his brood. The mines are safe for now.**

Reward: 500 experience, 10 gold, improved morale in the village, improved relations between Hayden's Knoll and the Bugtug tribe.

Congratulations! You have reached Level 5. Please open your character sheet to review changes.

While the soldiers finished their tasks, I opened my character sheet to level up. Luckily, I was able to set a filter so that my character sheet would only show things that had changed or new abilities I needed to review.

Player: Raytak.

Class: Commander (Imperium).

Rank: Lieutenant.

Level: 5 (5180/8000).

Attack: 5.

Defense: 11.

Health: 675.

Class Ability Upgraded:

Command Presence: Creates an aura in a 25-yard radius that inspires troops and allies under your command: +2 to attack, +2 to defense, and improved morale. The commander must concentrate on inspiring his forces and takes a penalty to attack and defense while the aura is active.

Honor Guard: This ability will now summon 2 copies of your advanced troops instead of regulars.

Unit Ability Unlocked:

Thrust: Soldiers will automatically activate the Thrust ability once every 30 seconds in combat. Thrust adds a +5 bonus to the next attack and has a 10% chance to cause a bleeding wound for 1 damage per second for the next 10 seconds.

It looked like my abilities were upgrading nicely. The damage increase from the new thrust ability would be a big help, as DPS continued to be our weak point. I also hoped we could find and afford some better weapons soon.

You have looted 5 gold, 22 silver, and 44 copper.

You have looted Goblin mining pick ×12, goblin shovel ×12, copper ore ×33, tin ore ×4, fangweb spider carapace ×14, fangweb fangs ×2, spider silk ×11, ribbon (unidentified).

While I gathered the loot, the rest of the men had cut the victims from the spiderwebs. Most of the victims, including the villager Jimmy, were dead, but we were able to save four more very sick goblins that should be okay once the spider venom wore off. I sent some of our soldiers to escort the wounded goblins back to their people. I also had them tell Bugtug that he could have the mining picks and shovels. The tools were crude and nearly worn out, but the goblins might find some use for them. Sergeant Ty detailed another group of soldiers to carry the rest of the loot back to our barracks.

You have returned wounded goblins back to their tribe and have given back the mining tools. Reputation with the Bugtug tribe is now Neutral.

Sergeant Ty looked at the blue vortex in front of us. "I guess there's just that left. Where do you think it goes?"

"I don't know. Only one way to find out." With that, we walked into the portal.

CHAPTER 30

"Hey, Lou, remember the anomalous power usage from the first medpod that we recorded?" Dave, Lou's assistant, asked while looking at the latest readings on his screen in the Qualitranos medical division's server room.

"Yeah, Dave. What about it? It was an issue with Clio's early calibration. Everything should be fairly stable now. Doesn't take much processing horsepower to project a comforting environment and replay memories, does it?" Lou answered.

"Well, buddy, the new pod has been doing it for the last hour, and the first pod is showing it again, too. It's still minuscule amounts of processing power, but I knew you wanted us to keep an eye on it," Dave said while swiping his screen over to Lou's device.

Lou read the data, then ran a few queries. "No way . . . It can't be. Dave, get the Limitless Lands VR gear we have stored in the back and load up full admin privileges on it, pronto!" Lou looked at the data again one final time before placing the helmet over his head. The light turned green, showing Lou was in-game. The admin privileges allowed the user to monitor any other gamer's activity. It was rarely used and was one of the few non-AI controlled features that allowed the company to police potentially harmful activity. After ten minutes (nearly an hour in-game), Lou logged out. He had a blank expression on his face as he activated his phone.

"Phone, dial Trey Raytak. Indicate it's an emergency." Lou waited for the call to connect while Dave stood there, stunned, not sure what the emergency could be.

"Trey, it's Lou. Sorry for waking you up, but this is important. Remember the anomaly with CPU usage and the medpods? We found the source tonight. The extra CPU usage is from Clio porting the medpod patients into the game. Trey, Mr. Ty and your father are both in the game right now . . ."

AFTERWORD

Thank you for taking the time to read Limitless Lands. I hope you enjoyed your journey, and if so, be sure to continue with Raytak's adventures in Limitless Lands Book 2: Conquest, which is out now. Limitless Lands is the product of the time I spent in the waiting room of the VA hospital in Johnson City, Tennessee. If you ever want to see real heroes, you need to go no further than the waiting room of a VA hospital to find them. While listening to the old war stories from some Vietnam veterans, I thought about what we were losing as these men aged and died. I had just found LitRPG as a genre and was intrigued by what would happen when you sent an old combat veteran into a game. I finally, one day, sat down and started writing. This book is the result.

I wanted to also take a moment to thank my family for supporting me during the time I spent away from them while tapping away at the keyboard, my sister Renee Kelly for using her mystical teacher powers to improve this work, Bodie Dykstra for his excellent editing and formatting work, and finally Charles M. Province for allowing me to use his inspiring poem in the forward. The talented Jack Voraces will be updating the audio version of this work and you can find it here https://www.amazon.com/dp/B07JJLPFZJ.

If you enjoyed the book, please take the time to leave a favorable review. Doing so helps the authors more than you know.